Out of Body

by

Kimberly Baer

Out of Body

Cover Art by *The Wild Rose Press, Inc.*

The Wild Rose Press, Inc.
PO Box 708
Adams Basin, NY 14410-0708
Visit us at www.thewildrosepress.com

Publishing History
First Edition, 2024
Trade Paperback ISBN 978-1-5092-5307-4
Digital ISBN 978-1-5092-5308-1

Published in the United States of America

Dedication

In memory of my mother, Donna Williams, who taught me to love books—and encouraged me to write them.

Whoa.

I was on the ceiling. Suddenly I was on the blinkin' ceiling, and I had no idea how I'd gotten up here or how to get down.

What the heck?

A moment ago, I'd been lying there thinking my thoughts, but now somehow I'd shrugged off gravity like an astronaut on a space mission. I was staring down at a girl on a bed, a sleeping brown-haired girl wearing mud-crusted jeans and a hoodie, who looked a little bit like me.

Actually, a lot like me.

Holy crud, it *was* me! The sleeping girl was me!

I must have dozed off. I was so exhausted, I'd fallen asleep, and now—

Now I was having an out-of-body experience.

Praise for Kimberly Baer

OUT OF BODY

"Fans of young adult fiction will devour this gem. Alongside the story's fantastical aspects, Abby faces real-world anxieties adolescent readers will readily identify with."

~ Dan Rice,
Author of The Allison Lee Chronicles series

"I highly recommend this work to anyone who enjoys YA sci-fi and fantasy. You will be hooked from page one."

~ Mark Rosendorf,
Author of The Witches of Vegas series

THE HAUNTED PURSE

"…a beautiful standalone story that teens and adults alike will enjoy. Recommended!"

~ Dr. Who Online Review

MALL GIRL MEETS THE SHADOW VANDAL

"A lively, jaunty mystery with a terrific cast of characters."

~ Kirkus Reviews

Chapter 1

Dad's recliner was rocking by itself again.

I could see it from the corner of my eye—the smug, seesawlike bounce of it. Rhythmic as windshield wipers, creepy as witchery.

I stared at the TV, my lips pressed tight. *I will not look*, I told myself. *This time I won't look. I absolutely, positively will not—*

And then I looked.

The recliner wasn't rocking. There wasn't so much as a lingering wobble to confirm it had rocked in the first place. But then, what had I expected?

This had been going on for the past fifteen minutes—strange movements that taunted me from the outermost edges of my vision. Rippling curtains, jiggling lampshades, that self-rocking rocker. Movements that stopped the instant I turned to confront them.

My anxiety level inched upward, a rising fever of dread. Was I having hallucinations? Some weird variety of migraine aura? Or was it something more ominous— an intruder in the house, a stalker, someone or something that was toying with me the same way a cat torments a mouse before the kill?

I muted the TV and rose from the couch. I turned slowly in a circle, letting my eyes rove across the house wall to wall, floor to ceiling. This took a while because the kitchen, dining area, and family room shared one large space. I'd turned on every lamp and all the overheads, but there were deep places the light didn't touch, shadowy nooks where who-knew-what could be lurking.

My gaze landed on the fireplace mantel, where a dozen framed photographs were lined up at different heights, like city buildings. Three-month-old me in a lacy, ruffly, bow-infested dress that I personally would never have inflicted on a helpless infant. A faded 80s studio portrait of toddler Mom and baby Aunt Lisa, chubby-cheeked caricatures of the ladies they would grow up to be. A scrunchy-faced newborn photo of their brother, Cody, born a decade later. A snapshot of my cousin Logan and me in matching NASA spacesuits, our Halloween costumes the year we'd been eight.

It was that fourth picture that snagged my attention, the one of my cousin and me. While all the other pictures were facing forward, that one was crooked. Turned nearly sideways, in fact. This was highly irregular—my mother did not allow *crooked* in our house. Plus, I was seventy-eight percent sure that picture had been lined up with the others a few minutes ago. I chewed my lip, wondering if I was seeing the first hard evidence of an uninvited guest. A burglar, a serial killer. Maybe a malicious ghost.

Four out of five moms would have said I was letting my imagination run away with me. After all, it was trick-or-treat night and I was home alone watching a scary movie. There was even a full moon. Still, I just couldn't convince myself the movements weren't real. And now there was that crooked picture to consider...

I grabbed my cell phone off the coffee table and tapped in 9-1-1. My forefinger hovered over the *send* button. It wasn't hard to imagine the conversation.

Nine-one-one, what's your emergency?

Um, hi, I'm home alone, and my dad's recliner keeps rocking by itself. Also, a lampshade jiggled. Oh, and a picture on the mantel is crooked.

[A reproachful pause.] Miss, are you aware that making prank nine-one-one calls is a federal offense?

I didn't know if it was a federal offense. It had to be some kind of offense. And the last thing I needed was trouble with the law.

I x'ed out 9-1-1 and punched in Logan's cell phone number.

Two rings. Three rings. Four. I hung up as my call went to voice mail and immediately dialed his family's landline number.

Three rings. Four rings. Five—

"Hello?"

"Aunt Lisa?" I said, relief coursing through me like warm milk. "Sorry to be calling so late. Can I talk to Logan?"

"Abby—hi, honey. I'm sorry. Logan's in bed."

This wasn't a big surprise, but my heart plummeted anyway. It was only 7:20 here in northern Oregon, but in Pennsylvania, where Logan and his parents lived, it was after ten.

"Are you sure he's asleep," I pressed, "and not, like, reading or something?"

"I'm pretty sure. He had a long day, got up really early to finish some big geography project. But I can check. Hang on."

She was gone for an eternity, and I spent that time

3

glancing around the house yet again, wary as a deer sniffing for hunters. My eyes couldn't be everywhere at once. An attack could come from any direction, at any time.

Or not. Just-my-imagination remained a possibility, which was why I needed to talk to my cousin. He would help me figure this out.

Finally, I heard a fumbling at the other end of the line. I waited for Logan's calm, drawling voice to fill my ears, but all I got was more Aunt Lisa. "Sorry, hon. He's snoring like a hibernating bear. I'll tell him to call you tomorrow, okay?"

"Okay," I mumbled, my sense of dread deepening.

There was a short pause. "Abby? Is everything okay?"

For a moment, I considered telling her just how far from okay everything was. But she was practical like my mother—it was in their genes. If I told her my crazy tale, she'd say I'd given myself a case of the Halloween heebie-jeebies. And for all I knew, maybe I had.

I forced a smile, knowing she'd hear it in my voice. "Everything's fine. Tell Logan I'll talk to him tomorrow." I tapped *end call* before she could say another word.

I settled back into the couch, clicking the remote to unmute the TV. I tucked my knees up inside my T-shirt, compressing myself into a tight ball of apprehension. The house was as still as death—for the moment. I shuddered and turned my attention back to the TV.

Tonight's movie was a scary outer-space flick from the 1970s. I'd seen it before, so I knew to cover my eyes just before the alien burst out of the guy's stomach. Now the creature was loose on the spaceship, slaughtering crew members one by one.

I was so jumpy that when the doorbell rang, I shrieked out loud. I patted my chest, trying to settle my racing heart, and sock-scurried across the fake-hardwood floor to open the door.

Standing on my porch were three life-sized crayons—purple, green, and yellow. They wore pointy hats that matched their respective colors, but no masks, so it was easy to recognize them as three of my ninth-grade classmates.

Sophia Travers, Emma Levy, Lanie Chobany—the golden girls of my class. They'd been stars since fourth grade, when they'd won the school talent show doing a synchronized dance routine in glittery leotards. Now in junior high, they'd moved on to bigger things—singing (Sophia), gymnastics (Emma), cheerleading (Lanie).

My eyes flicked from girl to girl to girl. In their form-fitting minidresses, they were the sexiest crayons the world had ever seen.

Lanie's eyes skimmed down the length of me, a faint smirk on her face. I thrust my chin out and stared back defiantly—*Go ahead, judge me*. I was wearing my nicest T-shirt, the gray one that said LOVE with a pink lace heart in place of the O, and jeans that made my hips look narrow. Sweats would have been fine for this occasion, but I wanted to look my best. You never knew who might show up on trick-or-treat night, their identity concealed under yards of mummy wrappings or a furry werewolf mask.

"Hey, Abby," said the green crayon.

"Hey, Emma." My gaze moved to the purple and yellow crayons. "Sophia. Lanie. You guys look great."

"How come you're not trick-or-treating?" asked

Emma.

Because I'm not seven.

I almost blurted it out but then realized how insulting that would sound. Anyway, I was only pretending I was too old for trick-or-treating. Halloween was a big deal in Eerie, Oregon, named for black-magicky events that had allegedly occurred a hundred and fiftyish years ago, when the town was young. There was an annual parade, parties galore, and a scariest-yard contest. If you were under eighteen, it was pretty much a given that you'd go trick-or-treating. Even parents donned costumes to make the rounds with their little ones.

The truth was, I wanted to be out there with everybody else, roaming the streets in some crazy get-up. I was practically breaking the law by staying home. But for the first time in my life, I had nobody to go with. And going trick-or-treating by myself would have been pathetic, even for me.

The three crayons were staring at me, waiting for my response.

"My parents went to a party," I said, rolling my eyes like the long-suffering daughter I was. "*Somebody* had to be here to hand out candy."

I grabbed the bowl of fun-size bars from the foyer table, and they each snatched up a fistful. They were all wearing the same sparkly blue nail polish. I aimed my brightest smile at Sophia. I imagined her tilting her pointy purple head and saying, "Hey. Why don't you come with us?"

A few weeks ago I'd assembled a costume, just in case somebody requested the pleasure of my company on T-or-T night. It consisted of a black dress my mother had bought for my grandpa's funeral (and refused to wear again because of the sad memories), a black witch's hat from some previous Halloween, a black half-mask, my black winter boots, and a beat-up broom from the garage. If the crayons asked me to go with them, I could transform from a jeans-clad homebody to a witch in sixty seconds flat.

But they didn't ask. And that was probably for the best. I mean, a witch and three crayons? That didn't make sense thematically.

"Okay, then," said Sophia. "Bye."

The three of them clomped down my porch steps, Emma and Lanie flanking Sophia like she was the gold medalist to their silver and bronze. From the window I watched them stroll down the sidewalk. Matching ponytails trailed down their backs, Emma's sleek black hair a striking contrast to Sophia's and Lanie's golden tresses.

I sighed as I stepped away from the window, and I got even more depressed when I thought back to last Halloween. Logan had still been here, and we'd done the T-or-T thing together. I'd been Little Red Riding Hood, and he'd been a wolf dressed up like a grandma. He'd stolen the show in his pink flannel nightgown and matching bedcap, with an old pair of his dad's glasses perched at the end of his rubber wolf snout. People had given us extra candy, probably because we (okay, *he*) had made them laugh.

The candy bowl was down to a handful of fun-size bars, just enough for one last trick-or-treater. But trick-or-treaters never came alone—they traveled in packs. Time to turn off the porch light.

Back in the family room, I gobbled up all four

candy bars. Fun-size my butt—I was not having fun. Between the candy bars and the two brownies I'd eaten earlier, I felt like I'd swallowed a bucket of mud.

I fetched a glass of water from the kitchen. I plopped down on the couch. I stared morosely at the TV.

And then it happened again.

Chapter 2

It was the teensiest movement at the far end of the couch, a half-hearted flutter, like a wounded bird flopping around, trying to fly. But just as I whipped my head in that direction, the movement stopped.

I pressed the *mute* button on the TV remote, bringing on a silence as heavy as white noise. I could almost hear the dust falling. Our five designer pillows were piled untidily at the opposite end of the couch, just where I'd tossed them when I'd first sat down. We weren't allowed to actually use those pillows, meaning we couldn't lie on them, prop our feet on them, or use them as plush food trays, because they were decorative, not functional. That was one of my mother's strictest household rules.

The pillows were freeze-tag still under my gaze. I stared for another minute, sizing up the situation. And then I relaxed, just a little, because this time there was a logical explanation. The pile of pillows had shifted, that was all. One or more of them had surrendered to the tug of gravity, like rocks sliding down a mountain.

I was sixty-seven percent sure about that.

I scooted across the couch and tossed the pillows onto the floor one by one. There. If pillow slippage was what I'd seen, it wouldn't be happening again.

I unmuted the TV just as a commercial came on. A fluffy-haired mom was raving about laundry detergent like it was a new religion. I watched raptly, wondering if there were actually people in the world with nothing more pressing to worry about than how to get grass stains out of jeans. I wished my life was that simple.

The other commercials were equally cheery, featuring puppies and babies and crinkle-eyed older folks sipping coffee. When the movie came back on, its grimness was a jarring contrast to the overflowing joyfulness of commercial land. I tensed up instantly.

It occurred to me that watching a scary movie in my state of mind wasn't the best idea. Why hadn't I thought of that sooner? I started clicking through channels, looking for a sitcom. Sure, it was Halloween in Eerie, but I was surprised and frustrated by how many channels were airing scary movies. Then there were the news channels, which were even scarier. Finally, I found a teen drama I'd never really cared for. It would have to do.

The show had been in progress for maybe five minutes when there was another movement from the end of the couch. I snapped my head around so fast, I nearly gave myself whiplash. My heart lurched in horror.

One of the pillows was back on the couch, nestled squarely in the corner as if arranged there by my mother. But...that was impossible. I'd thrown those pillows on the floor. At least I was eighty-two percent sure I had. There were five of them. Maybe I'd missed one.

But what if that wasn't it? What if something more sinister was going on, some weird Halloween mojo that had brought our designer pillows to life? I had to confess, sometimes when my mother wasn't around, I broke the rules. I'd dribbled potato chip crumbs on those pillows. I'd fallen asleep and drooled on them. What if they'd been waiting for their chance to get even? What if they were planning to creep across the couch and smother me?

Okay, now I was really freaked out. I dashed to the kitchen and pulled a garbage bag from the box under the sink. I grabbed a carving knife from the utensil drawer. If one of those zombie pillows came at me, I would slice its sorry designer butt to smithereens.

Back in the family room, I stuffed the pillows into the garbage bag, counting twice to make sure all five were accounted for. After double-knotting the bag shut, I tossed it into the coat closet in the foyer and slammed the door. For an extra measure of protection, I slid the foyer table in front of the door.

The next ten minutes were peaceful if you didn't count the teen angst oozing out of the TV. Then, in sync with a burst of melodramatic background music, something rose and quickly fell near my dad's recliner, in the corner by the fireplace. I gasped and jumped to my feet in a battle-ready half crouch, the carving knife in my hand.

Everything looked normal. The recliner sat in the corner like a patient dog, waiting for my dad's butt to return and give it a reason for living. Dad's jacket was sprawled across the back, sleeves splayed as if it had tried to catch its balance while somersaulting through the air. My mother had foisted it on him as they were heading out the door—"It's going to be chilly later"— but he'd tossed it on the chair when she wasn't looking.

I marched to the recliner and peeked behind it. I stooped down and peered beneath it. One of my dad's black plastic combs was there, along with some errant coins, but nothing else.

What was going on? I was now ninety-nine percent sure I wasn't seeing things. But if that was true, if the movements were real, why couldn't I figure out what was causing them?

The house suddenly seemed too big, too menacing. *A residential gymnasium*—that was what my dad called it when he wanted to passive-aggressively insult my mother's taste for open floor plans. Not that our house was actually large, but the lack of interior walls in the main living area made it feel that way. I decided I'd feel safer in my room, with the door locked.

I strode back to the coffee table and pressed the *off* button on the remote. Instantly the TV went blind and silent, like a lopped-off head. But I didn't make it to my bedroom. Before I could take another step, I saw it again, that flitting movement near the recliner. This time there was an accompanying noise—the unmistakable rustling of clothing.

I turned in dread, and at long last there was something to see. I felt the briefest flicker of triumph— *Ha! Caught you!*—before the horror of the situation thumped me in the chest.

My dad's jacket had come to life. It was floating in the air beside the recliner, puffy and solid as if inhabited by a body. The sleeves were waving: *Hey, look at me!*

I couldn't speak, I couldn't breathe, I couldn't move. My vision darkened as if I was going to pass out, but if I did, that would be the end of me, because that thing would come over and strangle me. It was a *disembodied jacket.* It couldn't be up to any good.

The jacket's sleeves reached down. They bent at the elbows. Up went the jacket's zipper with a *z-z-zip* sound.

Somehow I managed to draw in a big, rasping breath, and I screamed. I screamed loudly enough to wake the Halloween dead.

Then I ran for the front door.

Chapter 3

"Your parents are on their way," Mrs. Benson said, hobbling into the living room. Her arthritis made her walk stiff-legged, like a toddler with a loaded diaper. "Your dad said they'll be here in fifteen minutes."

"Thanks for calling them," I said hoarsely. "And for letting me stay here."

"Of course, dear. That's what neighbors are for."

She handed me a glass of water. I thanked her and took a gulp. The silky coolness soothed my throat, which was raw from all the screaming.

Mrs. Benson, a widow in her seventies, lived five doors down from us. That was how far I'd had to run to find somebody at home. Not that I'd minded putting some distance between me and The House of the Self-Zipping Jacket.

This was the first time I'd been inside Mrs. Benson's house. I glanced around discreetly, judging the decor. The tiny living room was crowded with furniture—a couch, a love seat, an easy chair, three tables, two bookcases, and an overstuffed footstool. Even the walls were cluttered—with paintings and plaques and colorful tapestries. All the wall art hung at the same angle of crookedness, which made me wonder if maybe I was the thing that was crooked.

"Abby, I'm not entirely sure I understand the situation," Mrs. Benson said, easing her saggy body onto the equally saggy couch. "You weren't making much sense when you got here. Can you tell me again what happened?"

"Yes, ma'am." Mrs. Benson was a retired elementary school teacher. She hadn't worked for over a decade but still had that teacherly air that made me sit up very straight and remember my manners.

"What happened," I said, "is I was home by myself, and I heard noises, and I got scared that somebody was in the house."

I'd come up with that story while she was in the kitchen calling my parents. I couldn't bring myself to say that my dad's jacket was aiming to murder me and the couch pillows were in on it.

Mrs. Benson nodded sympathetically. "You were right to come here. Those noises were probably nothing, just the house settling. But better safe than sorry. Now," she said brightly, slapping her thighs with her wrinkly hands. "Tell me how that cousin of yours is doing. Such a nice young man! I do miss him. I suppose you do, too, dear."

I told her Logan was doing great in Pittsburgh. He had friends, he was in a soccer league, and he'd just made the debate team. He'd even been elected to student council after the previous rep moved to Arkansas.

Logan was doing much better in his new life than I was in my same old one, but I didn't get into all that.

"Good for him," said Mrs. Benson. "Wonderful sport, soccer. My grandson plays. Little Garrett. Have I ever showed you pictures of my grandchildren?"

"Um, no," I said, thinking how great it would be if we could keep it that way, but she was already bending toward the coffee table, grunting a little as her belly flattened against her thighs. She pulled a fat fake-leather photo album from the lower shelf.

"Come closer, dear." She patted the couch cushion next to her as if summoning a pet dog. Resignedly, I scooted over. The faint smell of b.o. overlaid with talcum powder wafted up my nose.

Mrs. Benson kept up a running commentary as she turned the pages. Ah, there was Garrett in his pee-wee soccer uniform. And wasn't little Cassandra a doll in her flower girl dress? How about that little Carter with his spelling bee trophy? I smiled and nodded and made admiring clucking noises, like I'd observed my mother doing in similar situations. I said how cute everybody was, even though little Carter looked like an alpaca.

Finally, I heard my parents coming, their car zooming up our quiet street like a speedway competitor. I was ninety-nine percent sure my mother was driving, and I could almost hear my dad griping. *For God's sake, Leah, slow down. Do you want to get another ticket?*

Through the gauzy curtains fogging the picture window I watched the car lurch to a stop at the curb. My parents jumped out, not even bothering to close the car doors. Oh crud. I'd forgotten they were coming from a Halloween party. Which meant they were in costume.

Their costumes might have been cute on a younger couple, but on two people in their late thirties who happened to be my parents, they were just plain embarrassing. My mother was a sexy wand-wielding magician dressed in a silky white blouse, black shorts, fishnet stockings, and a cape. A shiny black top hat completed the outfit, though she must have left it in the car. Dad was a big, goofy white rabbit who presumably had gotten abracadabra-ed out of Mom's hat.

Thankfully, none of the neighbors had been around to see them leave for the party. But now Mrs. Benson was going to get an up-close look, so I just might get to die of embarrassment after all.

The doorbell rang three times in rapid succession. It took Mrs. Benson a minute to hobble over and open the door. My mother rushed past her with barely a hello.

"Abby! Are you okay? What's going on?"

"I'm fine," I mumbled, rising heavily from the couch. "I'll tell you everything in the car."

Mrs. Benson was staring at my mother's fish-netted legs. Then her gaze went up, up, up to my dad's pinkened nose and floppy bunny ears. Her lips tightened like she was trying to hold in a comment. Or, more likely, a snicker.

"Seriously?" I grumbled as the three of us walked to the car. "You couldn't have taken those costumes off before you left the party?"

"What, and drive here in our underwear?" my mother snapped.

My dad tugged half-heartedly at his bunny ears. "I tried to take this ridiculous headpiece off. It's stuck."

"It is not stuck," said my mother. "You just have to undo the snaps and the zipper. And the button. Here— let me." She fiddled around at his neck and pulled the headpiece off. My dad sighed in exaggerated relief. His hair, damp with sweat, stuck up in discrete peaks, like meringue on a pie.

Once we were in the car—them in front, me in

17

back—my mother scootched around so she could see me. "What's going on, Abby? Mrs. Benson said something scared you?"

"Yeah," I said. And then I told them what had happened. The real version.

When I'd finished, my parents glanced at each other. Then they looked at me. Then back at each other. It seemed I'd stunned them speechless. Dead silence from my dad wasn't unusual—he was an introvert like me. But my mother? I'd never seen her at a loss for words before.

"I know it sounds crazy," I said. "But, hey, our town has a history of crazy happenings. Brooms sweeping by themselves, pots and pans levitating."

"I wouldn't call it a history," said my mother. "More like colorful stories passed down through the generations."

I glared at her. "Well, mine isn't a colorful story. It actually happened."

Dad asked, "Why'd you go all the way to Mrs. Benson's house?"

"Nobody else was home."

"Not even the Murrays?" asked my mother. "They don't go out much now that they have the baby."

I shrugged. My parents exchanged another look.

"So, what do we do now?" I asked. "Call the police?"

Dad gave me a sympathetic smile. "The police wouldn't come for something like this, sweetie."

"Couldn't we say somebody broke into the house?"

"Lying to the police is never a good idea," said my mother. She sounded so bitter, I had to wonder if she was speaking from experience.

A car cruised by and turned into the driveway next to Mrs. Benson's house. It was the Martinez family, back from their annual trick-or-treating-by-car excursion. The car doors flew open, and four little Martinezes spilled out. They were in costume—witch, vampire, ghost, skeleton—and clutching bulging trick-or-treat bags.

My mother said, "Something like that happened to me once."

I blinked at her. "Something like a jacket coming to life?"

She was watching the Martinez kids zip around their driveway, clearly buzzed up on sugar, while their dad unlocked the front door. Mrs. Martinez dashed after the kids and eventually managed to herd them toward the house. I could almost hear my mother thanking her lucky stars that she didn't have four kids. The one she had was trouble enough.

"I was about your age," she said. "I woke up in the middle of the night, and right above me was this huge spider rappelling down from the ceiling. When I say 'huge,' I mean a body as big as a grapefruit. With legs as long as celery stalks."

"Interesting visual," Dad commented.

"I screamed bloody murder. I jumped out of bed and turned on the lights, but I didn't see the spider. My parents came running. We tore the bed covers apart. We looked under the bed, behind the dresser, everywhere. There was no spider."

She turned back to me, her face iced white by the moonlight streaming through the car windows. "It took my parents hours to convince me I'd dreamed the whole thing."

I made a huffy noise. "What happened to me wasn't a dream! I wasn't even asleep."

"You must have nodded off without realizing it. That happens to me sometimes when I'm watching TV."

"I did not nod off! I wasn't even sleepy. It was, like, eight o'clock."

But even as I protested, I wondered if she might be right. With every minute that ticked by, my experience seemed more surreal, a plot straight out of dreamland. Even a grapefruit-sized spider seemed more believable than a jacket that floated in the air and zipped its own zipper.

"How about we go home," said my dad. "I'll make a thorough search of the house. You two can wait in the car."

My mother turned the key in the ignition, and the car's engine started up with a roar. "I'll help you search. Abby can wait in the car."

"Nobody's waiting in the car," I snapped. "We'll all go in together."

The drive home took all of ten seconds. As we neared the tall hedge separating the Calvertons' property from ours, a crazy image popped into my head—Dad's jacket and the couch pillows marching across the porch in a conga line. But in reality, nothing like that was going on. With the golden lamplight spilling from the windows, the house looked peaceful and inviting, a place of hot tea and warm baths and clean, cool sheets. The only creepiness came from the Halloween decorations in the front yard—grim reaper, bloody bodies, resin gravestones—but that didn't bother me.

My mother parked in the driveway and turned off the car. "Let's go see what that crazy jacket is up to."

Chapter 4

I started to lose my nerve as I got out of the car. "Do we have a gun? I'd feel better if we had a gun."

"We do not have a gun," said my mother. "Besides, how would that help? A jacket doesn't have a heart or a brain or blood vessels. Would a bullet even stop it?"

I didn't know whether she was mocking me or pretending she suddenly believed me. I wasn't sure which made me madder.

"It's not just the jacket," I said. "I didn't lock the door when I left. Anybody could have walked in. A burglar, an ax murderer…"

"We'll go in through the garage," said my dad. "We can grab some tools to use as makeshift weapons."

The three of us went shopping in Dad's carpentry area. I grabbed a hand saw. I figured that if the jacket came at me, I'd get it tangled up on the sharp blade teeth. Mom opted for a nail gun. Dad chose a crowbar.

Mom pushed past Dad and me and flung open the door to the kitchen like some fish-netted federal agent. I half-expected her to yell, "FBI! Freeze!" She held the nail gun in front of her, ready to fire at a moment's notice. I made sure to stay behind her. I didn't want to end up with a nail in my butt.

I figured the jacket would be either missing or crumpled on the floor. But when I glanced into the family room, I saw it sprawled innocently across the back of the recliner, just where Dad had thrown it before he'd left the house.

Which seemed to support the dream theory.

Then that awful zipping sound tore through my memory, and I shuddered. If what happened had been a dream, it had been a very realistic one.

Dad snatched his jacket off the recliner and headed for the coat closet.

"Could you put it on the porch instead?" I asked. "And make sure you bolt the door when you come in."

"Of course, sweetie."

"Take the couch pillows, too," I called as he opened the front door. "They're in the closet."

When Dad came back inside, we started our search. Mom looked in the powder room, Dad tackled the laundry room, and I checked unlikely (but possible!) hiding places like the cupboard under the sink and the triangle of space behind Dad's recliner. We teamed up to do the bedroom wing. We looked in every closet, peered under every bed, scoured all the nooks and crannies. Then Dad pulled the hidden ladder out of the ceiling and clomped up to the attic, his crowbar clanking dully across the wooden rungs. When we were finally done, Dad returned our weapons to the garage and the three of us met up in the kitchen.

"Are we ready to declare this house free of burglars, ax murderers, and rampaging outerwear?" Dad asked.

I shrugged morosely and slid into a chair at the kitchen table.

"Well then. If you ladies will excuse me, I'm going to take a shower. I'm sweating like a pig in this furry jumpsuit."

The zipper on the jumpsuit was stuck, so my mother had to help him unzip it. Dad loped toward the bathroom, his furry bunny feet slapping against the floor.

My mother poured me a glass of milk, and I sipped it while she washed the few dishes I'd left in the sink.

"Are these brownie crumbs?" she asked, using a fingernail to scrape at a dark spot on a plate. Her tone sounded innocent. The question was anything but.

"If you don't want me to eat brownies," I said, "maybe you shouldn't make them."

She widened her eyes at me. "Did I say I didn't want you to eat brownies?"

"Not this time," I said. "Not technically."

She opened her mouth and then shut it. And then opened it again. "It's just—your dad's sisters are both so hippy. I don't want you to end up like them."

If I hadn't already finished off the brownies, I'd have had one now, just to spite her.

The dishwater drained down the sink with a loud slurping noise. My mother came over and plunked a bottle of ibuprofen down on the table.

"Take one of these."

"I don't have a headache."

"It's the p.m. kind. It'll help you sleep."

"Fine." I swallowed a tablet with a swig of milk.

She slid out a chair and joined me at the table. She clasped and unclasped her hands several times before saying, "I think part of the problem is, you're alone too much."

I eyed her warily. "Part of what problem?"

"When you spend too much time alone, it's easy to let your imagination run away with you."

"Oh, so now it's my imagination, not a dream? Jeez, Mother, make up your mind!"

"I worry about you, Abby. You've gotten so isolated since Logan moved away. You don't have any close friends. You never talk to anybody."

"I talk to people," I argued. "Just tonight I was talking to three girls from my class. Three really popular girls."

"Yeah?" She tilted her head, as if viewing me from a different angle would help her see past my b.s. "So, these girls, these 'really popular' girls, did they call you on the phone? Did they come over to hang out? Did you meet them at Ghastly Gabe's to share a plate of nachos?"

I looked away, wilting under the intensity of her gaze. It was like a police interrogation light.

"I mean," she went on, in a slow, sardonic voice, "they weren't just trick-or-treating—*were they*?"

Why was she bothering to ask? She already knew the answer.

I picked up my glass and took several big gulps. Milk was supposed to have calming properties, but tonight it didn't seem to be working.

My mother was using a forefinger to trace the curlicue pattern on the placemat in front of her. "You know what you should do? Join some clubs at school."

"I'm already in clubs at school. The math club, anyway. You know this."

She waved a hand dismissively. My mother had never been that impressed with the fact that I was the top math student in ninth grade. "I'm talking about *real* clubs, like the ski club, the drama club. The group that plans dances and things. You need activities that'll give you opportunities for socializing. A chance to make friends."

"I don't want opportunities for socializing. I don't need to make friends. I like things the way they are."

I didn't mean that. But when my mother went into attack mode, I went into contrarian mode. It was a pattern we'd been stuck in for years, but she never tried to break out of it.

In fairness, neither did I.

"God, Abby," my mother said, rubbing her eyes with the palms of her hands. "You're going to turn into one of those weird old ladies who live alone with a bunch of cats."

"Sounds good to me," I declared. "I love cats."

When she moved her hands away from her face, I saw that she'd smeared mascara around her eyes. It gave her a theatrical look, like a vampire from an old movie.

She said, "It's not totally your fault, you know."

"What's not totally my fault?"

"Your social shortcomings."

I blinked in disbelief. "My social—"

"Your dad and I, we blame ourselves. We treated you and Logan like twins. So did Aunt Lisa and Uncle Dirk. It just kind of happened. I mean, you were born only three weeks apart, and we lived right next door to each other. We'd stick the two of you in the same playpen, put you down for naps in the same crib. Feed you in side-by-side highchairs. You used to cry for each other at night when you had to go home to your own beds."

"What does any of that have to do with what happened to me tonight?" I couldn't even look at her, so I stared at the refrigerator, where a late-fall housefly was creeping across the door as if it knew life-sustaining food was inside but couldn't figure out how to get to it.

She ignored my question. She was off on a tangent, talking fast, deaf to anything I might say. "I should have encouraged you to make friends, back when you were little. I just didn't realize. I thought you already had friends, because you and Logan were always at the center of a mob of kids. I didn't know Logan was the one forging all those friendships. You just kind of tagged along. You never had to make friends, because Logan did it for you."

This wasn't news to me. It had become especially apparent after Logan moved away. The kids in our neighborhood had always gravitated to our end of the street to play flashlight tag or hold roller-skating races or put on magic shows for the younger kids. But the true hub of the neighborhood had never been a place. It had been Logan. After he left, people drifted away, like birds abandoning an empty feeder.

My mother was looking at me in an intense, predatory way that made me feel like I was being bitten to death by a thousand tiny spiders. "You need a few close friends to hang out with, that's all I'm saying. People you can invite over for sleepovers, go to the mall with. Tell your deepest secrets to. I had two best friends when I was growing up. Courtney and Allison. God, we had fun together. The three of us were inseparable."

"Well, good for you!" I shouted. I stood up so abruptly, my chair fell over. My mother jerked like she hadn't seen this reaction coming. "I'm sorry you ended up with a daughter like me. Why don't you put me up for adoption and pick out a better kid at some orphanage!" I stalked away toward my bedroom, not even bothering to pick up the fallen chair.

"I just want you to be happy," my mother called feebly.

I slammed my bedroom door.

Mad as I was, I knew she was right. I needed to get a life, seeing as how mine had packed its bags and moved to Pittsburgh. I was flat and empty, more a shadow than a real person.

I just didn't know how to become real.

Chapter 5

The p.m. pill did its job, delivering a solid night's sleep free of nightmares. When I got up at a quarter after nine on Saturday, the house was empty. I wandered into the kitchen, the lingering smells of burnt toast and strong coffee wafting up my nostrils. I found a note from my mother on the kitchen table. At first I thought it was an apology, but I should have known better. "I'm hitting the gym as usual, then meeting a friend for lunch. Dad's running errands. Call my cell if you need me. P.S. Logan called after you went to bed, will call back today."

Logan had called? That was odd, considering he'd been asleep last night when I'd called him. He must have woken up at some point and seen my missed call on his cell phone. But why had he decided to call me then instead of waiting till morning?

I was mildly uneasy about being home alone again, though the melodrama of the previous evening had receded, chased away by the passage of time and the friendly glimmer of daylight beyond the windows. I opened the front door and stepped onto the porch. The couch pillows were in the far corner, still secured in the garbage bag. Dad's jacket lay on the swing, limp and lifeless. I eyed it for a minute, daring it to rear up, but it didn't so much as twitch.

A chill wind curled around me like tentacles. I

shivered and retreated into the house. I made breakfast—cereal, peanut-butter toast, and orange juice—and took it into the family room so I could watch TV while I ate. I clicked through channels until I found an old show Logan and I used to watch, the one about people going boldly on a starship.

In grade school, the two of us had been obsessed with outer space. We'd spent a lot of time in the woods pretending to be space travelers exploring an alien planet. We'd pooled our money to buy space movies, which we'd watched over and over on Logan's DVD player. We talked our parents into taking us to a planetarium—*four times*—despite the fact that the place was three hours away. One Halloween we were astronauts; another, space aliens.

This show was comfort food for the soul. I settled back to watch.

My cell phone was on the coffee table, where I'd left it last night. During a commercial break, I clicked it on. I was surprised to see a bunch of missed calls and text messages from Logan. I spooned cereal into my mouth as I scanned the texts.

—*Abs are you there*—

—*I'm calling back in ten seconds please pick up*—

—*Are you getting these messages??? Please reply!*—

—*I'm sorry!!! Sometimes I do dumb things*—

—*I'm sorry Abby really sorry call me as soon as you can*—

I read the messages several times, struggling to understand. What was Logan sorry about? That he'd been asleep when I called? That didn't make sense. I scrolled through the calls and messages again, noting their times. About half had come last night, the others at various times this morning. But why was Logan so desperate to reach me?

I called his cell phone. He picked up before the first ring faded.

"Abby, finally! Listen, I am so, so sorry."

"You keep saying that. What are you sorry about?"

"For scaring you."

"Scaring me?" I shook my head in bewilderment. "When did you scare me?"

"Last night. The thing with the jacket. That was me."

My breath faltered. "How—how do you know about the jacket? Did my mom tell you?"

"Nobody had to tell me. I was there. I was the thing inside the jacket. Making it move, zipping it up."

I could feel my brain straining to make sense of his words, but there was no sense to be made. "You couldn't have been here. You're in Pittsburgh."

"That's true."

"I called you last night. Your mom said you were in bed."

"I *was* in bed. Here's the thing, Abby." He paused, and I could almost see him gazing upward, groping for the right words. "I have this…I don't know. Power, I guess you'd call it. When I'm sleeping, I can turn into this kind of ghost and fly away to different places. I was at your house last night. I made things move—the lampshades, the recliner, those fancy pillows on the couch. Then I put on your dad's jacket and zipped it up. It was me, Abs, all of it."

31

Chapter 6

For the longest time, I couldn't think of anything to say. Finally, I croaked, "That wasn't you. It couldn't have been."

"Except it was. I was there last night, at your house. You were handing out trick-or-treat candy. You were wearing that 'love' T-shirt, the one you wear when you think you might run into Austin Oliver."

"Austin Oliver! That is totally—"

"You were watching that old movie *Alien.* Sophia, Emma, and Lanie came by. They were dressed up like crayons."

"What colors?" As if he hadn't already given enough proof.

"Purple. Green. Yellow."

I shook my head, dazed by the impossibility of what he was telling me. "How do you know all this? Did you put a hidden camera in my house?"

"I told you, I was there. In spirit form."

"So…you're a ghost. Is that what you're saying?" I gasped as the full implication of that hit me. "Logan, are you dead?"

He barked a laugh. "I'm not dead. I guess you could say I'm a living ghost. You've heard of out-of-body experiences, right? Astral projection?"

"*That's* what's going on? But that's science fiction!"

"So were cell phones and virtual reality fifty years ago."

I closed my eyes, trying to let his words sink into my brain. *I was there. In spirit form. I'm a living ghost.*

It was crazy. Impossible.

But so was a levitating jacket.

I said, in a shaky voice, "Assuming this is true, and I'm not saying I think it is, how long has it been going on?"

"A couple of months. It started with these weird dreams. They felt—different. Like real life. Later I'd find out they actually happened. Like, there was this one day when I was home from school with a cold. I took a nap in the afternoon, and I dreamed I was in history class. After school my best friend, Charlie, brought me my homework and gave me his history notes. The notes said the same things I heard the teacher talking about in my dream."

My best friend. The words bounced between my ear drums like a gunshot echoing in a canyon. Logan had a best friend and it wasn't me.

"Abs?" said Logan. "You still there?"

"Yeah," I said. "This is a lot to take in."

"Tell me about it. Before this, I would have lumped OBEs in with all that other woo-woo stuff—alien abductions, Bigfoot, parallel universes."

"OBEs?"

"Out-of-body experiences."

My gaze drifted to the recliner. I could still see that creepy puffed-out jacket, its shoulders sagging as if a younger, narrower body than Dad's inhabited it.

I'd grown up with Logan. I knew him better than I knew myself. I could usually tell when he was lying.

He wasn't lying.

I slumped against the back of the couch. "So I have a cousin with a superpower."

There was a moment of wary silence. "You believe me?"

"Yeah. I believe you."

He blew out a heavy breath.

I asked, "Do your parents know?"

"No. And I'm not going to tell them. If they knew that the kid they think is sleeping peacefully in bed is actually flying to the top of a mountain or chasing a jaguar through the Amazon jungle—well, let's just say they would not be okay with that."

"The Amazon jungle! You've actually been there?"

"I've been all over. There's nowhere I can't go."

Something in his voice, an unbridled enthusiasm, made me say, "Nowhere?"

"Abs." His voice went down to a whisper. "I've been to *the moon.*"

"The moon? The actual blinkin' moon? Wait, are you messing with me?" With Logan, that was always a possibility.

"No. Swear to God."

I let out a long, reverent breath. "Holy crud, Logan." But was I really surprised? As children, we'd dreamed of exploring space. It made perfect sense that he would seize the opportunity to actually do it. "Tell me everything! What's it like there?"

"Amazing. Well—it was at first. Now it's just boring. Nothing but rocks and dust and craters."

"The moon, though! That's so far away. How do you make it home in time to get up for school?"

He chuckled. "Distance isn't an issue. I don't have

a physical body holding me back, so I can go as fast or slow as I want. Like, last night, when I came to your house? I got there in seconds."

I picked up my piece of toast, contemplated it, and dropped it back on the plate. My appetite was gone, done in by shock. "Why didn't you tell me about this sooner?"

"I needed time to get used to it on my own. I still haven't told anybody else. Only you."

I felt a small rush of triumph, like I'd scored a critical point in some game. And yet, I wondered—if last night hadn't happened, would I still have been the first person he told? Or would he have confided in that new best friend of his?

"How'd you make stuff move?" I asked. "The jacket, the pillows, the other stuff."

"That took some doing. I didn't even know it was possible, not at first. But then I saw this movie about a ghost that would throw dishes to make itself known. And I got to wondering if I could do that. It took a while, but I figured it out. I started off practicing in my bedroom. Knocking things off my desk, moving books around. Then I decided to try it out on somebody else, to see their reaction."

"And you picked me! Hope I didn't disappoint."

"I was planning to call you right after I did it. But I can't always control when I come back to my body. Sometimes it takes a while. By the time I woke up, you were gone. And you didn't take your cell phone with you."

A sudden restlessness itched at my insides. I got up off the couch and paced around the room. "My cell phone was the last thing on my mind. I just wanted to get out of the house as fast as I could."

I squeezed my eyes shut, remembering the horror of those moments. "Why did you let it go on for so long? You shouldn't have even had to do the jacket thing. Wasn't the other stuff enough for your little experiment? The picture, the couch pillows, the recliner? Couldn't you tell that I saw those things? Didn't you see how scared I was?"

"Yeah. I did. The truth is—" He sighed resignedly. "—I guess I was having fun watching you get more and more freaked out. It kind of turned into a prank."

"A prank?" I stopped pacing, my arm hairs bristling. "Seriously?"

"Like the time I put the rubber snake in your bed. I mean, you have a good sense of humor. I figured once I called you and explained, it'd be cool. We'd laugh about it."

"Holy blinkin' crud."

The shock and wonder of his wild tale had slowly been wearing off, and now I was just mad. Madder, probably, than I'd ever been in my life. It had started with *my best friend* and gotten bigger from there, like a snowball rolling down a snowy hill.

"You are—such a jerk!" I said, unable to keep the tremor out of my voice. "Do you have any idea how scared I was? I didn't know what was in the house with me, a demon, a ghost, a serial killer—"

"Actually, it *was* a ghost," he said lightly. "Just not the usual kind."

"This isn't funny!" I shrilled. "Why didn't you warn me? Why didn't you tell me about this freak-show 'power' of yours before you came to my house and scared the living poo out of me?"

"I don't know," he said, his voice suddenly sober. "Yeah. I should have done that."

"And why me out of everybody you know? Why didn't you pick somebody else to be your guinea pig? Like that best friend of yours. Or, better yet, if you're going to do something so mean, why not do it to somebody you don't like?"

"Abby, I'm really—" he began, but I cut him off.

"No. I don't want to hear any more of your sorries. You weren't sorry last night when you were having your fun. I can't talk to you anymore. Just leave me alone."

I wished I had a receiver to slam down, but since I was on a cell phone, all I could do was tap the *end call* button extra hard.

It occurred to me that now I was mad at two of the three most important people in my life.

Chapter 7

Dad got home around ten thirty. He popped inside long enough to change his clothes before heading back out to mow the lawn one last time (he hoped) before winter. Give him an hour, he said, and then he'd whip us up some lunch, probably leftover lasagna.

Too restless to stay inside, I zipped myself into a hoodie and headed out for a walk.

Sometime during the night, the grim reaper had fallen on top of one of the bloody bodies in our yard. It looked like they were having a romantic encounter.

"None of that," I scolded, yanking Grim upright.

The trees up and down our street were flaunting their colors—red, rust, orange, yellow. I caught a whiff of woodsmoke, tangy and unseen. Something droned in the distance, a leaf blower or a chainsaw. Maybe a monstrous bumblebee. At Halloweentime in Eerie, anything was possible.

Turning from our driveway onto the sidewalk, I glanced at the Murrays' house, just next door. Mr. Murray, whose first name was Matt, was out front raking leaves. I cursed the bad timing and slunk backward, hoping I could sneak away before he spotted me. But he looked up. Our eyes met. He stopped raking.

"Hi, Abby. How you doing?" The halfhearted way he said it told me he really didn't expect a reply. I surprised him by chirping "Good" before continuing down the sidewalk.

My relationship with the Murrays was complicated. If they'd lived somewhere else, anywhere else, we probably could have been friends. But they didn't. They lived next door—in Logan's old house.

In the four months since they'd moved in, I'd barely spoken to them. I'd mumbled "Hi" when my dad had first introduced us and "ninth" when Matt asked what grade I was in. That was pretty much it. I knew that Matt and his wife, Koko, thought I didn't like them, and I supposed that was true. Every time I saw them, I felt like yelling, "Go away! That's not your house!"

Koko had given birth to their first baby a month ago. I'd been hoping for a girl, but she had to go and have a boy. It was like they were trying to give the neighborhood a newer version of Logan. They'd even named him Morgan, which was essentially *Logan* with a different first syllable.

I hadn't run to the Murrays' house last night, even though it was the closest place and the lit-up windows had told me they were home. I wouldn't have run there even if nobody else on the whole block had been home and the levitating jacket was hot on my tail.

Today, though, I was feeling kinder, mainly because I was so mad at Logan. I even felt bad about being so unfriendly. It wasn't Matt and Koko's fault Logan had moved away. On a whim, I stopped walking and turned toward Matt.

He stopped raking, his gaze on me apprehensive. What was the scary neighbor girl going to do? I let the suspense build for a few seconds before saying, "Did you ever find Holly? My mom said she got out of the yard a couple of days ago."

Matt looked startled by my query but recovered quickly. He leaned the rake against a tree. "No, we haven't found her. We put up flyers and took out a lost-dog ad in the newspaper, but so far no leads."

"Aw. That's too bad," I said, and I meant it.

Holly was a cute little Yorkshire terrier, the only member of the Murray family I was on friendly terms with. Before disappearing, she'd spent a lot of time in the Murrays' backyard. I couldn't have a pet of my own because of Dad's allergies, so Holly had become my surrogate pup. I used to scratch her head through a broken fence slat. Sometimes I would toss a small ball over, and she would fetch it and bring it back.

"Koko's devastated," Matt went on. "We've had that pooch since before we got married."

"Well," I said, "she's only been gone for a couple of days. She might still come back. I really hope she does."

"I hope so, too. Thanks for asking about her."

I gave a little wave and went on my way.

My neighborhood was a spooky wonderland. I passed yards cluttered with blood-spattered chain-saw killers, animatronic witches, life-sized vampires, and zombies bursting out of the ground. Porches populated with headless bodies and bodiless heads. Gauzy ghosts hanging from tree branches like Spanish moss. Gigantic inflatable spiders perched on rooftops. Most of the decorations would remain in place till at least Thanksgiving—that was how much my town loved Halloween.

When I got to the corner, I saw one of the missing-dog flyers tacked to a utility pole. It included two photos of Holly—a close-up of her grinning little doggy face and a wider shot of her whole body. A reward of fifty dollars was offered for information leading to her safe return.

I really did miss that little pup. The night after my mother told me she'd run away, I'd dreamed about her. In the dream, she was tied to a tree in the backyard of a house in a nearby neighborhood, a light-green house with maroon trim. I remembered wondering why anybody would paint a house such ugly, clashing colors. I was floating in the air, and Holly was barking up at me. Then somebody hollered out a window, "Shut up, you mangy mutt!"

I frowned. Remembering that dream was giving me a funny feeling. The same itchy feeling I'd gotten during this morning's phone call with Logan.

A small, thick cloud abruptly blotted out the sun, and in the grayed-out light, the world around me took on an ominous tone.

A black car with frowny-eyed headlights cruised past, its occupants—vampires? demons?—concealed behind tinted windows.

The season's last insects hummed urgently, like tense violin music in a thriller movie.

My heart pounded. My breath rasped.

I tried to think about other things, happy things—lasagna for lunch, just me and Dad; a movie I'd been wanting to see coming on TV tonight—but my mind kept snapping back to that dream. It had been a tiny, meaningless dream. Not much to offer plot-wise. Why was it thumping so insistently inside me?

You know why, said a firm, quiet voice in my mind.

But I don't.

You do. It's because—

I walked faster, trying to outrace the voice. Knowing I couldn't.

—because there was something different *about that dream.*

No, there wasn't!

Something strange.

"No," I said, as if uttering the word aloud would give it more weight. "It was just a dream. A normal, stupid dream that didn't mean a thing."

Except it didn't feel like a dream.

Yes, it did.

It felt like real life.

That's crazy! It's ridiculous! It's—

Like. Real. Life.

The words slammed into me like three bullets. I came to an abrupt stop.

Like real life. That was how Logan had described his dreams before he'd realized they were out-of-body experiences.

Had the Holly dream been an OBE?

"No," I moaned, sagging against a hefty oak tree in the Hoffmans' front yard.

It wasn't true. It couldn't be. Out-of-body travel was Logan's thing, not mine. I was letting my imagination run wild. My mother always said I was impressionable.

Then again, was it so crazy to think I might have the same weird ability Logan had? After all, we were cousins. Maybe it was a trait we shared, like our thin brown hair and knobby knees.

A violent shiver rippled through me, even though the sun was once more warming the air. The notion that

I might have left my body like a dead person and flown off into the night was terrifying.

And also exhilarating.

Something creaked nearby, a wooden swing suspended from a sturdy tree branch. A skeleton sat in the swing leering at me, a fuzzy black spider peeping out of its eye socket. *You live in Eerie,* the skeleton seemed to say. *Embrace the weirdness!*

I didn't realize I'd started walking again until I glanced down and saw my feet moving. Quickly, purposefully. They seemed to know where I was going, even if the rest of me didn't.

A second later, my conscious mind caught up with my subconscious, and I knew where I was heading. I was on the hunt for that ugly green house. If it existed, if I could find it—and, especially, if Holly was there— well, I would have my answer.

At the next street corner, I glanced around, getting my bearings. The dream had given me a rough idea of where the house was. I set off up the sidewalk, my heart thudding in suspense. I didn't know what I wanted the outcome to be—house or no house? Dog or no dog? OBE or plain old dream? I couldn't suppress a giggle-sob, thunderstruck by the outrageous sci-fi of this scenario. Yeah, I lived in Eerie, but this brand of weirdness was beyond anything I'd ever experienced.

I turned right at the next intersection and quickened my pace to a trot. After four blocks I was still going strong, fueled by my ongoing adrenaline rush.

After two more blocks I came to a street sign— "Sorcery Place." Somehow I knew to turn left. I passed a sign that said, "Dead End." It had a picture of a gravestone on it, like all the dead-end signs in Eerie.

I jogged to the very end of the street, and there it was—one house all by itself up a short driveway, sandwiched between a cluster of mature trees in the front yard and a thick woods in the back. Through late October's thinned foliage I could make out the house's color scheme.

Light green with maroon trim.

I was breathing hard now, more from astonishment than from exertion. I made my way up the crumbling asphalt driveway, hoping my trembling legs wouldn't give out. When I reached the house, I slunk through the side yard, stealthy as a cat stalking squirrels. As I edged around the rear corner of the house, I squeezed my eyes shut.

I knew what I would find in the backyard. I just wasn't ready to see it.

Chapter 8

When I opened my eyes, I saw Holly tied to a tree. She lay on the ground with her head on her front paws, looking glum. I slithered back around the corner before she spotted me. If I knew Holly, she'd start barking her head off the second she laid eyes on me. And then somebody would come bursting out of the house to investigate the ruckus. Maybe with a shotgun—it seemed like that kind of house.

I needed a minute to catch my breath. To at least begin to process the stunning truth I'd just learned. I slid down the side of the house until my butt hit the ground, and there I sat, staring at a smirking, green-eyed witch propped against a nearby tree.

I was a living ghost, just like Logan.

But I couldn't dwell on that now. I needed to figure out what to do about Holly. Should I go get Matt? Call my dad? Grab Holly and run?

I almost went with option three but in the end chose a fourth—appealing to the people who lived here. I intended to take Holly with me today, now, but I didn't want to be sneaky about it.

I got to my feet, uncomfortably aware of the cool dampness that had seeped through the seat of my jeans. The ground was still wet from the hard rain we'd had yesterday morning, though I hadn't thought about that when I'd sat down.

I plodded toward the front of the house, trying to work out what to say. Talking to strangers wasn't my thing, and even if it was, this would be a tough conversation. What if they refused to hand over Holly? What if they hauled out that shotgun and shooed me off their property?

I figured it would help my case if I had one of Matt's flyers to present as evidence. Holly's face was mostly whitish, but she had a splotch of gray fur above her nose, a sort of doggie birthmark that established her identity. I remembered seeing one of the missing-dog flyers a block or two back. I retraced my steps and untacked it from the utility pole. Then I jogged back to the ugly green house on Sorcery Place.

The porch was cluttered with junk—a cracked toilet, a broken lamp, some rusty mechanical thing that might have come out of a car. A worn, mildewed couch sat where most people would have put a swing.

I rang the doorbell and waited. When nobody answered, I rang again, three times in rapid succession. Finally the door swung open.

Framed in the doorway like living art was a boy of about sixteen in maroon pajama bottoms and a threadbare white undershirt. He held a cell phone. I thought I'd seen him around, though I didn't know his name. He might have played flashlight tag with us once or twice, back in the days of Logan. He had a tangle of dark hair and a browbone that jutted out like a visor, shadowing his eyes. A sour odor wafted from him, a combination of morning breath and needs-a-shower. I took a discrete step backward.

"Hi my name is Abby you have my neighbors' dog tied up in your backyard and I've come to take her home," I said, the words rushing out in one long, unpunctuated string. I rose on tiptoes to make myself more imposing. "She's a Yorkshire terrier. Her name is Holly."

I held up the flyer, but the boy didn't see it. He was thumbing away at the keypad on his cell phone.

"Yeah, I don't know nothing about that." His voice was still raspy with sleep. A musical tone sounded. He grinned at his phone and did some more thumbing. "You'd have to talk to my sister. It's her dog."

"Yeah, see, that's the thing. It's *not* her dog."

No response. This guy was totally into his phone.

I cleared my throat and spoke a little louder. "Can I talk to your sister?"

"She ain't home."

"How about your parents?"

"My dad's home, but he's sleeping. And, trust me, you don't want to wake him up after he's worked the night shift. Try back later, okay?"

He started to close the door. I stepped forward, thrusting the flyer in his face. "That dog in your yard belongs to my neighbors," I said firmly. "She ran away a couple of days ago. I'm here to take her home to her rightful owners."

I never said things like "rightful owners." I was glad I'd thought of it. It made me sound authoritative, like a police officer or a lawyer.

With a resigned sigh, the boy slipped his phone into a pocket of his pajama bottoms. He took the flyer out of my hand and studied it. "Okay, yeah, this does kind of look like her. But, hey." A defensive tone crept into his voice. "We didn't know she was somebody's dog. We figured she was a stray. My parents said my sister could keep her as long as she fed her and cleaned up her poop and stuff."

"Well, tell your sister thanks for taking care of her. I'm going to go get her now. Okay?"

I inched backward, hoping he wouldn't fight me on this. Praying he wouldn't wake his sleeping father to come deal with me.

The boy peered at me from his shadowed eyes. He said, in a grudging tone, "I'll be glad to see her go. Mangy mutt never stops yapping. My sister, though—she ain't gonna be too happy."

I shrugged in a not-my-problem kind of way. I heard the door shut as I tromped down the porch steps.

Holly was overjoyed to see me. She kept springing up to paw my thighs, muddying my jeans in the process. She yipped like crazy as I untied her from the tree. She was small enough for me to carry, though at first she was so wiggly with glee, I could barely hold onto her. She wouldn't stop licking my face, my neck, my ears.

I race-walked up the sidewalk, intent on getting Holly home before she could squiggle out of my arms and dash away again.

Two blocks from my street, I saw somebody up ahead loping down the sidewalk. As the distance between us shortened, my heart bounced into my throat and then plopped to the depths of my stomach.

Austin Oliver was headed my way.

Austin was a high school junior, which meant he attended classes in the senior high building. Whereas I was stuck at the junior high building, two miles away. Austin lived three blocks down my street, close enough that our addresses were similar but far enough away that I rarely saw him. He'd occasionally participated in our neighborhood games, though he'd stopped showing up a year or two ago. Logan said he'd outgrown us.

I hated the mute, quaking blob I turned into when Austin was around. I could never think of a thing to say. Except for today! Today I had lots to say, a riveting tale to tell. Today, finally, I could make Austin see what a take-charge, fascinating girl I was.

Abby Kendrick, hey! I haven't seen you in ages.

Oh. Hi, Austin.

Did you get a dog? Hi, poochie!

Actually, she isn't my dog. Holly, no! Sorry, she likes to lick people's faces. Holly belongs to my neighbors. She ran away a couple of days ago, and I just found her.

That's great! How'd you find her?

Well, I was taking a walk, and I recognized her bark and followed it. I found her tied up in somebody's yard. They were planning to keep her.

Oh, wow. How'd you get her away from the people who took her?

I just went to the door and told the guy I was taking Holly back to her rightful owners. And then I went in the yard and took her.

Wow, Abby, that was so brave. Hey, mind if I come with you? I'd love to see your neighbors' reaction when you show up with their dog.

Of course. They're going to be so happy.

And after that, would you maybe want to have lunch with me at Ghastly Gabe's? My treat. I think it's time we got to know each other better, don't you?

Austin, that would be lovely...

Austin was staring at his phone as he walked, his

golden-brown bangs hanging over his eyes like drawn curtains. When we were a few yards apart, he must have heard my feet thudding up the sidewalk. He glanced up. His blue gaze met my brown one. Something electric zinged through me.

I put on my most dazzling smile and came to a stop. "Austin—hi!"

"Hey." It was barely a word, more of a mumble. He ambled on by, his eyes already back on his phone.

I stood there for a minute, trying to remember how to breathe. My armpits were damp. My heart was thumping. Another unrealized conversation disintegrated like brittle autumn leaves.

Did Austin even know my name? Was I nothing to him but a vaguely familiar neighborhood face?

Would I ever have a boyfriend, let alone a husband?

I buried my face in Holly's soft fur, seeking comfort there. When she let out a muffled yelp, I realized I was squeezing her too tightly. I released my grip and set off again, trying to push Austin out of my head. I forced myself to focus on the joyous reunion ahead.

Matt had been busy. A pile of leaves sat in the front yard, and the rake was propped against a tree, though Matt himself was gone. I rang the doorbell.

Matt opened the door. His gaze went from my face to the squirming bundle in my arms. "Oh my God. I can't believe it. Oh, Abby!"

He leaned into the house and yelled, "Koko! Get over here!"

He pushed open the screen door, tears glistening in his eyes. "Come here, Holly, you bad girl!"

I handed over the wriggling dog. Matt gestured me into the house, but I shook my head. I could see past him to a brown leather couch that was nothing like the blue and tan plaid sofa I'd curled up on so often with Logan to watch movies or play video games. I looked away, wishing I could unsee it.

"What's up, hon?" Koko pattered barefoot to the door, baby Morgan nestled in the crook of her arm. When she saw Holly, she let out an ear-piercing shriek. The baby jerked, arms flailing, and started bleating frantically. "Oh, Holly!" cried Koko. "I thought you were gone for good!"

Matt and Koko did an awkward switch—he took the wailing baby while she gathered Holly into her arms. They thanked me over and over. They wanted to know the wheres and hows of the rescue. I told them the untrue story about how I'd been walking in a distant neighborhood and recognized Holly's bark.

Matt held up a forefinger. "Don't go anywhere." He disappeared into the house. When he came back, he thrust two twenty-dollar bills and a ten at me. The reward money. I protested, because that was the polite thing to do, and tried not to look too relieved when Matt insisted I take the money.

"You've earned it, Abby. If it wasn't for you, we probably wouldn't have gotten her back."

"Come over anytime to play with Holly," said Koko. "She really loves you!" She giggled as Holly fidgeted in her arms, straining toward me.

"Well, I love her, too," I said, giving Holly's forehead a vigorous scratch.

Chapter 9

"That is utterly astounding," Dad said, a forkful of lasagna poised midway between his plate and his mouth. "Recognizing a pooch by its bark? I don't think I could do that."

"I play with her through the fence sometimes," I said. "I guess I've just gotten to know her bark really well."

My mother came home as we were loading the dishwasher. "Hey, guys. Have you eaten? I've got half a turkey club and some leftover fries you can fight over." She rustled a white paper bag, trying to entice us.

That was Leah Kendrick in post-quarrel mode. No apologies, no conciliatory hugs. Just pretend everything is back to normal, and pretty soon it will be.

"Thanks, I think we're good," said Dad, patting the slight paunch above his beltline.

My mother tossed her restaurant bag into the fridge and turned abruptly, aiming both forefingers at me like an Old West gunslinger. "Hey. We need to start planning your birthday party. Have you thought about a guest list?"

All the good feeling from the Holly rescue drained out of me. I'd known this was coming. I just wasn't ready for it.

Every year from kindergarten on, there'd been a joint birthday party for Logan and me. A big party, with lots of guests and a noise level loud enough to cause hearing loss. The parties had been held at various venues over the years—Logan's house, my house, the roller rink, a video arcade. Last year we'd rented a laser-tag facility, and people had said it was our best party yet.

This year? Forget it. No way was I doing the party scene without Logan.

"You know what I'd really like?" I said, doing that obnoxious double-forefinger thing right back at my mother. "A nice, cozy family celebration. Just us and Grandma and Uncle Cody. I was thinking we could all go out to dinner."

My mother's eyes went unfocused, and I knew she was trying to think of something to say that wouldn't steer us back into last night's argument.

"Sure, we can do that," she said in a tentative tone. "In addition to the usual party."

"The usual party?" I snorted. "What would be usual about it? Logan's gone."

"But you're still here." She moved closer, invading my personal space. I took a step backward.

"I know you miss Logan," my mother went on. "I miss him, too. But you deserve a party, just like any other year. I was thinking we could rent the fire hall and hire a DJ. Wouldn't that be a great way to ring in your fifteenth birthday?"

"The fire hall! A DJ! What a fabulous idea!" said Dad. But I heard the dismay in his voice. Dad hated spending money, and *DJ* plus *fire hall* was bound to equal *expensive.* Especially since we no longer had Logan's parents to split the bill with.

My arm muscles were throbbing, and I realized I'd

been clenching my fists. I shook my arms to loosen the kinks. "I don't want a big party. It's *my* birthday. I should get to choose how I celebrate it."

"But parties are so much fun," said my mother.

"For *you*."

"Think of the food, the music, the—"

"Opportunities for socializing?"

"*Presents*," said my mother, her eyes blazing. "I was going to say *presents*."

Dad moved to her side. She made a gesture like she was literally handing something over to him. A problem named Abby. Now Dad was the one trying to figure out what to say. My mother and I stared at him, waiting for his paternal words of wisdom, and finally he offered, with an apologetic shrug, "We just want you to have a good birthday."

Now that was a statement I could work with. "Great! That's what I want, too. Glad that's settled." I grabbed a banana from the fruit bowl on the counter and scurried off to my room.

I slammed my door and laid the banana on my dresser. If I got hungry, it would tide me over till dinnertime. I was not leaving my room till then.

I flung myself onto my bed so hard the box springs groaned. I stared up at the ceiling, my chest heavy, my limbs loose. I was exhausted—physically spent from all the running around I'd done today, mentally weary from the stunning events of the past twenty-four hours. The levitating jacket, the fight with my mother, Logan's revelation, our subsequent fight, my realization about my own OBE, the Holly rescue, the encounter with Austin, and now a possible birthday party. It was too much.

I wished I wasn't mad at Logan. I needed to talk to somebody about this out-of-body business, and he was the only person who would understand. I had so many questions.

How many OBEs had I had? Surely the Holly incident hadn't been the only one. My heart thumped as I thought back on my dreams from the past month or so. I couldn't deny it—some of them had been tinged with that same vivid quality as the Holly "dream." Most had been undramatic, forgettable, and so I hadn't given them much thought. But now that I knew the truth, it seemed clear that they'd been experiences, not dreams.

Like the "dream" I'd had a few nights ago. Not much to it—I'd been wafting around on the front porch like a dying helium balloon, and I'd watched Matt drive up and take a box of disposable diapers into his house.

Another time I'd been at my grandma's house, watching her sleep, which was even less exciting than watching Matt bring diapers home.

My heart jolted as I recalled a third instance. A few weeks ago, I'd dreamed I was at a sleepover at Sophia's house, and Emma and Lanie were there. I'd never been to Sophia's house, but in the dream I could see every detail of her bedroom. The matching white-wood furniture, the royal-purple bedspread and curtains. The hardened blob of orange nail polish on the bottle-cluttered dresser. The odd combination of rock band posters on the wall and stuffed animals on the bed, as if Sophia couldn't decide whether to advance through teenhood or go back to being a little girl.

The three of them were sitting on Sophia's bed, their gleaming heads bent over last year's yearbook, and they were writing COOL or NOT COOL above everybody's picture. I was kind of floating above them. I kept trying to throw in my two cents, but they wouldn't pay attention to me.

I was startled when my name came up. "Guys, seriously? I'm right here." But they didn't seem to hear.

"Fill in the blank," said Sophia. "Abby Kendrick is..."

"Quiet," said Emma.

"Mean," said Lanie.

"Weird," said Sophia.

Those three words hung in the silence that followed, heavy as fruit rotting on a tree. I didn't even try to defend myself. I had no words.

"I get *quiet*," said Sophia, twirling her purple pen between her fingers. "But *mean*?"

"Trust me." Lanie's nasal voice scratched at my eardrums. Nails on a chalkboard, that voice. "She's sneaky about it, so maybe you've never seen it."

"Why'd you say *weird*?" Emma asked Sophia.

"Because of that, like, sad look she's got going on." Sophia made her eyes big and drooped her mouth, demonstrating. "And because she doesn't have any friends." She looked from Emma to Lanie. "I mean, does she?"

"Abby's too weird to have friends," said Lanie.

"Hey!" I said crossly. "I sit with Pia Hockenberry every day at lunch."

They ignored that.

The truth was, I wouldn't have called Pia a friend. Outside of school, we never hung out. We didn't call or text each other. Pia had a boyfriend in a different school district and spent all her free time with him. Every day at lunch, she yakked on and on about Boyfriend and the wedding she was already planning. She never showed the slightest interest in me or anybody else, which was probably why no one but the socially desperate would sit with her at lunch.

"Guys, let's just decide." Sophia moved her pen toward the yearbook page. "Abby Kendrick—cool or not cool?"

The dream had ended there. Except now I was ninety-six percent sure it hadn't been a dream.

I wondered how they'd rated me. Had Lanie talked the others into NOT COOL?

Lanie Chobany. God, how I hated that girl! And yet I needed her approval, because Lanie wasn't just Lanie. She was part of Sophia-Emma-Lanie, the three-headed monster that ruled the school. Those girls had power. If they considered you NOT COOL, other people did, too—at least the ones who were too wishy-washy to think for themselves.

I might have a chance of getting into Emma's and Sophia's good graces, but Lanie was never going to like me. And that was a problem.

The trouble between us dated back to first grade, to that day in art class when I'd drawn a blue cloud in a white sky instead of a white cloud in a blue sky because I didn't want to color the whole big sky with my broken stub of blue crayon, and Lanie told me my picture was stupid. And I said right back to her, "*Your* picture is stupid, and so is your hair!"—because while all the other little girls, including me, came to school with our hair braided or pony-tailed or banana-curled, and embellished with barrettes and ribbons and colorful scrunchies, Lanie's hair was always unadorned and in need of a good combing—and that was the part Mr.

Grandy heard, and he yelled at me.

Things never really got better between us. In the lower grades, Lanie mostly ignored me. By the beginning of fourth grade, the Sophia-Emma-Lanie alliance had been formed, and if Lanie paid me any attention at all, it was to give me contemptuous sideways glances while whispering in Sophia's or Emma's ear. Lanie did a lot of whispering in grade school.

And yet she'd been popular, even back then. Maybe it was her name that drew our classmates to her. People liked the built-in rhyme, so they said it a lot, which meant Lanie Chobany was constantly on the tips of our tongues, at the forefront of our awareness, and…and…

Whoa.

I was on the ceiling. Suddenly I was on the blinkin' ceiling, and I had no idea how I'd gotten up here or how to get down.

What the heck?

A moment ago, I'd been lying there thinking my thoughts, but now somehow I'd shrugged off gravity like an astronaut on a space mission. I was staring down at a girl on a bed, a sleeping brown-haired girl wearing mud-crusted jeans and a hoodie, who looked a little bit like me.

Actually, a lot like me.

Holy crud, it *was* me! The sleeping girl was me!

I must have dozed off. I was so exhausted, I'd fallen asleep, and now—

Now I was having an out-of-body experience.

Chapter 10

For the longest time I stared down at the sleeping girl. I stared, and then I wondered how I could be staring when I didn't have eyes. I was up here. My eyes were down there. With *her*.

The girl slept on, never stirring, breathing deeply. Arms and legs akimbo, hair spread out like disconnected wires, mouth hanging open. Was that how I looked when I was sleeping? It wasn't pretty.

Something twinkled below me, a translucent silvery cord tethering me to my body. I'd never noticed it in my dreams-that-weren't-really-dreams, maybe because I hadn't realized I was out of body. The cord, thick and round as Italian sausage, was weird but reassuring. I assumed it would keep me from getting lost, because no matter where I went, I could simply follow it back to my body.

But how did the cord work? Was it retractable like the cord on our vacuum cleaner? Stretchy like a bungee cord? If so, how far could it stretch? All the way to the moon, apparently! I wanted to test it for myself, but before I could do that, I needed to figure out how to move. For now, I was stuck in place like a stalled weather front.

A few nights ago, I'd traveled all the way to Sorcery Place. I'd gone to Sophia's house, to Grandma's. How had I done it?

More important, how could I get back into my body? I gave a psychic grunt, straining toward that sleeping form, but nothing happened. I was anchored to the ceiling as firmly as my physical body was anchored to the bed.

What if I couldn't get back? What if I was stuck up here forever?

Now I was in full-blown panic mode. I was totally helpless. Paralyzed, voiceless, nothing more than a disembodied tangle of thought.

Time passed—five minutes or ten or maybe an eternity. Gradually, I started to calm down. My thought processes dialed back to rational. I'd left my body before, and I'd always returned. The same thing would happen this time.

I needed to believe that.

The forced-air heat came on with a gushing sound, and I went wafting across the room, borne by that artificial breeze. I bobbed above my desk, staring at the poster of the solar system mounted on my wall.

Knowing what it felt like to move was helpful. Now I just had to figure out how to do it on my own. I thought about how athletes were taught to visualize success. I concentrated hard and finally felt myself rotate—slowly, like a ship changing course. I heaved a big *oomph* and finally started to drift toward my bedroom door. Success!

I winced as I approached the closed door, expecting to bump into it and bounce back to the center of my room. But that didn't happen. I wasn't a balloon—I was a spirit. I had no substance. I passed right through that solid wood.

Now I was in the hallway, moving a little faster. I

remembered learning to roller-skate as a child, those early days at the rink when I'd clunked along at a snail's pace, veering in unplanned directions and colliding with people. I'd fallen down a lot. But I'd gotten better with every lap.

I would get better at this, too.

My parents were in the family room, sitting at opposite ends of the couch. My mother flipped through a magazine while Dad worked a crossword puzzle in the book I'd given him for his birthday. It was a comfortable domestic scene, one that temporarily assuaged the divorce fears that were always simmering at the back of my mind.

Every few minutes, my mother piped up, recounting some intriguing bit of gossip she'd learned from her lunchtime friend, and Dad said, "Hmm, interesting."

I flitted in front of them, waving my arms. "Mom? Dad?"

No response. It was obvious that they couldn't see or hear me.

I was invisible to myself, too. I waved a hand in front of my face but saw nothing, not even a shadow. I kicked my legs out in front of me. Nothing. The silvery cord leading back to my physical body was the only part of me I could see.

My mother looked up from her magazine. "Joe, what are we going to do about Abby's birthday? I think it's so important for her to have a party this year. She needs to start building a life without Logan."

I fully expected Dad to murmur, "Hmm, interesting," which would have proved he wasn't listening. Instead, he said, "We can't force her to have a party. I think we should give her the space she needs to figure this out on her own."

My spirit swelled with gratitude. *Thanks, Dad.*

My mother turned several magazine pages in quick succession. "The thing is, I've already booked the fire hall."

Dad looked up from his puzzle book. "What?"

"I had to, Joe. The fire hall is a really popular venue. People snatch it up six, eight, nine months in advance. I didn't call the reservations manager till August, and I was darned lucky they'd just had a cancellation in December. It's two weeks past her birthday, but I figured *close enough.*"

Dad slapped his puzzle book shut. "You've had the fire hall reserved since August and you never told me? Or Abby?"

"I guess it slipped my mind."

"Slipped your mind?" Dad's voice grew louder. "Come on, Leah. Things don't slip your mind. You're sharp as a tack."

My mother pursed her lips as if trying to decide whether to thank him for the compliment or bristle at the accusation. In the end, she did neither. "Okay, okay—I didn't tell Abby because Logan had just moved away, and I knew she wasn't in the right frame of mind to think about her birthday. And I didn't tell you because—because…"

Dad raised his eyebrows, waiting.

The rest of the sentence came out in a rush. "…because I had to make a nonrefundable deposit and I knew you wouldn't like that."

Dad's eyes got very narrow. "How much of a deposit?"

"A hundred dollars."

"Jesus," muttered Dad. "If you wanted to throw away a hundred bucks, why didn't you just flush it down the toilet? That would have been easier."

My mother pressed her lips together, nodding bitterly. "I knew you'd freak out."

"You bet I'm freaking out! Who wouldn't?"

"Somebody who isn't a tightwad." She mumbled the words, but loudly enough for him to hear.

"Oh, here we go again. That's me, the big, bad tightwad."

"Admit it, Joe. You don't want to throw Abby a big party because of the expense."

"Expense has nothing to do with it. I only want what's best for Abby."

"Sure you do. It just so happens what's best for Abby is also good for your wallet."

Dad tossed his puzzle book onto the coffee table with so much force that it slid the whole way across and dropped to the floor. "I will not apologize for being careful about money. Did you ever think maybe you're the problem? Your spending sprees, your extravagant tastes? If I didn't rein you in, you'd bankrupt us."

"Bankrupt? Oh my God. What a gross exaggeration."

They glared at each other. If they'd been two alley cats, their tails would have been switching, their ears flattened against their heads.

After a minute, my dad said in a thin voice, "What's happened to us, Leah? We're partners—we're supposed to make decisions together. Remember how things were when we first got married, all those long talks we used to have? We had our whole marriage mapped out, how it would work, all the great things we'd do together."

A long silence followed. I watched my mother's posture soften in a way that made me think of a wicked witch melting into a puddle. She said, "You're right, Joe. You're absolutely right. I'm sorry. I should have talked to you before I rented the fire hall."

Dad shot her a suspicious look, like he wasn't sure she meant it. Leah Kendrick rarely backed down that quickly. But she looked genuinely contrite, her head bowed, hands folded in her lap. The fire faded from Dad's eyes. He shifted his body around so he was facing her more directly.

"I didn't expect the nonrefundable deposit to be an issue," she went on, "because I never imagined we'd end up canceling. But you're right. Abby would hate us if we forced her to have a party."

Dad reached out to clasp her hand. "It's okay. A hundred bucks won't make or break us. I'm sorry I got so worked up."

"You don't have to apologize. You had every right to get worked up."

I glided hastily to my room as they moved in for a kiss. Didn't need to see that! I returned to my spot on the ceiling and stared down at my sleeping self.

Knowing I was off the hook for the party was a big relief. But it spurred an interesting counter-thought— *would a party be so bad?*

I'd done the party scene with Logan enough times that I knew the drill. Surely I could handle it alone. I would never be as popular as my cousin, but maybe it was time to remind people that although Logan was gone, Abby was still here, a person in her own right. A person who knew how to throw a party.

And the party wouldn't have to be totally Loganless. I could call him on my mother's laptop and let all the party guests talk to him.

I returned to my body abruptly with the sensation of being sucked through a tunnel. Suddenly I was lying on the bed with my eyes open, staring up at the blank ceiling.

I sat up slowly. I felt groggy and unsettled, like someone recovering from a fever. But I remembered every bit of what had just happened. And I knew it hadn't been a dream.

I ran my hands over my arms, patted my cheeks, wiggled my toes. Everything seemed to be intact and working properly. And really, what had I expected? It wasn't like I'd teleported from a starship and left pieces of myself behind.

I grinned at the empty air. OBEs were amazing! I couldn't wait to have another one.

Chapter 11

Over the next week, I had an OBE just about every night. Knowing I had this ability seemed to have brought it fully to life. My spirit was eager to roam.

The first two nights I stayed in my house, wafting from room to room as I got more comfortable with my spirit form. I zoomed from the front door to the back. I haunted the attic. I infiltrated the locked cabinet in the garage, where I found one of my birthday presents—the boots I'd been wanting.

On the third night I ventured outside. At first I hovered above my roof, too nervous to go farther. I found that if I went totally limp and still, air currents would toss me around like an empty grocery bag.

That was fun, but only for about two minutes.

Eventually I left my roof and drifted down the deserted street. On a whim, I veered into the Martinezes' house. Everybody was asleep, the youngest child sprawled across the middle of her parents' bed while her mother and father clung to the edges. I left in a hurry when the family dog padded into the room and started growling at me.

I worked my way down the street, visiting random houses. Most people were asleep, though a few were watching late-night TV or hunched over laptops, their faces illuminated by the flickering bluish light.

I hovered outside Austin Oliver's house for the

longest time before deciding to go in. Austin was asleep on top of his bed covers, wearing only a T-shirt and underpants. My whole spirit blushed, but I couldn't look away. He was snoring loudly, his mouth hanging open. Austin, a snorer? I never would have thought. He seemed above it somehow.

I flitted around his room, snooping. His bookcase contained the entire *Harry Potter* series and some sports biographies. But the shelves and the books themselves looked dusty and abandoned, as if Austin didn't do much reading these days.

On the dresser was a framed snapshot of Austin with his arm around Gabriella Fitz, both of them squinting in bright sunlight. They'd dated over the summer, but I'd heard they'd broken up a few weeks ago. Why did he still have her picture on his dresser? Wasn't he over her yet?

I moved back to the bed and hovered above Austin's face. What bliss to just gaze at him. This boy was as elusive as a wild animal. He'd lived a few blocks away from me my whole life, yet we barely knew each other. We'd never really talked, except in my imagination.

So, Austin. Ever been there?
Been where?
Austin, Texas, silly!
Oh, right, ha-ha. No, I've never been there.
You should go.
I should, shouldn't I? I mean, I was named for the place.
Right?
No, you know what? We should go together, you and me.

What? All the way to Texas?

Yes, yes—let's take a road trip, just the two of us. I've been wanting to spend more time with you, Abby. I guess I've always wanted to. I was just too shy to—

Austin stirred, and I gave a guilty start. He couldn't see me, but what if he sensed my presence, the same way Holly and the Martinezes' dog had? In a mild panic, I zoomed out of the house.

I hung out on Austin's roof for a while, appreciating the owl-like night vision my astral eyes afforded. There wasn't much going on in the neighborhood—everyone was in for the night. Eventually my gaze drifted to the moon. A thin cloud diffused its light, the same way a lampshade would.

Euphoria swept me as I realized I could go there. I could go to the moon. Or beyond! Logan had launched himself into space, and I could do the same anytime I wanted.

Except…except the moon was so far away! I knew the exact distance—238,855 miles—because that was one of the facts I'd memorized in my space-obsessed days. I shuddered at the thought of traveling so far from my body. And at the same time, I thought, *Someday I will go there.*

Heading back up the street, I saw a light in an upper window of Mrs. Benson's house. I melted through her walls and found her in bed, holding a framed, faded photo of a bride and groom. I was disconcerted to see that she was crying—silently, forcefully, tears streaming down her cheeks. I felt a stab in my heart as I realized this was her own wedding picture, taken decades ago. She was crying over her dead husband, gone for nearly a year.

I slipped back outside, suddenly ashamed of myself for spying on my neighbors, observing them in their most private moments. Not that I meant any harm. The universe had given me this power. Surely I was meant to use it.

On the fourth night, I ventured farther from home, and with the whole world spread out before me, I went a little crazy. I rocketed from one end of my street to the other, a trip that took a split second. I soared above rooftops, a strange, invisible bird caught between the starry sparkle of the sky and the twinkling lights of the town. I did loop-de-loops. I zoomed down the length of the river that divided our town into a good section and a bad section and hovered under a bridge like a hummingbird, inches from the rippling water.

Eventually I ended up at Sophia's house. If I'd had any doubts that my previous visit was an OBE, they vanished the second I saw those royal-purple fabrics, the white-wood furniture, the rock band posters on the wall.

It had really happened—the yearbook ratings, the things those girls had said about me.

Quiet.
Mean.
Weird.

Sophia was asleep, bedcovers pulled up to her chin. I flitted around like a moth until I found the yearbook. It was on her desk, partially hidden under a pile of beauty magazines. I tried to push the magazines away, first through force of will and then by ramming them with my spirit-self. Neither method worked.

I flew home in frustration. I needed to see what Sophia had written above my picture, but I wouldn't be able to do that unless I learned how to move objects. I knew it was possible. Logan had done it.

I spent Saturday afternoon doing Internet research. I entered various search terms—"how to move objects during out-of-body experience," "interacting with the physical world during astral travel"—but the results weren't helpful. The closest thing I found was a how-to article about telekinesis.

That night, before I went to bed, I lined up some objects on my dresser to practice on—a hairbrush, a pen, a paperback book. Over the next few days, I spent all my OBEs trying to move those objects, using the tips in the telekinesis article. But I couldn't get so much as a bobble from any of them.

It looked like I was going to have to talk to Logan.

I hadn't planned to make up with him so soon. I wanted him to stew in remorse for a while longer. But I really needed to get into that yearbook, and Logan was the only person who could help me do it.

On Sunday afternoon I shut myself in my room and made the call.

"Hi, it's me. You want to hear something crazy?"

Chapter 12

"No way," said Logan. "Are you serious? This is crazy!"

"Told you."

"And you're sure these aren't just dreams?"

"Hundred percent."

"This is insane! It's wild! Incredible!"

I let him go on like that for a while because it felt good to shock him. After he stopped exclaiming, I said, "You realize what this means. This thing runs in our family."

There was an airless silence, like he'd stopped breathing. He said, in a dazed voice, "I thought it was just me. I thought I had, like, a birth defect or something. But you're right. It has to be hereditary."

"So who do you think we got it from—Grandma or Grandpa?"

He let out a short laugh. "Somehow I can't picture either one of them flying around Eerie in their pajamas. Not that they ever did. This is probably like certain diseases. Not everybody gets the disease—some people just pass the gene on to the next generation."

"Disease," I repeated. "Is that what you think this is?"

"No, Abs. I'm just making a comparison. I'd say it's more like a gift."

For a while, all I heard was our breath, his and

mine, flowing in and out in perfect rhythm. Then Logan said, "Oh wow!"

"What?"

"This astral projection thing, this gene or whatever it is—I'm betting it goes back a lot further than Grandma or Grandpa. It probably goes back to the very beginning of Eerie."

I knew right away what he was getting at. "All that paranormal stuff!"

"People claimed they saw pots and pans floating in the air, doors slamming by themselves. A flag marching down the street like someone was carrying it. But it wasn't witches or poltergeists, like everybody thought. It was—"

"—somebody having fun with out-of-body experiences," I finished breathlessly.

Our family's roots in Eerie went deep, all the way back to the town's earliest days. In fact, the founder, Rupert Kellerman, was Grandpa's direct ancestor. Our town had originally been called Kellerman Springs, though that name had lasted only a few years. The paranormal goings-on had earned it the nickname *Eerie*, and pretty soon everybody was calling it that. Eventually, Eerie became the official name.

"Looks like we got this from Grandpa," said Logan.

"Grandpa." I said his name like a caress, picturing his kind, ruddy face. "Do you think anybody else in the family has it? My mom, your mom, Uncle Cody?"

"If they do, they're not letting on."

"Maybe some of our distant relatives have it." Distant relatives were the only kind we had. Grandpa had been an only child and so had his father, so we had no immediate relatives on that side of the family.

"Maybe," said Logan. "But those families moved out of Eerie generations ago. I wouldn't even know how to track them down."

He started to say something else but then interrupted himself with a muffled yell. "Be right down!"

To me, he said, "Sorry, Charlie just got here. We're going over to the school to shoot hoops with some other guys."

This was nothing new. Even when Logan had lived in Eerie, he'd often gone off with his guy friends, leaving me behind. I'd never liked it, but that was how it was. Now that he was 2,500 miles away, I didn't like it any better, though part of me recognized how irrational that was.

"Well then," I said. "I guess you have to go."

"In a minute. Have you told anybody else about your OBEs? Your parents?"

"God, no."

I felt the same way Logan did. My parents would freak out if they knew what was happening to me. They'd consider it dangerous. They'd take me to doctors, trying to get me "cured." I'd be poked, probed, turned inside out. Written about in medical journals. Treated like a lab rat.

I heard a drawer slide open and thunk shut. I pictured Logan's nicked-up oak dresser and wondered if he'd pulled out the sweatsuit I'd given him last Christmas. He'd worn it a lot while he still lived in Eerie. Did it still fit?

Logan said, "So, uh, I guess you're speaking to me again. Does this mean you're done being mad?"

I didn't answer right away. I wanted him to think I was still deciding. Finally I said, in a begrudging tone, "I guess."

"Look, I'm not going to say I'm sorry again, because that seems to make you mad. But I promise, I will never do anything like that to you again. Okay?"

"Okay." And, really, all the steam had gone out of my mad. It was silly to stay upset over something that had happened more than a week ago, something that had been scary while it lasted but had turned out fine in the end.

"Before you go," I said, "can you tell me how to move things? Like you did at my house with the pillows and the jacket and stuff?"

"Oh, that. It's not too hard. It just takes concentration and practice. You know what helped? Thinking about brain hockey."

"Brain hockey?"

"Remember? That game we played at the science museum when we were, like, ten?"

"Oh, right."

Brain hockey involved two people seated on opposite sides of a table. Both were hooked to a device that measured electrical signals from their brains. The players tried to move a small ball across the table, using only their brain waves. The first one to get the ball across the other player's goal line won.

I'd won the first game. Logan had won the second.

"I mean, it's not exactly like that," said Logan. "You're not actually using brain waves. But the way you concentrate is basically the same. Just try it. When you want to move something, focus on it like you're playing brain hockey."

"Thanks. I'll give it a try." I hesitated and then decided to end the call on a gracious note. "Hey, have fun with your friends."

But I was still jealous of my cousin's booming social life.

Chapter 13

Once you know how to do something, it seems easy, no matter how hard it was to learn. Like whistling. Riding a bike. Or moving objects when you don't have hands.

Using the brain hockey method, I mastered object-moving in a single session. I'd probably been trying too hard before. Concentrating in that brain hockey way forced me to relax my mind. I went from not being able to move things at all to doing it every single time, with ease.

On Friday night I celebrated my new ability by going to Austin Oliver's house and turning the picture of him and Gabriella Fitz face down on his dresser. Then I visited Sophia's house, intent on opening that yearbook. It was only a little after ten, but she was already in bed, rustling around under the covers. I couldn't even be sure she was asleep. I was afraid to move anything because what if I made noise? I was a spirit, not a ninja. I needed to do this when she wasn't in her room.

I didn't feel like going home yet, though I couldn't think of anywhere else I wanted to go. Maybe back to Austin's house for another imaginary conversation?

As I glided down my street, I saw a sparkly golden light hurtling toward me from the direction of my house. Before I could so much as flinch, the thing was directly in front of me. It stopped abruptly, as if it had slammed into an invisible wall.

"Hi, Abby. I've been waiting for you."

"Holy crud!" The sparkly thing was Logan! It looked like physical Logan, only translucent. And twinkly. Like a Logan-shaped jellyfish decorated with tiny white-gold Christmas lights. "What are you doing here?"

"I came to hang out with you."

Oh, that big, goofy grin! It had been too long since I'd seen it.

I drifted backward so I could take in the whole of him. "You're, like, all lit up and golden."

"That's my aura. Yours is a peachy shade, really pretty like a sunset."

"But how is it we can see each other?" This jellyfish version of Logan was wearing blue plaid pajama bottoms and a long-sleeved white tee. "That night you put on Dad's jacket you were totally invisible."

"That's because you were in the physical world and I was on the astral plane. Tonight we're both on the plane."

"I can't see myself, though." I waved an invisible hand in front of my face to reconfirm.

"Yeah, so when you're in the physical world and you look at something, you can't see your own eyeballs, right? On the astral plane, it's like your whole being is your eyeballs. That's how Jakob explained it anyway."

"Jakob?"

"A buddy of mine. Another astral traveler."

I looked at him in surprise. "You've met other

astral travelers?"

"Haven't you?"

"You're the first."

"Really? I mean, okay, you might be the only one in Eerie. But in other places, especially bigger cities—"

"I haven't been to any other places."

"Abby, Abby," he chided. "What are you waiting for? You can go anywhere. *Anywhere.* Come on, let's take a trip. Where do you want to go?"

"Now?"

"You got something better to do?"

"Not really." So where did I want to go? The moon came instantly to mind, but I still wasn't ready to venture into space, not even with an escort. Maybe a theme park? No, you needed a body to make the most of a place like that.

"How about Mount Rushmore?" I said, because it was on my list of Places to Visit Someday and was closer than the Great Wall of China.

"Rushmore it is."

"Wait. Are you sure my cord thingie will stretch that far?"

"You mean your sutratma?"

"My *what*?"

"Sutratma. The cord that connects you to your body. Don't look at me like that. It's a word. And, yeah, it'll stretch as far as you want to go."

I looked at the empty air surrounding Logan. "You don't have one."

"Sure I do. You just can't see it. You can only see your own. And don't ask me why, because I don't know."

I studied my sutratma, reassured by its sturdy

presence. It was thick like the braid that often trailed down Lanie Chobany's back. Silvery as fish scales but translucent. And constantly flickering, going nearly invisible one moment and emitting glints of light the next. It seemed durable, unbreakable. Impervious to any influences from the physical world. I traced it back to where it disappeared through the exterior wall of my house. Back to where physical me lay sleeping.

"Okay," I said. "Let's go."

Chapter 14

Moments later we were hovering in front of the four stony-faced presidents. I drifted from head to head, studying the intricate details. The hollowed eye sockets, the sculpted noses. "Wow," I finally said, feeling the inadequacy of that word even as I spoke it.

Artistic ability had always seemed like a superpower to me, mainly because it was a talent I didn't have. I couldn't imagine how Rushmore's creators had transformed a stony mountain into a dazzling work of art. They would have had to use clunky drilling equipment, not the delicate chiseling tools sculptors usually used. How had they gotten the enormous faces so perfect?

"It blew me away the first time I saw it, too," said Logan. "Take your time. I'll be on top of George's head."

I spent another minute marveling and then flew up to join Logan. We hadn't been together—physically together—for nearly five months. A surge of elation zinged through me as I realized we could hang out every night if we wanted to. When we'd been about six and joined-at-the-hip inseparable, we used to run around yelling, "Cousin power!" Astral travel was giving us the chance to recapture that closeness. To reclaim our cousin power.

"We should make this our regular meeting place," I

said. "Like, anytime I'm traveling, I'll stop here. You do the same. Then we can hang out."

"Yeah, maybe." He gazed into the night sky. Wistfully, like that was where he wanted to be. "But we won't always be traveling at the same time. It might not work out."

I quirked an eyebrow at him. I'd expected a little more enthusiasm. "Still. We should try."

"Sure. We can try."

We hovered in silence for a few minutes, taking everything in. The massive stone faces below us, the distant hills, the velvety sky. The moon was in one of its chopped-off phases, though it was bright enough to illuminate a passing cloud. *The moon*, I thought dreamily, wondering if I'd ever gazed at it when Logan was up there gazing back.

Logan said, "So, Abs. Have you been having any, uh, issues since you started traveling?"

"Issues?"

"Sleep issues. Like, trouble waking up after an OBE?"

"I don't think so. Have you?"

"Yeah, sometimes. Mom signed me up for a sleep clinic."

I looked at him uneasily. "All this traveling can't be good for our health. Think about it—are we getting a good night's sleep if part of us is out roaming the world?"

"Probably not. Still, roaming the world is a lot more fun than lying in bed unconscious for eight hours, wouldn't you say?"

"Sure. We just need to make sure we're not overdoing it." I shrugged. "Not that we can stop OBEs from happening."

"Actually—" He broke off, like he wasn't sure he should continue. But then he did. "There is a way."

"There is?"

"Yeah. Sleeping pills. Jakob told me about it. If you take a sleeping pill at bedtime, you won't have an OBE."

I did a quick mental inventory of my family's medicine cabinet. "Does p.m. ibuprofen count as a sleeping pill?"

"It should. I mean, it's supposed to help you sleep."

"Great. I can't wait to try it!"

I beamed at him, pleased to have an easy solution to an issue that had been troubling me—some nights I just wanted to sleep, not travel—but he didn't grin back.

"Have you tried it?" I asked, though I was ninety-five percent sure I knew the answer.

He gave me a wry look. "You know I don't do drugs."

"It's not drugs. It's just ibuprofen."

"Which happens to be a drug."

Logan was totally anti-drug, always had been, and his list included everything from baby aspirin to cocaine. As a small child, he used to clamp his lips shut when his mom tried to give him that delicious pink ear-infection medicine. I'd always offered to take his doses, but Aunt Lisa wouldn't take me up on it.

I said, "But if there's a chance it would fix your sleep issue—"

"The sleep issue isn't that big of a deal. It's only happened a couple of times." He rose into the air, like a magician's assistant levitating. "Hey. You ready to see some other places?"

He took me to the Australian outback, which was flat and desolate but populated with kangaroos and wild horses and types of birds I'd never seen before. We hung out there while I got Logan caught up on school gossip—who was dating who, which teacher had been spotted staggering out of a bar, who'd been passed over for a part in the school play.

Then we went to the tippy-top of the Alps, where there wasn't much to see except endless craggy peaks and barren white slopes. We did a swan dive into the clean air and zoomed down, down, down, riding an invisible roller coaster past isolated farmhouses and tiny Swiss villages and lakes made of blue glass. We startled a flock of sheep grazing on a hillside, and they dashed away like a single body.

"Where to next?" Logan asked as we soared back into the sky. "Any requests?"

I thought that over. "How about Paris?"

"Paris! The most romantic city in the world." He threw me a teasing look. "Have you been watching old romcom movies again? That one with Meg Ryan you like so much?"

"No," I shot back, though that was a lie. I'd watched *French Kiss* on TV two nights ago—maybe that was why Paris had come so readily to mind. "People are always talking about Paris. I want to see what all the fuss is about. Besides, I'm taking French in school, so Paris seems like someplace I should visit."

"Sure. That's fair," said Logan. "Me, I love the city—the old buildings, the museums, the whole vibe of the place. I go there a lot."

Moments later, we were perched atop the Eiffel Tower. The city sprawled below us in every direction, teeming like an ant colony. Skyscrapers jutted up in the distance, the same kind you'd see in any large American city. But closer to the Tower, the buildings were different—short and white and ornately embellished. They had an ancient dignity about them, and a firmness, too, as if they'd been there for so long, they'd put down roots.

The River Seine sparkled in the morning sun. Boats of various sizes floated along, keeping a respectful distance from one another. From up here, they looked like toy boats in a bathtub. The people roaming the streets were meandering dots. I wondered how many were lovers strolling along arm in arm. I wondered if I would ever have a lover to stroll arm in arm with.

"So, what do you think?" asked Logan. "Is Paris everything you imagined?"

"It's hard to tell from up here," I said, "but so far, I—"

I didn't get to finish that thought, because someone yelled, "Logan! Finally!" And then a giant bird sped toward us from below.

Except it wasn't a bird. It was a spirit, a boy a year or two older than us with light-brown hair and eyes that were gray or hazel or green or maybe golden-brown. I couldn't be sure, because he was looking at Logan, not at me.

I studied him in fascination. Like Logan, he was translucent and sparkly, though his aura was tinted a delicate purple that made me think of the lilac bush that bloomed every spring in Grandma's yard. He was wearing navy-blue silk pajama bottoms but no shirt. My gaze wandered to his bare chest, lean and muscular, and got stuck there.

It occurred to me that if an astral traveler slept in the nude, that was how they'd appear on the astral plane. Yikes! I made a mental note never to fall asleep in the bathtub.

"I've been looking all over for you," the spirit-boy said. "For weeks now." Reproach tightened his face. "Please tell me you haven't been—"

"Jakob, so good to see you, bro!" said Logan, plowing right over his friend's talk. "You're sleeping late today. What is it—like eight, nine a.m. here in Europe?"

"Something like that."

"How are you doing? What have you been up to?"

Jakob folded his arms, making it clear he wasn't interested in chit-chat. "I've been worried about you. Where've you been?"

"Oh, you know. Here and there."

"Yeah? Me too. Been visiting all our old haunts, looking for you. Strange we haven't run into each other till now, wouldn't you say?"

"Not really." Logan's eyes darted around, landing everywhere but on Jakob and me. "Your time zone is six hours ahead of mine, so we're not always going to be on the astral plane at the same time. And even if we were, what are the odds we'd show up at the same place? When you think about it, it's amazing we even met."

Jakob's lavender tint deepened into violet, making me think of the 1970s mood ring my grandma kept in her jewelry box. He said, "You've been going back there, haven't you? After we agreed not to. Damn it,

Logan!"

I couldn't stay silent any longer. I sailed into their airspace and said, "Going back where? What's he talking about, Logan?"

Jakob turned his gaze upon me. I saw that his eyes were light brown with golden flecks. The color was warm. The look he was giving me was not.

He said to Logan, "Who is this?"

Logan grinned contritely. "Sorry, I suck at introductions. Jakob, this is Abby—my cousin. Abby, meet Jakob."

"That's *Jakob* with a *k*," said Jakob, glowering at me like I'd already misspelled it.

"Jakob's from Germany," Logan went on, his congenial tone contrasting with Jakob's testy one, as if they were actors reading from two different movie scripts. "Rothenburg—right, bro?"

"Yes, Rothenburg," muttered Jakob, clearly peeved that the conversation had swerved back into chitchat territory.

I offered a tentative *hi* and, trying to jumpstart a friendlier vibe, said, "Germany, huh? You speak English really well. You don't even have an accent."

Jakob snorted. "I'm not speaking English. I'm not speaking any language. I'm not even speaking." He gave Logan a scornful look. "Doesn't she know anything?"

"Hey!" I said, scowling fiercely. I whirled toward Logan, waiting for him to put this rude interloper in his place, but all he said, with an apologetic *heh-heh*, was, "Abby's new to astral travel."

To me, he said, "Astral communication transcends language, Abs. That means all astral travelers can talk to each other, no matter where they come from or what language they speak. Of course, we're not actually talking. Astral communication is basically telepathic. It feels like real talk, though. All the inflections are there. Like, if you whisper, it comes across as a whisper. If you scream, it's a scream."

He flashed a charming grin, but I was in no mood to be charmed. "You could have told me that sooner. How am I supposed to know stuff like that?" My words were aimed at Logan, but I glared at Jakob as I said them.

Jakob's attention was back on Logan. "We talked about this. We agreed we wouldn't go back."

"No," said Logan. "You said we shouldn't go back. I never agreed."

"Go back where?" I asked again. "What's this about? Logan, are you in danger?"

"No," said Logan.

"Yes," said Jakob.

I glanced from Logan to Jakob, trying to decide who to believe. I couldn't make up my mind. With their crossed arms and mirror-image sneers, they looked equally convinced of their own righteousness.

"Oh my God," I said. "Will somebody please tell me what's going on?"

"What's going on," said Jakob, "is that your cousin has been playing astronaut."

I met his stare head on. "So?"

His eyebrows went up. "You knew about this?"

"I know he's gone to the moon."

Jakob gave a derisive laugh. "He's gone a lot farther than the moon."

"Oh?" I turned to Logan. He was staring off into

the distance, his aura pulsing like a car's four-way flashers. "Logan? Where else have you gone?"

"Where he's gone is only part of it," said Jakob. "The other part is what he's been doing there."

"Okay. What's he been doing there?"

Logan shook his head, a nearly imperceptible movement I wasn't meant to see. Jakob saw it. He said to me, "Why don't you go to Versailles?"

My whole spirit bristled. "Go to Versailles? Is that the European way of saying *go to hell*?"

"No, it's the European way of recommending a popular tourist site."

I blinked at him. "You want me to go sightseeing?"

"If you're going to visit Paris, you should see Versailles. It's the palace where Marie Antoinette—"

"I know what Versailles is. I'm just not going."

"Someplace else, then. A museum, an art gallery. Paris has plenty of both."

"No." I wafted close to Logan's side and folded myself up like a yoga instructor. "I'm staying right here."

"Fine," said Jakob. "You stay. Logan and I will go elsewhere."

"No," I said again, sounding to myself like a belligerent toddler. "I'm sticking with my cousin. Wherever he goes, I go."

Jakob's spirit seemed to grow puffier, like a male beta fish facing an adversary. "Logan and I have business to discuss."

"Really."

"Private business. It doesn't concern you."

"If it concerns Logan, it concerns me."

"That's where you're wrong."

Our gazes locked. His was made of iron, mine of steel. I felt the spark of metal striking metal.

"For your information, *Jakob-with-a-k*"—I spat the name out like a mouthful of watermelon seeds— "Logan and I don't have secrets from each other. Do we, Logan?"

Logan gave me a pained look. "Abs, just wait here, okay? I'll be back in a couple of minutes."

I gaped in outrage. Jakob smirked in triumph. Before I could say another word, he and Logan sped off, heading God knew where.

I zoomed round and round the Eiffel Tower, trying to burn off my fury. Eventually I calmed down and stopped flitting, though uneasiness still burbled inside me like greasy soup. Once we got rid of Jakob, I would talk to Logan. I'd always been able to get the truth out of him, even when he didn't want to give it up. He would tell me what was going on.

What was taking those guys so long? I surveyed the air around me and the city below, trying to spot them, and ended up distracting myself. Paris really was lovely. Even from up here I could feel its energy pulsing like blood through invisible veins. I wondered what it would be like to be here on a honeymoon…

Where do you want to go next, Austin? Versailles? A museum? An art gallery?

Anywhere is fine, my love, as long as I'm with you. I can't believe I'm in Paris with my new wife! I love you so much.

And I love you. *Or as the French say,* je vous aime.

Hey, you want to take a boat ride down the Seine?

That sounds lovely. After that, let's have lunch at that quaint little café we passed.

Perfect! And then we can go back to our room for a little—

Something bumped me so hard I went flying. It took me a few seconds to glide to a stop and whirl around.

Jakob was floating a few yards in front of me, that maddening smirk back on his face.

"What the blinkin' heck?" I yelled.

"You're welcome."

I stared at him in outrage. "You want me to thank you for knocking me halfway across France?"

"No. But you might thank me for saving you from *that*."

I followed his gaze and saw something strange wafting nearby. Not a bird, because it was the wrong shape, the wrong size. Not a drone either. And it didn't look like a spirit because it wasn't sparkly. But what else would be floating through the air at the tippy-top of the Eiffel Tower?

A soft winter wind blew, nudging the thing in a new direction. Now it was heading back toward me.

"Get out of the way, Abby," called Logan, appearing at Jakob's side. "Trust me, you don't want to bump into that."

I edged backward. I was close enough to get a good look as the thing breezed past.

"Oh God." I clamped a spirit hand over my spirit mouth.

I was ninety-six percent sure I knew what the thing was.

Chapter 15

The floating thing was another spirit, an elderly white-haired man, except this spirit wasn't bright and sparkly. It was as gray and dark as an unplugged lamp.

Logan floated over to me. "Do you know what that is?"

"A dead spirit?" I said, wincing.

"Yeah."

We bowed our heads in an impromptu moment of silence.

"So that's an actual ghost?" I said. "The kind that haunts houses?"

"Maybe. Probably. We call them lost souls."

"Where's he going?"

"Nowhere. Anywhere. He's probably trying to find his way to wherever he's supposed to go next. Sometimes deceased spirits get trapped in the physical world and can't move on."

The lost soul was still moving through the air, aimless as a bee separated from its hive.

"I've seen that guy before," said Jakob, drifting over to us. "He just travels around Europe, searching. Mostly here, though. I think this is where he died."

I found this unbearably sad. "Can't we, like, tell him to go into the light or something?"

Jakob snorted. "That wouldn't work. The dead, they're not like us. We can't communicate with them.

They don't even seem to be aware of us."

I watched helplessly as the dead spirit floated to the ground and disappeared into the milling crowd.

"Why'd you tell me to get out of the way?" I asked Logan. "What's so bad about running into a dead spirit?"

Jakob replied. "Dead spirits mess up your energy. Turn everything inside you dark. I've never experienced it, but an Italian guy I know did a few months back. Hasn't been the same since. He's moody, depressed. Sits home all day with the blinds drawn. I hope he'll get over it, but who knows?"

"That's scary," I said.

"The astral plane is a scary place. There are hazards. Not everybody is cut out for astral travel, even if they have the ability." He was staring pointedly at me now, that faint smirk back on his face. "Some people are better off spending their nights at home, safe in their bedroom."

Some people. I gave him a murderous look and said, "Why don't you go to Versailles."

He let out a hearty laugh, this one free of scorn. It gave me a hint of what Jakob-behaving-decently must be like, if such a creature even existed. "I've been there many times, thank you. But I do need to be getting home. Grandmother will soon be barging into my room to sweep me out of bed with her broom." He turned to Logan and said stiffly, "I hope you'll think about what I said."

"I hope you'll think about what *I* said," Logan replied, just as stiffly.

"So lovely meeting you, Jakob-with-a-k," I said, making sure the sarcasm came through, but Jakob was gone before I'd finished. To Logan I said, "Wow. That guy is a jerk."

"Jakob? No, no, he's basically a good guy. He's just a little snarky at times."

"A *little* snarky? The guy is *all* snark."

"He's taught me so much about the astral plane. His older brother's a traveler, too, so he's learned a lot from him. And he has a good heart, he really does."

"If you say so." But I wasn't buying it. Logan tended to see the good in people, even when there wasn't much good to be seen.

We hovered in silence for a while, watching the endless movement of the city below. I hated to fracture the quiet with talk, but our time together was coming to an end, and there were things I needed to say. Things I needed to hear.

"You know you can tell me anything, right?" I said. "I mean, we've always told each other our deepest secrets."

"When we were little, sure." He threw me a look that was two parts love and one part pity. "Did you really think we'd keep doing that forever?"

Ouch. I hung my head and watched a line of beetle-sized cars creep across a bridge. "Yeah," I said softly. "I guess I did."

"But you have secrets from me."

I frowned. "Not really."

"You like Austin Oliver."

"What! That's not true!" I hoped he couldn't see the blush spreading across my translucent face.

"You've never told me, but I know. That's okay. You're allowed to have secrets."

"I do not like—" I started, and then gave it up.

93

There was no fooling Logan. I let a few seconds tick by and asked, "What are you doing in outer space that Jakob doesn't think you should be doing?"

Now he was doing that darty-eyed thing again. "Nothing. Don't listen to what Jakob says."

I floated in front of him, trying to capture his gaze. He kept dodging me. "He said you might be in danger. He said—"

"I'm not in danger," Logan snapped. "Can we stop talking about this?" He brushed past me, heading west. "It's late. I'm going home, and you should probably do the same. Good night, Abby."

And then he was gone.

Chapter 16

I got up late on Saturday, ate a piece of toast, and went back to bed for a few hours. I was exhausted, and I had no doubt it was because of Friday night's whirlwind tour of the world. When you exercised really hard, your muscles were sore for days afterward. I felt like my spirit was sore.

All weekend Logan's secretiveness niggled at me like a rogue hair that had worked its way down my shirt. What was he up to on the astral plane? Why wouldn't he confide in me?

I texted him five times on Saturday and six times on Sunday, demanding to know what was going on. I thought I could wear him down, but after the first few messages, he stopped responding. I tried to call him on Sunday evening—three times—but he didn't pick up.

I took p.m. ibuprofen on Saturday night, and it worked just as Logan had promised—not a single OBE fractured my sleep. Sunday night, though, I skipped the ibuprofen and spent my OBE searching for Logan. I checked all the places we'd visited together but couldn't find him anywhere.

On Monday I reluctantly set my worries aside to focus on school and the yearbook situation. Mostly the yearbook situation. I was determined to solve the mystery of COOL versus NOT COOL, but first I needed to find out when Sophia would be away from home.

All week I tailed Sophia, Emma, and Lanie discreetly through the halls, straining my ears toward their conversations. Sixty percent of the time, all I heard were the sibilant sounds of whispering. Those three had a lot of secrets.

But on Thursday, I finally caught a break. I heard them making plans to go to a movie on Friday evening.

"What's wrong? Are you sick?" my mother asked when, a little after seven p.m. on Friday, I announced that I was going to my room for the night. She came at me with her hand raised, trying to feel my forehead. I ducked away.

"I'm not sick. I'm just going to read."

"Read!"

She looked so dismayed that I had to ask, "What, you'd like it better if I was sick?"

"Of course not. I'm just thinking you should go out instead. It's Friday night. Surely there's something going on at school. A dance, a sporting event, *something*?"

"No, Mother, there's nothing. Anyway, I have a book report due on Monday, and I have to finish reading the book."

Actually, I'd already finished the book *and* the book report, but she didn't need to know that.

I went straight to bed, though I left my bedside lamp on so my parents would see the strip of light shining under my door and assume I was reading.

Thursday evening I'd guzzled full-strength iced tea, which had kept me awake until after midnight. This morning I'd forced myself to get up at five. I'd spent a miserable day at school dragging myself from class to class, struggling to stay awake during the more boring lectures. But tonight the sleep deprivation was paying off. I conked out within minutes. When my OBE started, I flew straight to Sophia's house.

Sophia's room was unoccupied—at least it looked that way at first. Then I saw, in the glow from the lavender nightlight, a cat sleeping on the bed, a long-haired white cat as dainty and well-groomed as Sophia herself. The cat's head jerked upward, her ears turning toward me like radar antennas. She stared, intent and distrustful, at the spot where I hovered. I tried to beam friendly, cat-loving vibes at her, and after a minute she furled herself back into a tight circle, apparently satisfied that I was harmless.

I flitted to the desk. The yearbook was still there but was buried under layers of Sophia's possessions—a rumpled sweatshirt, a backpack, the pile of magazines. I lifted the sweatshirt into the air, intending to move it to the desk chair. It looked spooky drifting by itself through the air. On a whim, I slipped it on.

I glided to the mirror and watched with amusement as the disembodied sweatshirt waved its arms and clutched its missing head. I almost wished Sophia was here to see this. She'd be freaking out, just like I had the night Logan had spooked me with Dad's jacket.

It was weird, I thought, that I still felt like I had arms. And hands and legs and feet. *Ghost limbs*—that was what they called it when somebody lost their legs but could still feel them. Sometimes those missing legs even ached.

I didn't just have ghost limbs. I had an entire ghost body.

I flitted back to the desk and released my hold on

the sweatshirt, letting it flop like a carcass onto Sophia's desk chair. I tried to ease the backpack to the floor but lost my grip, and it dropped with a soft *whump*. I froze, waiting for someone to burst in to investigate the noise, but no one came. The cat didn't even look up.

Finally I reached the layer of magazines. I was straining toward them, ready to slide them away, when I heard a voice from close by.

"Abby!"

Chapter 17

"Abby. Abby! Come on, Abby—wake up!"

Whoosh! Talk about a rude awakening. Suddenly I was back in my body. I opened my eyes. My parents stood on either side of my bed, pale-faced and wide-eyed.

"Oh, thank God!" my mother said, pressing both hands to her chest.

"Wh—what's going on?" I asked groggily.

"You wouldn't wake up!" It sounded like an accusation, but I knew she was just worried. "We've been standing here for five, six minutes, shaking you, calling your name. We were ready to call 9-1-1."

"No, no, don't do that," I groaned. I glanced at my bedside clock. It was a quarter till eight.

"Are you sick?" Dad pressed a hand to my forehead. "You don't have a fever."

"I was just really tired. I woke up early today and couldn't get back to sleep." I sat up slowly. "Why were you trying to wake me up?"

"Uncle Cody's here," said my mother. "We wanted to see if you'd like to join us for a game of rummy. I didn't expect you to be asleep, because you said you were going to read. When you wouldn't wake up, I got scared."

"There's nothing to be scared about," I mumbled. "I'm just a really deep sleeper."

They were still staring at me, clearly unconvinced. My dad wouldn't stop wringing his hands.

"Uncle Cody's here?" I swung my legs over the side of the bed. "I haven't seen him for ages. And, yeah, I'm up for some rummy."

Getting dressed wasn't necessary because I was already wearing a T-shirt and sweatpants, my standard sleepwear. I'd sworn off pajamas years ago, having had enough of the cutesy prints my mother insisted on buying.

I cast a wistful glance at my bed as I left the room. I was too wired to get back to sleep anytime soon, but maybe later, after Cody left, I could complete my mission.

"Hey, Minutia," Cody greeted as I plodded out of my room. He must have been hovering in the hallway the whole time, keeping his distance as he waited to see whether an ambulance would need to be summoned. He gave me a quick hug.

"Stop calling her that ridiculous name," my mother snapped.

Cody just smiled. He'd been fourteen when I was born. I was only the second newborn he'd ever laid eyes on and by far the smaller. Logan had entered the world at over eight pounds, whereas I was barely six.

Cody hadn't realized that *minutia* meant "trivial details." He'd thought it meant "something tiny." At that stage of his life, he was big on assigning nicknames—his best friends were Goggs, Jabber, and Wormhead—and he decided that Minutia would be a fitting name for his new little niece.

He called Logan Rump Roast, because Logan had been very red and meaty at birth.

My mother should have saved her breath. Cody wasn't going to quit with the nicknames, and, really, I didn't want him to. I liked *Minutia*, the queenly heft of it. Besides, the meaning sort of fit, considering what a details-oriented person I was.

We walked to the kitchen two by two, Cody and me leading the way. We were practically shoulder to shoulder—he was just an inch or two taller. But what Cody lacked in stature he made up for in good looks. His face was a work of art, perfectly proportioned, with eyes like pools of molten chocolate, a small tight nose, and straight white teeth. Oh, and that lush crop of auburn hair. Aunt Lisa accused him of shampooing with rhododendron fertilizer.

"Well. That was interesting," Cody said to me with a wry grin. "Looks like you found a fun new way to mess with your parents."

"That's why I did it."

"Seriously, though. Does this happen a lot?"

"No, like never."

"Except tonight it did."

I shrugged like it was no big deal. But I remembered Logan telling me he sometimes had trouble waking up after an OBE. Was this going to be a new problem for me?

My mother fetched beverages for everyone—milk for me, a beer for Dad, sodas for her and Cody. Dad emptied a bag of store-brand potato chips into a bowl. A deck of cards sat in the middle of the table. I shuffled and then speed-dealt seven cards to each of us.

During the first hand, all three grown-ups kept throwing me anxious glances. Dad finally said, "You sure you're okay, sweetie?"

"I'm fine!"

"No headache, no stomachache—nothing like that?"

"Oh my God. Can we please just drop this? And will you all quit staring at me like I'm an aneurism about to burst?"

"Okay, okay." Dad held up his hands, palms out, as if begging not to be shot.

"How's everything going?" my mother asked Cody.

"Yeah, how's work?" Dad added.

"Work—is—great." Cody slapped three jacks down on the table. "I've been with Innovec for almost a year now. The money's good, and I think I've found my niche with cybersecurity."

"So you like that better than network administration?" Dad asked.

"Please," said my mother, pretending to groan. "You two aren't going to go off on one of your IT tangents, are you?"

Cody gave her an indignant look. "Of course not. I need to focus on the game so I can beat you poor saps."

Cody and Dad both worked in information technology, so they always had lots to talk about— WANs and WAPs and defrag ops. They did it at family gatherings, and it drove the rest of us crazy. Grandma usually banished them to a remote corner of the house where nobody could hear them—"You can come back when you're ready to speak English like the rest of us."

"So," said my mother. "Aside from work, everything's going well?"

"Yep," said Cody. "Rummy," he said, a second later, after my mother discarded a seven of diamonds.

My mother swore and then winced in my direction like she hoped I hadn't heard. Cody played the card on the four-five-six I'd laid down a couple of turns back.

Cody won that round, and I won the next. My parents fell further and further behind, and soon it was a contest between Cody and me. Cody ended up beating me by ten points.

By now it was a little after nine, and I was starting to get sleepy again. Dad invited us to join him in the family room to watch an action movie that had just started, but everybody declined. Cody checked his watch and said he had to leave. Amy was waiting for him.

My mother, whose eyelids had been drooping toward the end of our game, perked up. "Amy? Who's Amy?"

"Uh, my girlfriend?" said Cody.

Dad said to Mom, "You remember—we met her at Dirk and Lisa's Memorial Day cookout. Nice girl," he said, nodding at Cody.

Cody gave an awkward laugh. "That was Allie. This is Amy. Whole different girl."

"Well, when are we going to meet her?" asked my mother. "Is it serious? How long have you been seeing her? Where'd you meet her?"

"Soon," said Cody. "Yes. Five months. At a friend's party."

It took me a minute to match answers to questions.

When Cody asked my mother to walk him to his car, something in his voice snagged my attention. He was trying too hard to sound casual. I scurried to my room, which was at the front of the house, near the driveway. I kept the light off and silently slid my window up a few inches. Cold air wafted in along with two voices.

"—driving me crazy," Cody was saying. "She's always barging in, coming down the basement stairs without knocking. I need to get out of there."

"I agree," said my mother. "It's time you had your own space."

Cody lived at Grandma's house, though technically not *with* Grandma. When my grandpa was alive, they'd turned their basement into an apartment that they were planning to rent out. But Grandpa died just a week after the renovation was complete. Grandma, a scared and lonely new widow, didn't want a stranger living below her. Meanwhile, Cody was between jobs and short on money, so he moved into Grandma's basement. He'd been there for over three years.

"Last weekend," Cody said, "she caught Amy and me in, shall we say, a compromising situation."

"Oh dear."

"Yeah. Next morning I got a lecture about 'sins of the flesh.' "

"Why don't you put a lock on the door so she can't come down? It's your place. You're entitled to your privacy."

"But it's not my place. It's hers. I have no say in where the locks go."

"But if you're paying rent—"

"I'm not. I've tried to give her money, but she won't take it."

My mother laughed bitterly. "Of course not. As long as you're indebted to her, she gets to call the shots."

Cody said, "So listen, I need a favor. A big one.

There's this apartment I want to get, but they want first and last months' rent, plus a security deposit. I have most of it, but not all. Do you think you could spot me a loan?"

"How much?"

"A thousand bucks. I'll pay you back within the next month or two, I promise. I'm in good shape, finally getting my finances in order. I just paid off the last of my debts and made a big down payment on my new car. That's why I don't have enough cash for the security deposit."

My heart panged in sympathy because there was no way we could afford to give Cody a thousand dollars. So I was shocked when my mother said, "Sure, no problem. I have to run over to Ma's tomorrow. I'll bring you a check."

"Thanks a bunch, Lee. I owe you one."

"I'm just glad to see you getting back on your feet. I know it hasn't been easy."

"Yeah. But I'm doing better." A pause, then: "You sure Abby's okay? Is she always that hard to wake up?"

"No, no, she's fine. It's like she said—she was just extra tired tonight."

I heard a pattering sound as Cody walked to his car. "Hey. Cody?" My mother called softly. "Don't tell Joe about the loan, okay? He has some oddball notions about money. I'd rather he didn't find out about my secret stash."

"Not to worry," said Cody. "Your secret is safe with me."

Chapter 18

What the blinkin' heck.

So my mother had a secret stash of money, enough that she could afford to hand out a thousand dollars as casually as she might lend somebody a book? How, where, and when had she gotten it? She was an office administrator at the Community Foundation of Eerie, a nonprofit organization that didn't pay much more than minimum wage. I knew because she was always griping about the low salary.

The fact that my mother was keeping secrets from my dad was troubling. I'd figured the nonrefundable fire hall deposit was an isolated incident, but obviously that wasn't the case. And this was so much worse! I could only imagine how Dad would react if he found out his wife had secret savings, not to mention the fact that she was lending a chunk of it to Cody. Dad felt that any extra cash should be socked away for my college education or for his and Mom's retirement.

Then there were the other curious comments, about Cody getting back on his feet. When had he been off his feet, and why?

With these new issues to think about, I expected to have trouble falling asleep. I surprised myself by drifting off almost immediately and slipping into an OBE shortly afterward. Two in one night—that was a first. I zoomed off to Sophia's house.

When I entered her bedroom, I saw that the cat was gone, though a circular indentation on the bedspread marked the spot where she'd been sleeping. I moved to the desk and slid the stack of magazines away. At last, the yearbook was exposed.

I hesitated, gazing down at it. Eager to open it. Terrified to.

I reached down and flipped open the cover. The book's spine creaked like the door to a haunted house. The inside cover and front pages were crowded with handwritten messages from last year.

"Sophia, to a super hot girl. Hope you have a summer as amazing as you are. Darius."

"Hey, girl, it's been real. Never forget those crazy times in Brosky's class! Luv ya! Kinsey."

Et cetera, et cetera.

I flipped slowly through the book, trying to minimize the crisp sound of pages turning. When I reached the eighth-grade section, I followed the alphabetized listings to my name, my picture. And finally, there it was.

Abby Kendrick.
NOT COOL.

Chapter 19

Saturday morning, I woke up feeling like somebody had double-knotted my intestines and then tied the dangling ends into a tight bow. *NOT COOL* had been with me all night, prickling at my subconscious. Now it was all I could think about.

I didn't know which burned stronger—my anger at Lanie or my grief over the general situation. I'd totally expected NOT COOL from Lanie, but knowing that Sophia and Emma had agreed was a wallop to the gut. I hadn't realized till now how much their opinion mattered to me.

I hated Lanie Chobany. I really and truly hated her. She would pay for this, I vowed.

Midmorning, looking for a distraction, I went next door to play ball with Holly. But her heartfelt doggy kisses didn't cheer me up.

At lunchtime, my mother brought home a pizza covered in my favorite toppings—sausage, mushrooms, and green peppers. Even that didn't cheer me up.

I spent the afternoon in my room, a tornado of thought whirling in my head as I alternately paced around my bed and sprawled across it in anguish. By dinnertime, I'd come up with a plan.

That cheered me up.

I was itching to get started, but the next three nights passed without an OBE. Was I trying too hard?

Was my subconscious trying to tell me something—like, don't do it? If so, I didn't want to hear it. I was going through with my plan whether my conscience agreed or not.

On the fourth night, an OBE started around midnight. I rose triumphantly from my body and sped off into the night.

Lanie lived on Apparition Avenue, a street in the poshest section of town. The big, glamorous houses were owned by the Eerie elite—doctors and lawyers and corporate CEOs. Most of the residents sent their kids to private schools, which made me wonder how Lanie, whose father was a doctor, had ended up in a lowly public school.

I figured her bedroom was upstairs, but I glided in at ground level just to nose around. The place reminded me of a lobby in an upscale hotel, not that I'd ever been to one. My knowledge of how the other half lived came strictly from TV shows and movies.

Smooth white columns held up the ceiling and separated the gleaming kitchen from the spacious living area. A glittering chandelier dangled like jewelry above a dining table made of rich, dark wood. The couches were pristine white boats floating on a sea of lustrous hardwood.

I spent a minute imagining I lived here—and then remembered I didn't. The knot in my stomach tightened. Why did a beautiful house like this have to be wasted on a nightmare like Lanie Chobany?

I wafted upstairs. The first bedroom I entered was unoccupied but looked like the habitat of a teenage boy. Black walls, lots of video-game posters, a beanbag chair designed to look like a deflated soccer ball. The next room was occupied by a sleeping girl of six or seven. The third room contained Lanie's parents, facing away from each other like bookends and snoring loudly.

I found Lanie in the fourth bedroom, curled on her side in a bed that would have comfortably accommodated triplets. The room was decorated in shades of cream and palest pink, in fabrics ranging from delicate lace to shimmery satin. It was a room fit for a princess.

I hovered over the bed, staring down at Lanie. Sleep had erased the day-sneer from her face, making her look innocent and unspoiled. Worthy of her royal furnishings. But I wasn't fooled. The cruelty was still there, hidden like black rot inside a picture-perfect piece of fruit. That was why I didn't feel bad about what I was about to do.

I moved to the dresser. It was cluttered with makeup, including half a dozen tubes of lipstick. I found one in a dark shade that would work nicely and raised it to the mirror above the dresser. Then I hesitated, suddenly uncertain.

I'd been planning to write JERKS DIE on Lanie's mirror because I wanted to scare the living poo out of her, but now that I was here, that seemed extreme. I mulled over some options and decided on JERKS GET THEIRS. I wanted to let her know that her behavior had been noted and deemed unacceptable. As for who had done the noting and the deeming—I would leave that up to her imagination. That would be part of the fun.

Moving objects was one thing. Writing on a mirror was another. I should have practiced at home. My lettering was shaky and uneven, like a three-year-old's first attempt at printing. But it was legible, and that was all that mattered.

I'd just finished scrawling the K in JERKS when a car alarm shrieked somewhere down the street, startling me. I lost my grip on the lipstick, and it clattered down on the dresser, even noisier than that car alarm. Crud.

I heard a whispery breath as Lanie awoke. I watched in the mirror as she pushed herself to a sitting position, peering groggily around the dim room. I picked up the lipstick and rushed to finish my message.

The bedside lamp flicked on. Lanie gasped.

I hadn't planned on having her witness the writing of the message. I'd wanted it to just be there when she woke up. But I couldn't stop now. I scrawled the last few letters and set the lipstick tube on the dresser.

Lanie leapt from the bed with a strangled cry and raced out of the room. I followed. She stumbled down the hall to her brother's room and flung open the door. A sob bubbled from her throat when she saw he wasn't there.

She crept back up the hall to her parents' door and raised her hand to knock. But something stopped her. She lowered her hand and bowed her head. For a minute she just stood there, small and hunched, breathing in a shallow, ragged way that made me think of pneumonia.

Hovering above her, I felt more like a spectator than a participant. As if I was watching a horror movie on TV. Except I wasn't rooting for the victim.

Lanie sent a fearful glance toward her room and raised her hand again. This time she knocked. She waited for half a minute, her ear pressed to the door, but no one called to her. She knocked again, louder. Still no response.

She turned the doorknob and stepped into the dark bedroom. Raspy snores drifted from the left side of the bed.

"Dad? Dad, wake up!"

The snoring didn't falter.

"Dad!"

A husky female voice rose from the right side of the bed. "Lanie? What the hell."

"I need my dad."

"Your dad has an early surgery tomorrow."

"There's something in my room. A ghost or…something."

"A ghost? What are you, five? You had a nightmare."

"No, no, it wasn't a nightmare. Come see, I'll show you—"

"Go back to bed."

"No, listen, something really scary is going on. Please, can I wake Dad up?"

"No!"

"Please! I just need somebody to—"

"Oh my God. If you aren't out of this room in five seconds—"

Lanie let out a sob and left the room, pulling the door shut behind her. She leaned against the wall, despair emanating from her like musk. After a few minutes, she slunk up the hall to her bedroom and peeked around the doorjamb, wild-eyed as a spooked colt.

She dashed to her desk and grabbed a pair of scissors, which she held in front of her like a weapon. The room brightened degree by degree as she walked around turning on lamps.

Then the search began. She dropped to her knees and peered under the bed. She opened the closet door and looked up and down, left and right. She strode across the room and disappeared into her bathroom. I heard thuds as she slammed cabinet doors, a swish as she swept the shower curtain aside.

She scurried back to her nightstand and picked up her cell phone. Swiped at the screen and tapped some keys. "Oh, thank God you answered! I am *freaking out*. Something was in my room, something or somebody, like, *invisible*, and they... What?" She glanced at the clock on her nightstand. "Yeah, I know. I'm sorry, but listen! This is serious. Something was in my room and— What? You're what? Hello?"

She huffed and tapped in another number. She stood perfectly still for fifteen seconds, the phone pressed to her ear. Then she threw the phone on her bed with a cry of frustration and turned to face the mirror. She pressed a hand to her mouth.

She fetched a roll of paper towels and a bottle of window cleaner from her bathroom and sprayed the mirror until it was dripping. She scrubbed away every trace of those lipsticked words.

When she was done, she grabbed her pillow in one hand and the creamy satin bedspread in the other. I followed her out of the room.

She tottered silently down the hall, past her parents' bedroom, dragging the bedspread behind her. She moved slowly, like a sleepwalker. She pushed open the door to her little sister's room, threw her pillow on the floor next to the girl's bed, and lay down on the plush carpeting, covering herself with the bedspread.

Then she cried. She did it in a quiet, hopeless way that would have broken my heart if anyone but Lanie Chobany had been doing it.

I didn't feel one bit sorry for her. She'd brought this on herself.

Chapter 20

Back in grade school, I used to wish Lanie Chobany would go away. I used to pray for it.

Now it was happening—Lanie was going away. Not in a physical, moved-to-Mississippi kind of way. But she was losing her Lanie-ness, the invisible substance that made her who she was. And that told me I'd been right to scrawl that message on her mirror. I'd done the world a favor.

The girl was falling apart. In the days following my visit to her bedroom, the man-eating tiger turned into a fearful kitten. She got paler and paler, her posture more hunched. She gasped at small noises and whirled in terror toward every unexpected movement. I heard her sometimes, at Emma's locker. "Why can't you guys understand how scary it was?" "I'm telling you, it was something supernatural." "What if it comes back?"

This was not how cool girls behaved. Cool girls were regal and self-possessed. They didn't let themselves go to pieces, and if they did, they never, ever let the world see. Sophia and Emma knew this. They lived it.

I could see it in their body language, the coming rejection. Their subtle grimaces, as if Lanie had developed a stench they couldn't stand. The way the two of them walked side by side in the school halls, spreading themselves out but linking arms so there was no room for anybody else. Lanie trotting after them like an annoying little sister they couldn't get rid of.

But she *wasn't* their sister, and they *could* get rid of her. Lanie knew that, and so did I.

Chapter 21

Logan was really mad at me.

Since our trip around the world, I hadn't stopped pestering him with emails, texts, and phone messages, demanding to know his secrets. What was he doing in outer space? And why was Jakob so against it? But no matter how much I pleaded, he wouldn't talk. I'd gone back to Mount Rushmore and the Eiffel Tower multiple times, trying to find him. Thinking it would be harder for him to ignore me in person. But he never showed.

We'd never before had a fight that lasted this long. We were both being stubborn, but he was winning. So I was surprised to find him hovering above my bed one night as I rose up out of my body.

"Logan? What the—?"

"You want to know where I've been going? Fine. I'll tell you."

I pressed my lips together and waited.

"Jakob's right. I've gone a lot farther than the moon. There's this planet I've been visiting."

I nodded like I'd known this, and maybe I had. Or at least suspected. Considering how the moon had lost its appeal, visiting a planet was the next logical step. "Which planet? Mars? Saturn?"

"Mysterium." His gaze drifted upward, as if he could see past my ceiling into the depths of outer space. "That's what I call it, anyway. It doesn't have a name, not that I know of."

Mysterium. The name sent a chill through me, though I didn't know why. I managed to keep my tone light as I said, "I'm pretty sure that one isn't in our solar system. Unless it's, like, hiding behind Jupiter and nobody knows about it."

He waved away my sarcasm. "It's in a whole different galaxy."

"What galaxy?"

"I don't know, Abs. A really far-off one."

The girl in the bed moaned and flopped from her side to her back. Speaking for us both, I said, "I don't like the sound of this."

"I didn't think you would."

"What have you been doing there?"

"It's better if you see for yourself."

I gaped at him. "What, you want to take me there?"

"That's why I'm here."

I backed away, shaking my head. "I've barely gotten used to astral travel. I'm not ready for an outer space trip."

"Sure you are. You've dreamed about this your whole life."

"It doesn't sound safe," I said, hating how much I sounded like my mother. "Going to a whole different galaxy—"

"Why wouldn't it be safe? It's our spirits going out there, not our bodies."

He had a point there. In spirit form we didn't have to worry about running out of oxygen or colliding with asteroids. I glanced at my body, lying so still in bed, and swore I could feel my heart racing. But was it terror or excitement that was causing the uptick?

"I've been going there for weeks," Logan said. He spread his arms wide, inviting an inspection. "See? I'm fine."

And he did seem fine, mostly. I thought I saw a hint of smudginess beneath his eyes, like twin bruises starting to form, but I could have been wrong. The face I was looking at was translucent, a ghost-face, little more than a faded snapshot of Logan's actual face.

I said, "Okay, but why does Jakob think—"

"Jakob isn't always right. Who are you going to trust—some German guy you met once and can't stand, or your cousin?"

My gaze wandered to the poster of the solar system mounted above my desk. How many times had I gazed at it through cupped hands, pretending I was looking out the window of my spaceship? These days I wasn't as obsessed with outer space as I'd been as a child, but I was still interested. And now I had the means to actually go out there. To live that childhood dream. I could practically hear the ghost of my nine-year-old self screaming, "Yes! Yes! Do it!"

"Fine," I said, with a sigh of surrender. "Let's go to Mysterium."

We blasted off like olden-day circus performers shot from side-by-side cannons. Up, up, up we went, through some puffy cumulus clouds and into the great beyond. Behind me, Earth shrank to the size of a child's bouncy ball. I twirled in a circle, dizzied by the feeling of being surrounded by stars. Weightless, substanceless, truly one with the universe.

I asked Logan if we could stop off at the moon. Moments later, we were hovering above a lunar crater the size of a football stadium. I surveyed the desolate landscape stretching endlessly in every direction. It was weird to see no houses, no trees, not a single blade of grass. To hear none of the sounds I took for granted on Earth—birdsong, the roar of the wind, the swish of a passing car. The utter absence of life pressed against me from all sides, like claustrophobia. I could understand how Logan had gotten bored here and decided to move on.

We looked at artifacts left behind by astronauts—an American flag, a plaque, a pair of boots. And some ickier items—containers of pee, used barf bags. I was surprised to see a jumble of footprints and wondered if there'd been a recent moon mission. Logan said no, the footprints were from decades ago. They would probably be there forever because there was no wind or rain to obliterate them.

"So they really happened," I said.

"What really happened?"

"The moon landings. Grandma's always saying the whole thing was a hoax."

"I wish we could tell her we've seen proof."

"She wouldn't believe us. You know Grandma."

"Yeah, she's stubborn like you."

"You mean like *you*."

We exchanged grins, and I thought how good it felt to slip back into that old familiar cousin-teasing, if only for a moment.

When we blasted off again, we took a zigzagging route so Logan could point out Venus and Mars. Then we crossed an asteroid belt, though finding an actual asteroid took some doing. We had to veer pretty far off course before we spotted one. It was as big as my house, its surface pitted like the acne-scarred face of a giant. We burrowed inside to see if anything interesting was in there—an alien life form, a chewy nougat center. We found nothing but gray rock.

We passed Jupiter, huge and gassy and striped like a ball of variegated yarn. We saw a nebula in the distance, a lacy veil of pinks and blues.

I was having the best time.

And then it turned into the worst.

Chapter 22

As we approached Saturn, I started to feel funny. Sick, weak, wobbly. I chalked the feeling up to disorientation, a kind of cosmic carsickness, and slowed my pace, waiting for it to pass. But the feeling persisted. And it kept getting worse.

I glanced at my sutratma. It was barely visible. I gulped for air but found none.

Panic raced through me like adrenaline. I was drowning in the bottomless ocean of space, my lungs filling with invisible fluid, and I couldn't breathe, *I couldn't breathe*, and I kept reminding myself that I didn't have to breathe because my lungs were already doing it, far away on Earth, but that didn't stop the horrible breathless feeling.

Logan was sailing toward Saturn, unaware that I'd fallen behind. He prattled on like a tour guide, naming the various ingredients in Saturn's rings. I had to call out twice before he stopped.

"Abby?" His eyes widened as he sped back to me. "Oh my God. Abby."

"I don't feel right," I whispered.

"It's okay. You're going to be fine. We just need to get you home."

"What's wrong with me?"

"I don't know. Your aura is really dim. Like a flashlight about to go out."

That didn't sound good. I thought of the dead spirit we'd seen at the Eiffel Tower, the light of his aura forever extinguished. "Am I dying?"

"No! You are not dying."

But I saw the look in his eyes. He was as scared as I was.

I said, "I don't think I can make it back to Earth."

"It's okay. I'll tow you."

He reached for my hand, and I felt a mild zap as our spirits connected.

"Can we take it slow?" I asked. "I don't think I can handle zipping and zooming."

"I was going to say we should probably go fast. But yeah, we can try slow."

We took off. Logan's idea of slow seemed more like warp speed. I felt as if I was trapped in a car that had lost its brakes while zooming down a steep mountain road.

"Tell me about Mysterium," I murmured, trying to distract myself. "What's it like there?"

He was silent for a long time, his face pensive. I figured he was gathering his thoughts, preparing to launch into a lengthy description, but when he spoke, all he said was, "Different."

"Different how?"

"It's basically— Mysterium is— Wow." He gave up with a shake of his head. "I don't know where to start."

"Does it have intelligent life? How'd you end up there in the first place? What have you been doing there?" Asking those three questions wore me out. I couldn't suppress a groan of fatigue.

Logan glanced at me—and did a doubletake. "Abs,

we need to go faster."

He didn't have to tell me I was looking worse. I could feel it.

Logan's spirit-hand tightened around mine. I felt a whiplash sensation and saw a blur of movement, and suddenly Earth loomed before us, its darkened land masses glittering with splotches of light like embedded stars. I felt a swell of love for my home planet and wondered suddenly why we didn't have a planetary anthem to complement the world's many national anthems. If there'd been one, I would've been singing it now, or at least mouthing the words.

Logan flashed an encouraging smile, though it didn't mask the worry in his eyes. "Hang on. We're almost there." We accelerated again, and suddenly I was floating above my bed, staring down at a girl so pale and still, she might have been a corpse in a casket.

Logan released my hand. "How are you feeling?"

"Glad to be home." I still felt awful, sicker than that time last year when I'd had the flu. I could feel my body drawing me toward it, luring me with the promise of sleep and healing.

"Abby, I'm so sorry. If I'd known this was going to happen—"

"But you didn't."

"—I never would have—"

"I know. Don't beat yourself up. You'll feel better once you've made it up to me."

He raised one eyebrow. "And how would I do that?"

"By promising you'll stay on Earth from now on."

He gave an exasperated sigh. "Abby—"

"Space travel is dangerous! What happened to me

tonight, it could happen to you at any time. And if you're out there by yourself, there won't be anybody to tow you back to Earth."

"It only happened to you because you're a new traveler. You're not used to a trip like that. But me, I'm totally used to it."

"Then how come you look so terrible?" This was the truth I'd denied earlier. "You've got those dark circles under your eyes. You're skinnier than you used to be. And speaking of dim auras, yours isn't exactly stadium lighting."

"I'm fine."

"Plus—" I began, but then my spirit-voice faltered. I tried again. "Plus, there's that trouble-waking-up thing."

"Which doesn't happen all the time."

"Even *sometimes* is too often. Did you know the same thing happened to me two weeks ago? Mom and Dad—" My spirit-voice broke again, and I had to dig down deep to bring it back. "Mom and Dad…they couldn't wake me up for the longest time."

He pounced on that. "Two weeks ago? That proves it isn't caused by space travel. You were never in outer space before tonight."

"I'm sure space travel…makes it worse. Getting that far away from your body…it can't be good." My words were coming slow and thick now, each one a boulder I could barely lift. "Please, Logan…just promise me…you won't go out there…anymore."

"Okay, you need to stop talking and get back in your body." I heard the urgency in his voice. I saw it in the rapid tick of his aura.

"Not till…you promise me."

"All this talk is draining your battery! Your aura, it's so dim—"

"I won't...stop bugging you...till you promise."

"Come on, Abby! This is serious."

I folded my arms and drifted deliberately away from my body. Maybe I *was* as stubborn as Grandma.

"What are you doing?" Logan's voice was an incredulous squeak. "Are you willing to die to get your own way?"

"Are *you*?" I shot back, though not as forcefully as I would have liked. "Because...all that space travel...it'll end up...killing you."

"Abby, please! Be reasonable!"

"*You*...be reasonable. It's your fault...this happened. Can't you do...this one thing...for me?"

He stared at me wretchedly. Then he swore, something I'd never heard him do before. "Fine! Okay! I'll stop doing outer space travel."

"Promise?"

"I promise."

Something like a sigh flowed out of me.

"Now get back in your body," he said. The white-gold tone of his aura had deepened to a mournful amber, the hue of tarnished brass.

I nodded and glided closer to my bed. Then I glanced back at him. "Can you at least tell me...what you've been doing...on Mysterium?"

"No." He was studying the solar system poster above my desk, really scrutinizing it, like there'd be a test later. I knew he just wanted to plant his eyes on something that wasn't me.

"Oh...nice." I tried to bark the words, but they came out a soft coo, with no trace of the sarcasm I'd intended. "So this…is how…you get back at me."

"I'm not getting back at you. I just don't want to talk about Mysterium. At all, ever."

"But—"

"No, Abby." He turned back to me, and I was startled by the coldness in his eyes. "You got what you wanted. Don't ask me for anything more." He nodded toward my bed, and the angry glare of his aura faded slightly. "I'll stay here till you're back in your body. I'll call tomorrow to see how you're doing."

I knew he was punishing me, and maybe I deserved it. Now I would never learn his secrets, though I supposed that was a small price to pay for winning the battle. For keeping my cousin safe.

As soon as I sank into my body, I fell into a deep sleep, like Briar Rose after the needle prick. In the morning, I slept through my alarm clock. My mother had to shake me awake, but she let me skip school when I said I had a migraine.

I spent most of the day in bed, dozing on and off. And, during the awake times, stuffing myself with food, including the entire leftover pot pie my mother had earmarked for dinner. I was so hungry! Mom ended up working late, so she never found out about the missing pot pie, and Dad, who hadn't known about it in the first place, made the two of us spaghetti for dinner.

By the time I went to bed for the night, I was feeling mostly okay. By the next morning, I was back to a hundred percent.

But I stayed off the astral plane for a whole week after that.

Chapter 23

"Goodness gracious!" Grandma clucked, planting noisy smooches all over my face. "I can't believe I have a fifteen-year-old grandchild! I'm getting so old."

"You have two fifteen-year-old grandchildren," I reminded her. "Logan's birthday was three weeks ago."

She gasped in mock horror. "You're right! Merciful savior, now I feel twice as old!"

She smiled vacantly at my mother and slid into the chair Dad was holding for her, the one to my immediate left. A lady server materialized like a genie and asked if we were ready to order. My mother told her we were waiting for two more people. No sooner had the server left than I spotted Cody and a pretty girl across the room, winding their way to us through the maze of tables.

Cody came straight to me and planted a kiss on my forehead. "Happy Birthday, Minutia!"

He introduced Amy, who was essentially a female version of himself. Same age, maybe two inches shorter, with long dark hair, big dark eyes, and the same perfect smile. I couldn't stop staring—they were so pretty together. A bride-and-groom wedding cake topper come to life.

Amy was a nurse at Eerie Memorial Hospital. Her shift hadn't ended until seven, but she'd wanted to come and meet Cody's family, so we'd scheduled dinner late to accommodate her. It was nearly eight, and my stomach was snarling like a rabid animal. At home, we usually ate by six.

"So, Abby," Amy said, as she and Cody seated themselves at the table. "I hear you're having another party in a week or two." She had one of those soft little-girl voices that work well for the nurturing professions.

"Yeah," I said, rolling my eyes to show that it hadn't been my idea.

"Twenty-nine guests are coming," my mother said proudly. "There'll be a DJ and lots of food and some age-appropriate games."

Cody said excitedly, "Ooh, that one where two random guests get sent into a closet for five minutes to make out?"

Amy snickered. My mother pinned Cody with her I-am-not-amused stare.

"Actually, we won't be playing games," I said.

"What?" blustered my mother. "I was thinking a fun relay race, maybe some charades…"

"No games," I said firmly.

She started to say something else but stopped abruptly, throwing my dad a furious look. I had a feeling he'd kicked her under the table.

I'd never dreamed so many people would want to come to my party. I'd invited thirty-two, figuring I might get ten yeses out of that. Instead, I'd gotten twenty-nine, which, if you did the math, worked out to a ninety-one percent attendance rate, not bad for a quiet/mean/weird girl like me. I figured I was still coasting on Logan's popularity. Or maybe people were coming for the DJ, a well-known local radio personality. Oh, who cared why they were coming? At least they were coming.

Sophia and Emma had RSVPed yes, which gave me hope that they were reconsidering the NOT COOL rating. Lanie was coming, too, but I figured I could put up with her for a few hours. She was a lot easier to take in her new, humbled state.

After a lot of agonizing, I'd invited Austin Oliver. He hadn't RSVPed, which probably meant he wasn't coming. I tried to tell myself that was a good thing. I'd be nervous enough without him.

"Ma, what are you doing?" My mother's voice, hushed but exasperated, jolted me out of my thoughts.

Grandma had her head tilted back and was squirting eyedrops into her eyes. "Really, Leah? You have to ask?"

"What I mean is, why don't you do that in the ladies' room?" My mother glanced around the restaurant to see whether anybody was watching. Nobody was.

My mother had firm ideas about what people should and shouldn't do in public. She'd once chewed my dad out for sneezing in the supermarket checkout line.

"All done," announced Grandma. She slipped her eye drops back into her purse and poked me with a fleshy elbow. "Dry eyes, dry skin, dry hair. Nobody told me getting old turns you into beef jerky!"

"Aw, Grandma, you're not old," I said, even though sixty-four seemed plenty old to me.

She patted my hand. "You always know the right thing to say. That's why you're my favorite grandchild. You know you're my favorite, don't you?"

"Sure, Grandma."

She'd been telling me that since I was little. She also told Logan he was her favorite. Maybe it hadn't occurred to her that we would compare notes. We laughed about it, Logan and I. It was *so Grandma.*

Our server came back to take our orders and bring us each a glass of water. Cody, ignoring the glass, raised his clear plastic water bottle and said, "A toast to Abby. May fifteen be a time of growth, fulfillment, and adventure."

"But not too much adventure," my mother said.

"What's with the bottled water, Cody?" Grandma asked tartly. "Restaurant water not good enough for you?"

"This restaurant serves tap water," said Cody. "I prefer my special brand."

"Special brand?" Grandma scoffed. "For heaven's sake, it's *water.* It's not like they produce it in some factory."

She'd been picking on him a lot lately. My mother said she was mad that he was moving out of her basement. Slipping out of her clutches.

While we were eating, Grandma mentioned that she would be reading scripture in front of her church congregation on Sunday, and we were all welcome to come. Nobody responded. We were all hunched over our dinner plates, forking food into our mouths and trying not to make eye contact.

"You're a bunch of heathens," Grandma said sourly.

We ignored that, too.

Dad asked Cody whether he'd moved into the new apartment yet. Halfway through the question, he jerked and glared at my mother, which made me think she'd kicked him under the table.

We weren't supposed to talk about Cody's new apartment in front of Grandma. Dad had obviously forgotten that, and Cody made things worse by not only answering his question ("Not yet, unfortunately") but also describing the apartment's many wonderful features. He was sitting too far away for my mother to kick *him* under the table. She tried lasering him with her eyes, but he didn't notice.

Cody told us he'd be able to walk to work because the apartment was downtown, just three blocks from his office. Whereas the trip from Grandma's place took forty minutes by car. He wished he lived there now. He had to be at the office at five a.m. all week to work on a big project.

While he was speaking, Grandma's mouth got tighter and tighter. Eventually, her lips vanished altogether.

After the dishes had been cleared, four servers came to our table clapping in rhythm and singing a lively birthday tune I'd never heard before. It sounded like something they were making up on the spot. I slid lower and lower in my seat, waiting for it to be over. Finally, the singing stopped. Our server brought us each a piece of carrot cake with vanilla icing.

Grandma had gone unusually quiet. I sneaked a peek at her. Her chin was jutting out farther than the rest of her face, like an outcropping on a cliff, and her eyes were fixed on Cody. I sensed a restlessness in the air around her, like a thunderstorm brewing. Nobody else seemed to notice.

A memory flashed into my mind—me and Grandma walking along her road one day when I'd been about six. At one point the sidewalk ended abruptly in a grassy bank, and you had to cross the road to get to the next section of sidewalk. There was a pedestrian crosswalk but no stop signs or traffic lights for cars.

Grandma had me by the hand as we entered the crosswalk. I saw a car coming and tried to pull back, but Grandma yanked me forward. "We have the right of way," she growled.

"But Grandma—" I said, because even at six I could see that the car wasn't slowing down. The driver, a bald man, was half-turned toward the person in the passenger's seat, his mouth moving. He didn't see us. Grandma kept going, and the car kept coming until suddenly there was an ear-splitting screech as the driver slammed on his brakes. The car stopped so close to us, I could feel the heat from its engine.

Grandma didn't even look over. She just kept marching across the road, yanking me along behind her.

The driver stuck his head out the window. "Jesus Christ, lady! Are you insane?"

Grandma stopped and shook her fist at him, the Grandma equivalent of giving somebody the finger. "We're in the crosswalk," she snarled. "We have the right of way. And watch your language, young man!"

The language got much worse after that, and Grandma told the guy he was going straight to hell.

If I ever wanted to describe Grandma to somebody without using a bunch of adjectives, that's the story I would tell.

Now, watching Grandma, I saw that same resolute look, the one that had hardened her face the day she'd marched us into the path of that car. Something bad was

133

about to go down.

"So, Grandma—" I said, thinking I might be able to defuse the situation by asking which scripture she was going to read on Sunday. Not that I had any sort of familiarity with the bible. My dad often said he didn't know Matthew, Mark, Luke, and John from John, Paul, George, and Ringo. I was even worse. I knew a little bit about the Beatles, but I had no idea who Matthew, Mark, Luke, and John were. Friends of Jesus, maybe?

But "So, Grandma—" was all the further I got. Cody was taking another swig from his water bottle, and no sooner had he set it down than Grandma's hand shot out, quick as a lizard's tongue seizing a fly. She grabbed the bottle and, before anybody could blink, tilted it to her mouth. Almost immediately, she spewed the contents all over her cake.

"This isn't water!" she screeched. "It's vodka! I knew it, Cody—I knew you were drinking again. And you a recovering alcoholic. Shame on you!"

Now everybody was staring at us.

Chapter 24

"Oh God," I said, covering my face with both hands.

Grandma whirled on me. "And shame on *you*, young lady, for taking the Lord's name in vain!"

"I wasn't taking his name in vain," I retorted. "I was praying for help."

"Happy, Ma?" Cody said dryly. "Way to ruin Abby's birthday."

"I did not ruin Abby's birthday," Grandma bellowed. "*You* ruined it, with your public drunkenness."

"Public drunkenness? Seriously?" Cody got to his feet and walked in a straight line, placing one foot carefully in front of the other, like a gymnast on a balance beam. He pivoted deftly on the ball of his foot and walked back to the table the same way. "Would I be able to do that if I was drunk? How about this?" He closed his eyes and touched his two forefingers to his nose, one at a time. "Having a few sips of vodka does not make a person drunk."

The whole restaurant was gawking at us. Even the servers had stopped what they were doing to watch.

"Oh, Cody." My mother shook her head reprovingly. "You've started drinking again?"

"No! I mean, okay, yeah, every once in a while I'll have a drink. Like now. I'm in the middle of a big

135

project at work. I've been working twelve, fourteen, sometimes sixteen hours a day. A little nightcap helps me relax before bed."

"It's true," Amy said. "He hardly drinks at all. And I've never seen him drunk."

"Save your breath, Amy," muttered Cody. "Let's get out of here. Happy Birthday, Minutia."

"Amy—take his keys," Grandma yelled as they walked toward the exit. "Do not let him drive in that condition."

Cody shot her a murderous look. Amy glanced uncertainly at Grandma and then followed Cody out of the restaurant.

My parents and I just sat there, shell-shocked. Our table looked like a battlefield with all the plates of half-eaten cake, the forks at odd angles like abandoned guns.

"That boy," Grandma grumbled. "He sure knows how to make me see red."

And I'd thought this party would be the easy one.

Chapter 25

Logan was an expert mingler, always had been. At our joint birthday parties, he'd made it a point to walk around and chat with each cluster of guests. I'd be right behind him, tight as a shadow, happy to let him take the lead.

Tonight, for the first time, I was flying solo at the b-day bash. Doing a single-mingle. Preparing to channel my inner Logan.

I was well-armed with conversation starters, thanks to weeks of planning. I'd even written them down on index cards, which I'd studied in the car on the way to the fire hall.

So, who do you think soaped Principal Whittaker's car windows?

Did you see [popular TV show] this week? What did you think about [plot twist]?

What are you doing for your social studies project?

Et cetera, et cetera.

I also planned to remind people that DJ Rick took requests and urge them to try the Buffalo chicken dip.

Cody dropped by to say hi as we were setting up. Coming out of the kitchen with a bowl of potato chips, I spotted him across the banquet room chatting with DJ Rick. Cody and Rick had been college roommates, and Cody was the one who'd arranged for Rick to be here. He'd even gotten us a nice discount.

"Ah, here's the birthday girl," said Cody, striding up to me and snatching a potato chip out of the bowl. "Minutia, you look gorgeous. I just hope this party is better than the last one."

"I don't see how it could be worse," I said. I was aiming for flippant, but the words came out a little frosty.

Cody sighed heavily. "I am so sorry—"

"I know. You don't have to say it again."

He'd called the day after the party to apologize. And then texted me another apology. And then sent an email with an even longer apology. Meanwhile, not a word from Grandma, who'd started the whole thing.

I set the potato chip bowl on the table and moved some other bowls around like a shell game trick.

"Hey," said Cody. "I want you to know, you do not have an alcoholic for an uncle."

I met his eyes. "But I used to."

"Yes," he said, and I had to give him credit for not looking away. "Once upon a time, I did a lot of drinking. The important thing is, I don't now. It's like I said—I have a nightcap now and then. That's it. Okay? Are we good?"

"Yeah. We're good."

We hugged it out.

"So. First party without Rump Roast, huh?" Cody stepped back to study me, his eyes soft with sympathy.

"Don't get me started. I'm still mad at Uncle Dirk. I mean, 'great job opportunity' my butt. He had a perfectly good job right here in Eerie."

"I hear you. The thing is, high school principals make more than science teachers. It comes down to money."

"Eerie has principals. He could have found a job here if he'd just been patient. It was selfish of him to drag Logan and Aunt Lisa all the way across the country like that."

"He'd probably tell you he was just doing his best to provide for his family."

"Money isn't the most important thing. Family is. And he tore ours apart."

"Hey, I don't like it either," said Cody. "But I'm still here. So is Grandma." His mouth twisted on *Grandma*, like it was a hard-to-pronounce foreign word. "Look, I know how close you and Logan have always been. I know how you two used to talk stuff over. If you ever need an ear, I'm here for you. You can tell me anything, and I'll keep it in the strictest confidence."

"Thanks, Uncle Cody. That's really nice of you."

Guests were starting to arrive, so I got down to the business of mingling. I started with the less daunting people—some younger kids from my street, the members of the math club. The chatting got easier as my social muscle warmed up. A couple of people rushed off to try the Buffalo chicken dip at my urging.

"Hi, Abby." Sarah Palmer came strolling up to me. Sarah was a pretty Black girl, brand-new to our school. She sat at my lunch table and was also in my homeroom. "Thanks for inviting me to your party."

"Yeah, I'm glad you came."

I didn't look at her as I said it, because I was afraid she'd see my insincerity. I'd only invited her because I was ninety-nine percent sure she'd come. That was back when I'd been worried nobody would show up.

Sarah's family had moved to Eerie only a month

ago, so she didn't really have any friends. She was trying, though. Some of my classmates called her Number Two because she liked to hand out pencils to people who had lost theirs. The pencils were the old-fashioned wooden kind, and they had short bible verses printed on them.

She'd given me a pencil one day at lunch, even though I hadn't lost mine. It said, "He restoreth my soul." I'd thanked her, but after lunch I'd tossed the pencil in the lost-and-found box in the school office. I preferred mechanical pencils.

"I wouldn't have missed your party for the world," said Sarah. She grinned, showing teeth that looked like small white kernels of corn. "We biblical girls have to stick together."

I raised an eyebrow. "Biblical girls?"

Her smile faltered. "I just mean, you know, because our names came from the bible. Sarah, Abigail. Are your parents religious?"

"Oh," I said. "Actually, my name isn't Abigail. It's just plain old Abby."

Her cheeks went pink. "Sorry! I just figured— Sorry." She looked so mortified, I felt like I was the one who should apologize.

Instead, I told her to try the Buffalo chicken dip.

Sophia, Emma, and Lanie had arrived and were planted at the edge of the stage, ogling DJ Rick. I kept one eye on them, and when I saw Lanie heading for the restroom, I scurried over to Sophia and Emma to do the host thing. They both had cardigan sweaters tied around their shoulders like superhero capes.

"Hey, guys! Thanks for coming."

"Hi, Abby. Great party," said Sophia.

"How'd you get DJ Rick?" asked Emma. "I heard he's booked, like, a year in advance."

"Rick's an old family friend." I waved at Rick and blew him a kiss to show Sophia and Emma how tight we were. He gave me an uncertain wave back.

Family friend was a stretch. I'd never met the man before tonight.

"He's so cute." Sophia's green-gold eyes, still on Rick, held a dreamy expression. "I love his hair, the way it's, like, long but not too long."

"Longish," said Emma.

"Yeah, Rick's always had great hair," I said fondly.

Emma said, "My cousin tried to get him for her wedding reception. He said yeah, he could do it—in, like, eleven months. Well, *that* wasn't going to work, considering she was already three months pregnant! She would've been pushing a baby stroller up the aisle."

My initial *ha ha ha* came out too hearty. I tamped it down into a soft chuckle.

I felt like I was at a sports try-out or an audition for a play. Forget the food, the music, the presents. Today was all about showing Sophia and Emma how cool I was. They probably couldn't erase that purple-penned NOT COOL from Sophia's yearbook, but they could always white out the NOT with correction fluid.

"Oh. That weird religious girl is here." Emma pointed at Sarah, who was standing all alone at the refreshment table, dabbing a tortilla chip into the Buffalo chicken dip. "What do they call her? Number Two?"

Sophia fixed her eyes on me. "Are you friends with her?"

I let out another too-loud laugh. "Friends? God, no. I only invited her because she sits at my lunch table." I snorted. "If she starts handing out pencils, I might have to kick her butt out the door."

Sophia and Emma snickered, and I grinned at them, relieved that I'd said the right thing. But our conversation was making me sweat. I unbuttoned the top button of my shirt to let some air in.

Sophia said, "I think I failed the algebra quiz yesterday. God, that was hard."

"I'm glad I'm not taking algebra," said Emma. "Pre-algebra is bad enough."

Sophia turned to me. "How'd you do?"

I gave a squirmy little shrug. "Okay, I think."

"Hear that?" Sophia said, nudging Emma. "She thinks she did okay. The person who got the math award in seventh grade *and* eighth grade. You aced it," she said to me in an accusing tone. "You know you did. God, you're good at math. I wish I was. My parents said if I don't make the honor roll this marking period, I have to quit the band."

"Oh no!" said Emma.

I frowned. "You're in marching band? What instrument do you play?"

Emma slapped a hand over her mouth, chortling. Sophia rolled her eyes in an *as if!* way and said, "Not marching band. A rock band. These guys in my neighborhood started it. Chad's the guitarist, Kenny's on keyboard, Aiden's our drummer, and I'm the lead singer."

"Oh," I said, flushing at my own stupidity. "That's cool. What's your band called?"

"Galactic Scrimshaw."

I nodded like I recognized the meaning in those words. I didn't, though. To me they sounded like random words plucked from a dictionary.

"They played at my cousin's bar mitzvah," Emma told me. "They're really good."

"I'm sure they are," I murmured. Sophia was a phenomenal singer, the best in our class. She got all the solos in our choral programs. We had a couple of other really good singers, but nobody paid them much attention because their talent was a notch below Sophia's.

Emma said to Sophia, "Making you quit the band, though. That's a pretty harsh punishment for not making the honor roll."

"It's not really a punishment. We practice a lot. They think it's interfering with my schoolwork."

"Is it, though? You're doing okay in your other subjects, right?"

"Yeah. Algebra's the only thing that's messing me up. It's because of Mrs. Farkosh. She's such a bad teacher."

"I hope I don't get her next year."

"She's terrible at explaining things. I wish I had somebody who could explain things better. And, like, show me how to work the problems."

"You mean like a tutor."

"Yeah, I guess. Except not an official one from the school's tutoring program. I don't want my parents to find out how bad I'm doing."

My eyes were darting back and forth from Sophia to Emma, Sophia, Emma, as I followed the ping and pong of this exchange. Their words tumbled out like a poem they'd memorized.

Then Emma said, "Oh! You know who would be perfect?"

"Who?"

"Abby."

Sophia gasped dramatically. "Abby? Oh my God. That's brilliant!"

They turned to me in unison, beaming like they'd just solved world hunger.

"Me?" I croaked. "You want *me* to be your tutor?"

"Could you?" Sophia clasped her hands as if she was praying.

I was so breathless with joy I could only grin and nod.

Sophia said, "We're done with quizzes till after Christmas, so how about we start in January? You can come to my house every Tuesday after school."

"Okay, yeah, that'll work." Mrs. Farkosh introduced new concepts on Monday and Tuesday, we reviewed on Wednesday and Thursday, and we got quizzed on the new material every Friday. Tuesday afternoon sessions would help Sophia get familiar with the concepts before each week's review. And by Friday, she'd have a good chance of acing the quiz.

But tutoring aside—holy crud! Ever since fourth grade and that glittery dance routine, I'd daydreamed about these girls, about getting tight with them. Sharing clothes, sleeping at each other's houses, as intimate as sisters. I'd always known it was nothing but a crazy fantasy, and yet now, suddenly, it seemed within reach.

Sophia and Emma were used to being a threesome. If they were kicking Lanie out of the clique, they'd be looking for somebody to replace her.

Why shouldn't that somebody be me?

Chapter 26

I went into the restroom to refresh my antiperspirant. When I came out, I saw that somebody new had arrived.

Austin Oliver.

He was standing near the punch bowl, flashing that teen heartthrob grin as he talked to two of his buddies. I'd invited a couple of guys from his end of the street, even though they were more Logan's friends than mine. I figured Austin would be more likely to come if he knew his buddies would be here.

I really hadn't expected it to work.

My knees wobbled as I walked across the room.

Oh, hi, Austin. I didn't think you were coming. I mean, I didn't get your RSVP.

What? I told my mom to mail it. She must've forgotten. Sorry about that.

It's okay. I'm just glad you're here.

Me too. I wouldn't have missed your party for the world. [Looks around.] Wow, you sure have a lot of friends. I guess you'll be tied up for a while, but maybe after the party, if you're not busy, we could—

A burst of laughter jolted me back to reality. One of Austin's friends exclaimed, "I told you that would happen! Didn't I tell you?"

The guy standing to Austin's right spotted me and said, "Hey, guys, I think the birthday girl is coming over to say hi."

Six eyes zeroed in on me, including Austin's two blue ones.

"Hi." The word whooshed out of me like bus exhaust.

"Hi," said Austin.

"Hi," said his two friends.

And just like that, my brain shut down. I was an airplane that had lost its engines. An electrical transformer fried by lightning. My words evaporated, leaving behind nothing but frantic thoughts.

What was wrong with me? Was I having a stroke? Where were all those conversation starters I'd practiced? They had to be rattling around in my head somewhere. Where were my flashcards? I was eighty-two percent sure I'd shoved a couple of them into a back pocket of my jeans. Did I dare sneak a peek? Time was ticking by, the silence getting louder by the second.

"The punch is really good." The boy on Austin's left raised his cup as if to prove he'd had some. He had kind eyes, and I knew he was trying to fill the awkward silence. What was his name? I couldn't remember, even though I'd addressed his invitation myself. "What's in it? I'm guessing ginger ale and fruit drink?"

"I'm not sure." I finally managed to speak, but my voice came out croaky, like the early stages of laryngitis. "My mom made it."

"I heard the Buffalo chicken dip is really good," said the boy on Austin's right.

"Yes!" I said. "The dip! It's good!"

"We should get some before it's gone," said Austin. He nodded curtly in my direction and headed for the food table, his buddies right behind him.

Suddenly, my thoughts came flooding back. "DJ Rick takes requests," I called. I almost added, "So who do you think soaped Principal Whittaker's car windows?"—but they were too far away for that conversation.

Chapter 27

"Hey, everybody!" Logan said from my mother's laptop screen. "Chad, Daniel, Tao—miss you guys! Hannah, how you doing? Kalisha—you changed your hair! Hoo, it's so good to see everybody."

Logan-on-screen wasn't as good as Logan-in-person, but at least he was with us in real time. The party dynamic changed abruptly. What had been a pleasant, murmuring, low-key event suddenly became rowdy, raucous, full of hilarity.

That was the Logan Effect.

The call went on for more than half an hour. Logan listened attentively as, one by one, people told him what they'd been up to. Then he shared his own stories, an entertaining mix of serious, titillating, and funny. After everybody'd had a chance to say hello, I spirited the laptop away to the deserted kitchen for my own conversation.

"How's the party going?" asked Logan. "Looks like you got a good turnout."

"Yeah, better than I expected."

"How have you been? We haven't talked for a while."

We'd been in touch only a few times since that disastrous outer space trip, and when we did talk, our conversations were stiff and painful, like new shoes that didn't fit right. I figured he was still mad at me for

148

making him promise to stay on Earth. Or maybe he thought I still blamed him for my cosmic brush with death. Maybe both.

I was ready to forgive and forget. I could only hope he was, too.

I said, "Yeah, I've missed you."

"I've missed you, too." He sounded so heartfelt, I had to swallow hard to keep from getting choked up. "What have you been up to, Abs?"

"Oh, you know. The usual stuff."

"Been to any school dances lately?"

"No."

"Gone roller-skating?"

"Not for a while."

"Who are you hanging out with these days?"

I aimed my most severe frown at him. "What's with all the questions?"

He settled back in his chair and studied me the way I thought a psychologist might. "Your mom is worried because you don't have friends. I heard her talking to my mom about it. On speakerphone. They didn't know I was listening in."

"Oh my God. Don't pay any attention to that! You know how my mother exaggerates."

"So…you do have friends?"

"Yes, I have friends! Did you not see how many people came to my party?"

"I'm not talking about party guests. I'm talking about *friends*."

"Okay, well, I sit with Pia every day at lunch."

"Pia *let's-talk-about-me-me-me* Hockenberry? She hardly counts."

"And there's this new girl, Sarah, who sits with us.

149

She—she gives me pencils." I heard how feeble that sounded as it came out.

"Abby, I know it's been hard for you since I moved away—"

"Yeah, it's been hard. But you can't expect me to make new friends overnight."

"It's been six months."

"Really?" I said, though I knew exactly how long it had been. "Seriously, you don't have to worry about me. I have friend options. In fact, I might have a chance at getting in with Sophia and Emma."

I explained how Sophia had just asked me to tutor her. I told him how Lanie seemed to be on her way out of the clique, which would free up a spot I might be able to slide into. Then I backtracked and told him about NOT COOL and the message I'd written on Lanie's mirror.

"You should have seen her. She was totally freaked out. Still is," I finished, chortling at the memory.

There was a long moment of silence. Then Logan said, "Oh, Abby. That's terrible."

"What's terrible?"

"What you did to Lanie. It's just—wrong."

"Wrong?" I repeated, dragging out the single syllable. "Oh, you think it's *wrong*—Mr. Levitating Jacket?"

A flush spread across his cheeks. "Okay, that was wrong, too. But this—it's so much worse!"

"How is it worse?"

"Because you threatened Lanie."

"I didn't threaten her. How did I threaten her?"

"Hello! 'Jerks get theirs'? That's a threat. People get arrested for sending messages like that."

I made a dismissive *puh* sound. "That's nothing. I was going to write 'Jerks die.' "

" 'Jerks die'? Oh my God, Abby. What is wrong with you?"

"Nothing," I shouted. "Nothing is wrong with me! Why are you taking her side? Lanie's the one you should be mad at, not me. She's the one who acts like she's better than everybody else. I'm trying to help her be a better person. I did this for her own good."

"No," said Logan. "You did it for you. You did it to get even."

I started to protest, but then I realized he was right. "So what if I did? She had it coming. Lanie's a jerk. I hate her."

He clasped his hands on his desk and studied me soberly. "How can you hate Lanie after all she's been through?"

"What are you talking about? What has she been through?"

"Well, for starters, her mom died when she was in kindergarten."

I sputtered in outrage. "No, she didn't! I've seen Lanie's mom. Tall red-haired lady, always glammed up like a model? I remember in third grade, she brought these stale store-bought cookies to school for Lanie's birthday."

"That's the stepmom. The real mom died of cancer when Lanie was five."

A small shock wave rippled through me. "I don't remember that."

"You wouldn't. Lanie went to a different school back then. A private school. She transferred to Eerie Elementary in first grade."

"How do you know this?"

"She told me."

"Just now? When you were chatting?"

"No, years ago."

"Why didn't you ever tell me?"

"I thought you knew."

"Well, I didn't."

Logan said softly, "Everybody has a backstory, Abs. Everybody."

In the give and take of the conversation, it was my turn to talk, but suddenly I had nothing to say. Logan gave me a minute and then pressed on.

"Look, I know Lanie can be a jerk sometimes. It's probably because of what she has to put up with at home. Her dad's hardly ever around, and when he is, he doesn't pay any attention to her. The stepmother has a son of her own, plus she had a kid with Lanie's dad—a little girl, I think. She acts like her own kids are God's gifts and treats Lanie like dirt. She doesn't talk to her unless she has something mean to say. She's always telling her she's clumsy, stupid, ugly."

I just stared at him, trying to reconcile my image of Lanie with this new information. I felt as though we were talking about two different people.

"There was this one day last year," said Logan, "when Lanie fell down the basement stairs and landed on her arm. She tried to tell her stepmom it was hurt bad, but the stepmom just told her to quit being a baby and go to her room. Lanie finally got her stepbrother to drive her to the ER. Turned out she had a broken arm."

I remembered the broken arm. I hadn't signed Lanie's cast, but Logan had.

My chest felt heavy, as if Logan's words were

bricks piling up on top of it. I thought back to the night I'd lipsticked Lanie's mirror, the way the stepmother had treated her. Now it all made sense.

"Can you imagine?" Logan went on. "How would you feel if your mom died and your dad married a lady who hated your guts? Or if your dad died and your mom married some jerk? Somebody who didn't even pretend to like you?"

"Well, then. I would be very sad," I replied. "But I like to think I wouldn't take it out on other people."

"Yeah, well, you can't really know what you'd do, can you, because you're not in that situation."

I couldn't talk about this anymore. "You look tired," I said, noting the dark circles under his eyes.

"Thanks. So do you."

"You're not…"

"I'm not what?"

…*still going into outer space?* I almost said it but stopped myself in time. He'd promised me he was done with space travel, and he deserved to be taken at his word.

"You're not at Mount Rushmore," I said, "like, ever. I stop there just about every time I travel."

"Didn't I tell you that probably wouldn't work out?"

"I look for you at the Eiffel Tower, too."

"I don't go there as much as I used to."

"So where *do* you go?"

"Different places. Some nights I just hang out in Pittsburgh."

"Are you ever going to tell me what you were doing on Mysterium?"

He chuckled, though I didn't see anything funny

153

about my question. Then my mother pushed through the swinging door and announced that it was time to sing Happy Birthday and cut the cake.

"I guess you have to go," said Logan.

"I guess so." I didn't want to, though. I felt like we had more to say.

"Happy Birthday, Abs. It was good talking to you. And please, cut Lanie some slack."

I maintained a fake, stretched smile during the singing of Happy Birthday, counting the beats till it was over. Too many eyes on me, though Austin's burned deepest, searing my cheeks. I scanned the crowd, looking for Sophia and Emma. They were nowhere to be seen, though I did spot Lanie prowling through the crowd like a hungry predator.

As slices of cake were being doled out, Lanie rushed up to me. "Have you seen Sophia and Emma? I can't find them anywhere."

Standing so close, she seemed larger than life-sized, her blue eyes big as planets, her citrusy perfume wafting up my nose. I was dizzied by my conflicting feelings—lingering resentment, newfound pity, envy, compassion, hatred, shame. I grabbed the edge of the table to steady myself.

I asked, "Did you check the bathroom?"

"Three times. And the kitchen. I even went outside and walked the whole way around the building. They're, like, nowhere."

Pia Hockenberry was walking by, thumbing away at her phone. I said, "Hey, Pia. Have you seen Sophia and Emma?"

She glanced up. "Yeah, they left a little while ago. I saw them go out the back door."

"What?" Lanie gasped so theatrically that people turned to stare. "Oh my God. They ditched me. I knew it! I knew something like this was going to happen!"

This was the moment I'd been waiting for, yet I felt no triumph. Lanie was staring at me with a stricken look, her face getting blotchier by the second. I grabbed her arm and propelled her into the kitchen, away from prying eyes.

"They didn't—even tell me—they were leaving," she sobbed.

"They didn't tell me either." I plucked some tissues from a box on the counter and handed them to her.

"They hate me. They don't want to hang out with me anymore."

"I'm sure that's not true," I said, not very convincingly.

"No, it is." She dropped heavily onto one of four folding chairs lined up along a wall. She hunched over her knees and cried hard into a tissue for a couple of minutes. I stood in front of her chewing my thumbnail, not sure what to say, what to do. All I could think was, *I bet she cried like this when her mom died.*

Finally, she straightened up. She wiped her eyes and blew her nose. "Something happened a couple of weeks ago. Something—supernatural. It was so scary, it has literally ruined my life. I can't stop thinking about it. Last week I quit the cheerleaders."

"Oh!" Hot shame burned inside me.

"I just don't have the energy anymore. I can't concentrate at school. All I can think about is that—that *thing* that happened. Sophia and Emma don't get it. They think I'm crazy. They get mad every time I bring it up."

Bricks were piling up on my chest again. I dropped into the chair next to hers. "Well, I won't get mad. Tell me what scared you."

She did, the words coming out halting and slurred amidst fresh sobs. If I hadn't already known the story, I would have had trouble understanding her, she was crying that hard.

I felt like crying, too. I'd broken Lanie Chobany.

Chapter 28

I reached out and patted Lanie's hand. "I don't think you're crazy. You know why? Because something like that happened to me not long ago. At Halloween, actually."

I told her about the levitating jacket, leaving out the part where I'd found out it was just Logan having some out-of-body fun.

"It felt so real," I told her. "I would have sworn on my grandpa's grave it actually happened. But it was just a dream."

She was all wide-eyed and slack-mouthed, like a child listening to a fairytale, one so dark she could hardly believe it had a happy ending. "Oh, Abby. Do you really think mine was a dream, too?"

"I'm sure of it."

"Sophia and Emma think so, too. But there's no way to prove it. That next day, when I was at school? I thought of going through my bathroom trash to see if the paper towels were there. You know—the ones I used to clean the mirror? But by the time I got home, my waste basket was empty. I asked our housekeeper about it, but she didn't know anything. She was like, 'I don't memorize the trash, Miss Lanie.' "

"It's okay. You don't need proof."

"Maybe the witches or ghosts or whatever used to haunt Eerie are back. Maybe all that weird stuff is starting up again."

"No. You had a bad dream, that's all."

"I want to believe you."

"Then believe me."

"Okay. I'll try." Her eyes caught hold of mine. "You know, you're actually really nice."

I let out a short laugh. "You sound surprised."

She nodded sheepishly. "I guess I just—I always had this...this impression of you..." She hesitated and then blurted it out. "I thought you were mean."

"*You* thought *I* was mean?"

"Yeah. You probably don't remember this, but once, way back in first grade, you said my hair was stupid."

"Oh," I said, feeling heat seep into my cheeks. "You remember that?"

"Only because it made me cry and Seth McDaniel wouldn't stop calling me a crybaby."

I'd made Lanie cry? I didn't remember that part.

"I'm sorry," I said. "I was just mad because you said a picture I drew was stupid."

Her eyes widened. "I said that?"

I had to laugh again. "You weren't wrong. My picture *was* stupid."

She managed a tremulous grin. "So was my hair. I was just really touchy about it. See, my mom used to do all kinds of fancy things with my hair. After she died— well, my dad didn't know the first thing about fixing a little girl's hair. He'd try, but it always looked worse when he was done. Then he married Tina, and she didn't want anything to do with me *or* my hair." Her tone was light, but I heard the pain behind the words.

"So who fixed your hair when you were little?" I

asked. "Because after first grade, it always looked really good."

"I did." She tilted her chin up proudly. "I had to. Nobody else was going to do it. I started with ponytails because they were easy. Then I taught myself how to braid. Later I got into French braids, banana curls, crimping, you name it."

All I could think was, *who is this girl?* She was no one I'd ever met before. The Lanie I'd thought I knew didn't exist. She'd been born out of *your picture is stupid* and grew to malignant proportions in my imagination. And her impression of me was just as false.

"Well, your hair definitely isn't stupid anymore," I said. "That French braid is perfect."

"Oh. Thanks." She reached up to pat the back of her head. "Hey, I could French-braid your hair sometime. If you want."

My mother poked her head through the kitchen door at that moment, saving me from answering. "There you are. How about you and your *friend*—" She paused to beam in Lanie's direction. "—come out and have some cake."

In the banquet room, Lanie and I sat at a table with slices of cake in front of us, though she just picked at hers. The party was winding down. I got up to help people find their jackets, and Lanie followed me around like a baby duck who'd imprinted on me. I was glad Sophia and Emma weren't here to see this. I'd never get in with them if they thought Lanie and I were tight.

"Oh, heck!" Lanie said as I was waving goodbye to Kinsey Kowalski. "I just realized, I don't have a way home. Sophia's dad was supposed to give me a ride."

She turned pleading eyes on me. "Could you and your parents take me home?"

"Actually—" I made a regretful face. "—we're going to be here for a while. You know, cleaning up and stuff."

"I can help."

"No, no, you should go home. You're upset."

"No, I'm okay now, thanks to you."

"Seriously," I said. "I want you to sit down and relax. I will find somebody to drive you home."

Only a few party stragglers remained. I spotted Sarah Palmer at the front window, watching for her ride. Sarah had shoulder-length hair, just long enough to French-braid.

I opened my mouth to call out to her but shut it as I heard a voice behind me say, "So you don't need to have a degree in music?"

It was a voice I didn't hear very often, but I recognized it immediately. It was the voice of Austin Oliver, and he was talking to DJ Rick.

Rick said, "No, no. If you wanted to be a radio DJ, you'd major in something like broadcast journalism. If you just want to do weddings and parties as a side gig, you don't need a college degree at all. You just have to put in the time learning the ropes."

"Hey, Austin," I said, moving toward him before I could talk myself out of it. "I need a favor." He turned to face me, his eyebrows jerking upward as if he was shocked to learn I had vocal cords. "Would you be able to give Lanie a ride home?"

See, Austin? I can talk just fine when I have something to say.

Austin said, "Who's Lanie?"

160

I pointed her out. She was sitting by herself at a table. When she saw us looking, she smiled hopefully and waved.

"Her ride left without her," I said.

"Huh. Rude."

"Yeah. She's really upset."

Notice how I'm taking the initiative here, Austin, finding a ride for a stranded guest. See how caring I am, how competent? I am a girl who knows how to get things done. A problem-solver. An interesting person. Not the nobody you've always thought I was.

"She lives on Apparition Avenue," I said.

He flinched in an exaggerated way. "Whoa. That street's too bougie for my car."

I laughed, a tinkling *tee-hee-hee* that didn't sound like me at all. "Oh, Austin. You're so funny. Your car is just fine."

Austin drove an old compact coupe, silver with a black fabric interior and an off-center dent in the front bumper. He parked it on the street in front of his house, and that car and I, we were good friends. Every time I walked past it, I ran my hand along its smooth exterior. I patted its hood. Once I'd written *Hi Austin* on one of the filthy passenger windows and dotted each *i* with a heart.

"Uh, sure, I can take her," he said, "Just give me a minute."

"Really? Thanks, Austin—you're the best."

Austin turned back to finish his conversation with DJ Rick. I was trembling as I walked back to Lanie. My face felt hot. But I'd done it. I'd had a real-life conversation with Austin Oliver.

Maybe fifteen would be a good year. Maybe I

161

could show Austin the girl I really was.
Maybe he'd even like what he saw.

Chapter 29

"No, no, no!" cried Sophia. She threw her pencil on the floor. "This is too hard. I'm never going to get it."

I suppressed a sigh. I really didn't need this today. I'd spent most of last night on the astral plane, and I was exhausted.

I hadn't given up on Logan. I'd been hanging out at Mount Rushmore just about every night, but he never showed. When I asked him about it, he swore he swung by Rushmore every time he traveled. We just kept missing each other, he said. Astral projection wasn't like bus or train travel. There wasn't a schedule. You couldn't control the timing of an OBE, and some nights you didn't even have one. Plus, there was the three-hour time difference. No wonder our paths hadn't crossed.

It all sounded like excuses to me. Evasiveness. But why? Was he hiding something new?

I picked up the pencil and laid it on Sophia's desk. "Let's try a few more problems."

"No. I'm sick of doing problems." Her lower lip jutted out in a pout. "You need to explain things better. That's what being a good tutor is all about. If you would just explain things right, I wouldn't have to do all these practice problems."

She was wrong there, but I wasn't about to tell her

that. When it came to math, practice really did make perfect.

"Fine. Let's start at the beginning," I said. I went over the week's lesson again and picked out four problems in the textbook. She got stuck on the first two, and I had to walk her through the steps. She got most of the way through the third one before calling me over for help. The fourth one she did on her own.

"See?" I said. "You're getting it. Now how about doing two more problems, just to reinforce—"

"No." She slapped her book closed. "I'm done. You want a soda?"

"Uh, sure," I said. This was only our first tutoring session, so I supposed it wouldn't hurt to cut it short. Anyway, I wanted to be more than Tutor Abby. I wanted her to see me as Friend Abby.

Sophia led me downstairs to the kitchen, which wasn't as impressive as Lanie's but was definitely nicer than mine. Cabinets white as a movie star's teeth, a golden hardwood floor. Stainless steel appliances, which my mother yearned for with every fiber of her being but which, according to her, she would get only over my dad's dead body. I just prayed she didn't have murder on her mind.

As Sophia was getting sodas out of the fridge, Emma breezed in the back door without knocking. Logan and I had always done that. We'd considered my house an extension of his and vice versa. Would I ever feel comfortable enough to barge into Sophia's or Emma's house? I couldn't imagine myself doing that.

"Well, look at *you*," Emma said, swirling her forefinger in the vicinity of my upper torso. I was wearing the birthday present Sophia and Emma had given me—a mint-green cashmere sweater. But while I appreciated the gift and what it must have cost, I couldn't help feeling disappointed. Didn't they know I already had a mint-green sweater? I wore it to school just about every week—they must have seen it. The sweater was a cheap polyester thing from a discount department store, not nearly as nice as the one they'd given me. But the point was, nobody needed two mint-green sweaters.

I was also troubled by the birthday card I'd found inside the gift box. Sophia and Emma had signed it, but there was a lumpy area near the bottom that looked like they'd whited out a third signature. Since I hadn't received a separate card and gift from Lanie, I was ninety-eight percent sure she'd gone in on the sweater gift. And if she'd chipped in to pay for it, she deserved to have her name on the card.

"I really love the sweater," I said. "Thanks a bunch, guys."

We sat at the island bar in the kitchen, sipping our sodas through the little keyholes on the can tops. Emma said to Sophia, out of the side of her mouth, but loud enough for me to hear, "Has she texted you lately?"

"Not for a while," said Sophia. "I think she's finally given up."

They turned to me as if inviting an inquiry about this exchange. So I obliged.

"Are you talking about Lanie? She was pretty upset when you left my party without her."

Emma giggled. "Um, we've kind of dumped Lanie."

"She went bonkers," Sophia added, widening her eyes for emphasis. "She wouldn't stop talking about

165

how some ghost or demon or something is haunting her. It's tragic, really."

"We couldn't take it anymore," said Emma. "The girl is cray-cray. We only hang with sane people."

They beamed at me like I was the poster child for teen sanity. Their approval was what I'd been longing for, yet it suddenly felt wrong to accept it at Lanie's expense. I felt bad about her dead mother, worse about what I'd done to her. The least I could do now was defend her.

"I don't think Lanie is crazy," I said. "She told me about the ghost-slash-demon thing. At my party," I clarified quickly. "It's not like I hang out with her. Anyway, she realized it was just a dream."

"That's not what she told us," said Sophia.

"She changed her mind after she thought it over," I said.

"Too late," said Emma.

Sophia took a lazy swig of soda. "We were probably going to dump her anyway. I mean, big whoop, so we were in the same dance class when we were, like, nine. Does that mean we have to be squished together for the rest of our lives?"

"We've *outgrown* her," said Emma.

"Don't feel sorry for her," Sophia told me. "She's doing fine without us. Especially now that she has *him*."

"Him," Emma said in a scathing tone.

"Him who?" I looked from Emma to Sophia.

"That guy. That cute junior," said Sophia. "What's his name again?"

"Austin," said Emma. "Austin Oliver. The two of them are dating. Totally in *luhhhvvv,* from what I hear."

Sophia slid off her bar stool. "Hey, you guys want to order a pizza? My mom's working late, and my dad's out of town. Or we could heat up leftover tuna casserole."

Emma made a face. "Tuna casserole, ew. Let's do pizza."

They looked at me, waiting for my vote.

"Pizza," I whispered, though when it arrived, I couldn't eat a bite.

Chapter 30

Hi, Austin.

Hi, Abby.

I just want to understand. Why couldn't you love me?

I don't know. I guess I never saw you as anything more than some girl who lives on my street.

Is it because I'm not pretty enough? Because I'm so shy around you?

I don't know what it is. People can't control who they love and don't love. Think about it—did you decide to fall in love with me?

No. It just happened.

Well, same here.

But why Lanie? Out of all the girls in Eerie, why did you have to fall in love with Lanie Chobany?

Because she's pretty and funny and easy to talk to.

So are lots of girls.

She makes me feel special.

I *would have made you feel special.*

Come on, Abby. It's because of you that Lanie and I got together. If you hadn't asked me to drive her home from your party—

I know. I guess this is what they call poetic justice.

Besides, if Lanie hadn't come along, I would have fallen in love with some other girl. Somebody else who wasn't you.

I know.
Goodbye, Abby.
Goodbye, Austin.

Chapter 31

I fell into a funk that lasted most of the week. My mother thought I was fighting off a virus and practically force-fed me orange juice and ibuprofen. She even let me skip school on Wednesday. I stayed in bed all day, curled like a dying insect under my blankets.

I wondered if, somewhere, God or the universe or whatever entity was in charge of The Big Everything was having a good laugh at my expense. Entertaining stuff, my heartache. Who doesn't love irony?

There was nothing I could do about this. Nothing. Love couldn't be destroyed or postponed or transferred to a different person. Time couldn't be turned back so that someone else, not Austin, could drive Lanie home from my party. Not that I would have altered reality even if I could. I'd hurt Lanie enough. She deserved a little happiness—and I deserved to have my heart shattered like a fallen icicle.

Thursday. Friday. Saturday. Sunday. My misery dragged on like a stretch of bad weather. Then, on Sunday night, I turned a corner. Suddenly, I was sick of wallowing. It was time to pull myself together. But I needed a distraction—and what could be better for that than astral travel?

I flew straight to Rushmore and settled in to wait for Logan. I wasn't surprised when he didn't show. Disappointed, but not surprised. Next I flew to Paris.

He wasn't there either, though I did see the dead white-haired man, still searching for that elusive portal to the next world.

With nothing better to do, I went exploring. I knew I would pay the price the next day, but I wasn't ready to go home.

I visited Stonehenge, which was as impressive in its own way as Mount Rushmore. I stayed for a long time, flitting from stone to stone, marveling. How had the long-ago builders, with no modern construction equipment to aid them, managed to stand those huge slabs of rock upright in a circle and lay equally huge slabs across their tops? It was a mystery worthy of Eerie, Oregon.

Flying over the English Channel, I met two other astral travelers, dark-skinned twin girls who appeared to be a year or two younger than me. But they were shy and flitted away before I could even ask their names.

I flew to Venice and followed the tight, mazelike passageways through the crowded interior of the city. In one of the shops, I saw a colorful pendant necklace that I would have bought if I'd been there in person. Astral projection was great, no doubt about it, but it had its limitations.

On a whim, I dove down into the ocean. I explored a sea cave, chased colorful schools of fish, and met a pair of whales who parted to let me pass between them.

Everything I saw was fascinating, and yet I couldn't recapture the sense of joy and wonder I'd felt while traveling with Logan. Seeing the world was an empty experience when you didn't have someone to share it with.

I finally decided to call it a night. Wafting wearily

up my street, I saw an unexpected sight—a dead spirit floating steadily upward. As I got closer, I was stunned to see who it was.

Mrs. Benson.

I chased her into the night sky. "Mrs. Benson! Mrs. Benson, wait!"

She didn't even look my way. When I reached her, I saw her darkened face turned upward, her eyes fixed purposefully on something I couldn't see.

Jakob had said astral travelers couldn't communicate with dead spirits, but I had to try. "Mrs. Benson? It's me, Abby. Oh, Mrs. Benson, I'm so sorry you died!"

Still no reaction. I scanned the ground, checking for an ambulance in her driveway, for lights blazing from her windows, something to indicate that her death had been discovered. But the house was dark, the street quiet. Mrs. Benson lived alone. I was probably the only person who knew she was dead.

When I turned my gaze back to the heavens, Mrs. Benson was gone. I glanced wildly in every direction, but she was nowhere. She must have reached her destination, the place her spirit was meant to go next.

I wished I'd seen her go. Had there been a bright light? A beckoning spirit guide? Was the portal to the next world something astral travelers could see, or only the dead themselves?

I swooped down and entered her house through the roof. I hovered above her bed, staring somberly at her body. If it hadn't been for the blue lips and grayish face, I might have thought she was sleeping. One arm dangled over the side of the bed. I lifted it and laid it gently across her stomach.

Both of Mrs. Benson's children lived out of state. She had no family nearby. How long would it be until somebody discovered her body? Days? That wasn't acceptable. It needed to happen sooner.

I picked up the receiver of her bedside phone and dropped it onto her pillow, next to her head. Then I dialed 9-1-1, though it took me a few tries to hit the right numbers. When I heard the operator answer— "Nine-one-one, what's your emergency?"—I left the room. I'd watched enough cop shows to know that when nobody replied, the authorities would trace the call. They would send someone to the house—a police officer, most likely.

Downstairs, I unlocked the front door to make things as easy as possible for whoever responded.

Back in my bedroom, I landed in my body with a jolt that awakened me. There was no way I'd be able to get back to sleep anytime soon. I paced around my room, chewing my thumbnail and gasping "Sorry! Sorry!" toward the ceiling.

Mrs. Benson was only the second person I knew who'd died. The first had been my grandpa, who'd passed away when I was eleven. When my mother had told me about the stroke that killed him, the first thing I thought of was how awful I'd been to him that time when I was five. Grandma and Grandpa were visiting, and I was mad about something, and Grandpa, trying to help, scootched over on the couch and said, "Come sit with Grandpa, Abby," and I yelled, "No, Grandpa! I hate you!"

Six years passed, and in all that time, I never once said, "Hey, Grandpa, remember that time I said I hated you? I didn't mean it." Then he died, and I couldn't.

Now I was in a similar situation. Hadn't I learned anything?

When Logan and I used to see Mrs. Benson weeding her flower bed or raking leaves, we would stop to chat. That had been Logan's doing. But when I was outside alone, I would cut through the Martinezes' backyard to avoid her. I didn't want to get stuck listening to her dull, drawn-out stories about her grandkids, her heating and ventilation issues, the new pill that wasn't doing a thing for her arthritis. Logan knew the right things to say to gabby neighbors. I didn't.

Mrs. Benson had been a nice lady. A good neighbor. She'd taken me in when I was scared about the levitating jacket. She used to bring us tomatoes from her backyard garden. I liked her a lot, but I'd never told her, and now I never could.

Chapter 32

"This is stupid." Sophia threw her pencil on the floor. "Why do I have to learn about quadratic equations? Am I ever gonna use this stuff in real life?"

She was wearing a T-shirt that said, "I'm Your Worst Nightmare." I wondered if she'd put it on specially for me.

I picked up her pencil and placed it on her desk. "Probably not. But if you want to pass algebra, you have to learn it."

"I wish I was still in pre-algebra like Emma. That was easier."

"Well, you're not in pre-algebra. You're in algebra, so let's get back to it."

I explained the concept of quadratic equations for the third time, though Sophia interrupted twice to answer text messages. I gave her some problems to work through. While she was occupied with that, my thoughts drifted to Mrs. Benson.

I'd tried to act shocked when my mother had told me the news. I didn't have to fake my sadness, though. The funeral had been this morning, and both of my parents had attended. I'd wanted to go, too, but my mother said that Mrs. Benson, being a retired schoolteacher, wouldn't have wanted me to miss school on her account.

"Oh my God! I am so not getting this!" Sophia

cried, flinging her pencil to the floor yet again. "Jeez, Abby. I thought you'd be a better tutor."

And I thought you'd be a better student. I pressed my lips together so I wouldn't accidentally say it out loud. She'd gotten a C-minus on last week's quiz.

"I need to get a B or better on Friday's quiz. If I don't bring my grade up—"

"I know."

"Maybe I need a different tutor," she said savagely. "Brent Lamar is good at math. Maybe I'll ask him."

Deep in my stomach, a fist clenched. "Come on, Sophia. You have to give this a chance. This is only our second session."

"Well, it's no better than the first."

"Let me think. I'll figure something out."

"You'd better."

Her phone rang, its pulsing hip-hop ringtone lashing the quiet like a siren. I could tell that the caller was Emma from Sophia's tone as she launched into a scornful blow-by-blow of a conversation she'd had with the girl whose locker was next to hers. She plopped down on her bed, chattering and giggling like I wasn't there.

Meanwhile, I was racking my brain for a new teaching method, something that would turn *I'm not getting this* into *now I understand.* Was there an *Algebra for Dummies* book? Probably, but Sophia would be offended by the title. A step-by-step video? I shook my head. Nothing was going to help if Sophia wasn't willing to put in the work.

I heard Sophia say, "And then her friend walks over—you know, that girl with the annoying eyebrows? And she says…"

I was thinking so hard, my head was starting to ache.

Finally, an idea popped up out of nowhere, though it wasn't a teaching method. It wasn't any kind of method. It was an idea straight from the dark side of my soul. God, what was I thinking? I couldn't do that.

Could I?

Abruptly, Sophia's tone changed. Her responses became clipped and cryptic. My ears prickled. I was ninety-nine percent sure she and Emma were talking about me.

"Yeah, like, right now. …Um, pretty bad. …No—opposite, opposite. …I thought so, too, but… I know. …Yeah, I might have to. We'll see."

When she got off the phone, I walked over to her. "I might have a way to get you through Friday's quiz."

"What is it?"

"I'll tell you tomorrow. I have some work to do first."

This had to be the worst idea I'd ever had, but if it worked, Sophia would ace the quiz, and I'd be a hero—in her eyes, anyway.

To the rest of the world, I'd be a villain.

Chapter 33

My OBE began, and though I was itching to fly off to Mount Rushmore to look for Logan, I went to school instead.

I entered through the front doors, which was silly, because I could go in anywhere—through the roof, a window, the sturdy brick walls. Force of habit, I supposed. The school had a postapocalyptic feel with everyone gone, with the lighting dimmed. I half-expected to see a zombie lurching down the hall.

Mrs. Farkosh was not only my algebra teacher but also the adviser for the math club, so I knew a lot about her practices and routines. She created our weekly algebra quiz every Tuesday and stored the printout in the bottom drawer of her desk. On Thursday afternoons, she went to the office to make photocopies. At this late hour, her classroom door was shut and probably locked, but that didn't stop me. I sailed straight through.

I inserted a tendril of myself into the lock on her desk and jiggled it till I heard a click. A bunch of manilla folders were inside the bottom drawer, arranged alphabetically. I flipped through them until I came to one labeled Weekly Algebra Quiz - Ninth Grade. Just inside was this week's quiz, a single sheet containing five problems. Behind it was the answer key.

This was turning out to be easier than I'd expected.

I slid the answer key under the classroom door.

Back in the hall, I picked up the paper and wafted it above me like a kite. As I flew to the school office, I made sure to stay out of range of the security cameras. If someone viewed the video footage, I didn't want them spotting a sheet of paper floating through the air. I doubted that anybody watched the security videos on a regular basis, but you never knew.

The school office was locked up tight, so once again I inserted the paper under the door. I went to the photocopier and made a copy of the answer key.

Sophia's locker was just up the hall from the office. I folded the copy in half vertically and slid it through one of the vents. It hit the floor of the locker with a loud *ping*.

Down the hall I saw a light shining from a classroom door. A yellow cart was parked outside, cluttered with mops and brooms and cleaning supplies. Out of sight, someone was whistling, undoubtedly old Moe, the nighttime janitor. It would take him a while to work his way up to this part of the building. Still, I shouldn't dawdle.

I hurried back to Mrs. Farkosh's room, where I slipped the original quiz key into the folder and locked the drawer. Then I flew home.

The return to my body woke me up. Nausea rose inside me like a tidal wave. I ran to the bathroom and threw up.

Today's headline: *Abby Kendrick hits a new low.*

Chapter 34

"Abby, this is fabulous! It's exactly what I need."

Sophia was standing at her locker, folding the bootleg quiz key into a small square. I'd made sure I was waiting for her first thing in the morning, before she opened her locker.

"How'd you get this?" she wanted to know.

"That's not important. Listen, this is a one-time thing, okay? It'll get you through this week's quiz, but after that, you're going to have to work really hard and actually learn the stuff."

"I will," she promised.

I didn't feel good about helping Sophia cheat, but I didn't feel totally bad either. Studying the answer key would help her learn this week's lesson. We had to show our work for each problem, so she would have to memorize all the steps. That would involve study and repetition—the very things she'd been avoiding—so in the end she was bound to have a better grasp of the concepts. And that made it more likely that she'd understand next week's lesson, since each lesson built on the previous one.

On Saturday, I got invited to the mall with Sophia and Emma, my first friend-type outing with them. I told my mother I was going to the library—alone. I didn't want to jinx anything.

We got our nails done in matching colors, a rich

purple that was actually called "Rich Purple"—*so* unimaginative, we agreed—and tried on some outlandish designer clothes we had no intention of buying. Sophia mentioned a weekend ski trip her family would be taking in February. Her parents had said she could bring a friend along, but she was pretty sure she could talk them into two. She didn't say I was the second friend, but the implication was there.

On Monday, Sophia practically floated out of algebra class. Mrs. Farkosh had handed back our quizzes, and Sophia had aced it. Mrs. Farkosh was happy, too. "I think you people are finally getting it," she said, throwing a bright glance around the classroom.

But on Tuesday we were back to pencil tantrums. Sophia wasn't getting it, my tutoring skills weren't up to par, et cetera, et cetera. She cried prettily into a wad of tissues. She *needed* that answer key, just this week, just one more time. Please, she begged. *Please.* If she had to quit Galactic Scrimshaw, she would literally die.

So I gave in. I got her the answer key that week. And the next week and the next.

How gullible *was* I? Had I really thought this would be a one-time thing? I'd given Sophia an easy way to sail through algebra, and she'd latched onto it with tiger teeth. But although her grade was stable for now, what would happen when it was time for the multichapter exam at the end of February? Memorizing the solutions to a five-problem quiz was one thing. But a whole exam? Even somebody with a photographic memory would have trouble retaining that much information. Would she blame me if she failed?

I couldn't shake a feeling of impending doom. I

felt as though I was sliding down an icy slope that ended in a cliff.

Chapter 35

"Abby. Abby, wake up!"

I lurched upward as if hurled from a catapult and found myself eyeball to eyeball with my mother. Talk about disoriented. A second ago, I'd been hovering above Mount Rushmore yet again on the off chance that Logan would show up. Now I was back in my bed. I wondered if astral travel jet lag was a thing.

"Why are you always so hard to wake up?" my mother yelled.

"I'm not always hard to wake up."

"And why are you sleeping on a Saturday afternoon?"

"I needed a nap. People take naps."

"Not you. You never used to. That does it. I'm making an appointment at a sleep clinic like Lisa did for Logan."

I gave her a dry look. "And how did that work out?" I already knew the answer.

"The results were inconclusive," she admitted. "Still. If this keeps happening, we need to do *something.*"

I slid off the bed and hiked up my droopy sweatpants. My legs, no longer in spirit form, felt heavy, like weights dragging me down. "Did you want something, or do you just enjoy interrupting my sleep?"

"Your friend is here. A pretty blonde girl. I think I

remember her from your birthday party." She didn't even try to hide her grin. A friend had come to visit!

"Why didn't you say so?" I bounded to my dresser to run a brush through my hair. Then I changed into my nicest jeans.

Based on my mother's description, I was picturing Sophia, so it was a shock when I saw Lanie sitting on the couch in the family room, sipping lemonade from one of our good glasses.

"Hey," Lanie said when she spotted me. Her hair was tousled in that messy-chic style I'd never cared for.

"Hey," I said warily, perching on the edge of Dad's recliner. "What are you doing here?"

"I was taking a walk and thought I'd stop by to say hi."

"I didn't know you knew where I lived."

"My boyfriend showed me. Austin Oliver? He lives down the street. He said he used to come up here to play flashlight tag."

"Right." I couldn't stop staring at Lanie's hands, with their dainty, tapered fingers. Those hands had privileges mine would never have. I pictured them stroking Austin's face, playfully patting his biceps, sliding up his chest as he pulled her in for a kiss.

"We usually spend Saturdays together." She grinned and corrected herself. "Well—all our spare time, actually." She sighed blissfully. "Austin's so great."

I managed to keep my face neutral—but *ouch*. I looked down at my own hands, which were squarish and short-fingered and would probably never stroke a boy's face. Was Lanie about to thank me for getting her and Austin together? If she did, I just might throw up.

"You want something to eat?" I asked. "I think my mom made chocolate chip cookies. We might have potato chips, too."

"No thanks, I'm good." She sipped her lemonade. "Austin and his whole family are out of town right now. His aunt from Tennessee died."

"Aw, that's sad. Is your lemonade okay? Does it need more sugar?"

"No, it's fine." Lanie set her glass on the coffee table, taking care to center it on the coaster my mother had provided. "Austin and I, we were together on Tuesday. We went to the mall. We saw you with Sophia and Emma."

Ah. This was why she'd come.

I said, "Huh. I didn't see *you.*"

That wasn't true. Sophia and Emma and I had been heading toward the food court when Emma said, "Here comes Lanie with that new boyfriend of hers. Walk fast so we don't have to talk to them."

I'd looked away as soon as I spotted them, but the afterimage lingered—the glowing faces, the clasped hands. When Lanie called my name, I pretended not to hear.

Now she was sitting on my couch, waiting for an explanation. I didn't owe her one, but I gave it anyway. "I'm tutoring Sophia in algebra. Sometimes when we're done, she invites me to do stuff with her and Emma. Like get pizza or go to the mall. That's all it was."

That was the truth. We still hadn't crossed the line into true friendship territory. It was frustrating. I happened to know that Emma had slept over at Sophia's house last night. I hadn't been invited.

"That's cool," Lanie said with a shrug. "If you

want to hang with them, I'm totally, totally fine with it."

The double *totally* told me she wasn't fine with it.

Which made us even because I wasn't fine with everything she was doing.

"I just want to warn you," she went on, "in case it turns into something more."

"Warn me?"

She leaned forward and spoke softly, as if afraid of being overheard. "Sophia and Emma—they're not the nicest girls. They're mean, and I'm not just saying that because of what they did to me. They've always been mean. Their favorite thing to do is talk about people. Put people down."

"So?" I shot back. "You used to be like that. You used to put people down."

For a second, Lanie looked startled, and maybe even hurt, but then she nodded heavily. "I know. It's not something I'm proud of. I did what I had to do to fit in."

"I saw Sophia's yearbook from last year," I told her. "She told me how the three of you went through and rated everybody cool or not cool." Now I was flat-out lying. Sophia had never mentioned the yearbook ratings. "In fact," I said, watching her carefully, "she said you were the one who wanted to rate me not cool."

"That's true." Her gaze on me didn't waver. "But I only said that because Sophia said you were weird. I was trying to agree with her. When you're with those two, the safest thing to do is just go along with whatever they say. Anyway, that was back when I didn't like you, so no way was I going to say you were cool."

I had to give her points for honesty. And I realized she was right. That night when they'd been going through the yearbook, it was Sophia who said I was weird, right after my name came up. I'd forgotten that part. It suited me better to pin the whole thing on Lanie.

"I don't know why I stuck with those two as long as I did," Lanie said, shaking her head ruefully. "They were always ganging up on me. They used to put me down for being just a cheerleader."

"Just a cheerleader?" I frowned. "Most people think being a cheerleader is cool."

"Not those two. They don't think it's as good as being a gymnast. See, I tried out for the gymnastics team the same time Emma did, but I didn't make it. They never let me forget that. They were always saying how singing and gymnastics take real talent, but anybody can be a cheerleader. All you have to do is jump around yelling preschool words. 'Go team go. Get that ball. Fight, fight, fight.' "

"I'm sure they didn't mean it," I said half-heartedly. But I had to wonder—if Sophia and Emma looked down on Lanie for being a cheerleader, what did they think of me? I was good at math but not much else.

"The only reason we came to your birthday party," Lanie said, "was so Sophia could get you to be her tutor. You know that, right?"

Something sharp twisted in my heart. I'd suspected as much but had chosen not to believe it. Now that Lanie had said it out loud, I could no longer deny it.

"Yeah," I mumbled. "I know."

"You're a nice person, Abby," Lanie said, getting to her feet, and I had to look away because I wasn't a nice person, not at all. "Don't let them turn you into one of them."

Chapter 36

It was 6:47 p.m., and I was tucked into bed for the night.

My parents didn't know I'd turned in early, because they weren't home. They'd gone to the Community Foundation's annual banquet. That meant I didn't have to worry that somebody would come at me with ibuprofen and a thermometer, demanding to know why I was in bed so early. My plan was to head to Pittsburgh as soon as I had an OBE.

If I had an OBE.

Please, God, let me have an OBE.

In all the time I'd been searching for Logan on the astral plane, I'd had no luck. Sometimes I spent my whole OBE at Mount Rushmore, flitting back and forth above the presidents' heads. I'd also continued to visit the Eiffel Tower. One night I met another astral traveler there, an Israeli woman who said she knew Logan but hadn't seen him for months. She asked me to tell him hello from Talia. Twice I saw the dead white-haired man, still wafting aimlessly through the air.

Logan, though? He never showed.

This made me very uneasy. I often found myself gazing into the night sky, wondering if Logan was up there doing God-knew-what, despite his promise to stay on Earth.

Last week, I'd started making nightly treks to

Pittsburgh, hoping to catch him as his OBE was starting. Somehow I knew where his house was, even though I'd never been there before. Astral travel seemed to come with its own magical GPS.

But I was always too late. The time difference gave Logan a three-hour head start that thwarted me every time. I finally realized that if I wanted to catch him in Pittsburgh, I was going to have to go to bed super early.

Last night I'd inflicted some serious sleep deprivation on myself. I'd been in a zombielike daze all day and had even nodded off in French class. Tonight, though, my fatigue was paying off. I'd barely closed my eyes when I found myself floating above my bed, looking down at that sad, sleeping girl with the gray hollows under her eyes. I zoomed outside and headed east.

Logan was in his bedroom talking on his cell phone. Laughing, flirting. His room looked a lot like his old one in Eerie. Same furniture, arranged similarly. But the comforter on his bed was different, a solid hunter green that seemed more grown-up than the colorful geometric patterns he'd favored in the past.

I drifted around, browsing the framed photos on display throughout the room. They cluttered his desk, his dresser, his nightstand. Logan always said it didn't make sense to keep a bunch of photos stored on your phone, invisible and largely forgotten. Better to print them out so you could enjoy them every day.

Most of the pictures were snapshots from his new life in Pittsburgh. Logan on the soccer field, a blur of movement. Logan at a Halloween party, dressed like a gangster in a dark suit. Logan laughing with three other guys, all of them wearing Santa hats. A bunch of photos of Logan standing next to a particular guy with tortoise-shell glasses and a shock of dark hair. I was ninety-nine percent sure the guy was Charlie.

I found my school picture from this year on his dresser, half-hidden behind a picture of Charlie.

A thought hit me with the force of an epiphany: *maybe Logan was better off without me.* Had I held him back from living his best life? I thought back on all those Halloweens we'd shared, our coordinated costumes. Our joint birthday parties. Would he have preferred to go it alone?

And a related, equally troubling thought: was *I* better off without *him*?

I was trying not to listen in on Logan's phone conversation, but when I heard him say, in a husky voice, "You're the one who started it. Not that I'm complaining," I slipped outside to give him privacy. I hid behind the chimney of the house next door while I waited.

Who was he talking to? Someone he liked a lot, obviously. It was weird not knowing everything that was going on in my cousin's life.

Half an hour later, Logan's spirit shot through the roof and soared up into the sky. I followed, keeping my distance. I kept waiting for him to arc back toward Earth, but he never did. I followed him up through a puffy cloud. We passed a jetliner cruising at altitude. And still he kept going, pushing past the last layers of Earth's atmosphere.

A heaviness settled into the core of my being. I called out, "Logan, stop!"

He came to an abrupt halt and whirled to face me, his face registering surprise, guilt, and anger, in that

191

order. "Abby! What the—? Are you following me?"

I caught up with him, frowning like a stern parent.

"I can't believe this. You *promised.*"

His shoulders slumped. "I know, Abs. I'm sorry. I meant to stay on Earth, I really did. I just couldn't do it."

"Where are you off to? Mysterium?"

A shrug. Those darty eyes. "I'm going to Jupiter. To get more stupider." It was a silly rhyme we used to say when we were little.

I didn't crack a smile. I just stared at him.

"I like to hang out in space, okay?" he said, sounding defensive. "A couple of times a week I come out here and zip around the solar system, checking out different planets. It's no big deal."

"No big deal? Have you forgotten what happened to me the last time we were out here together? We talked about this, you and me. How hard astral travel is on our bodies."

Another shrug. "That's why I don't stay out here for too long."

"Well, you look terrible." Even in the void of space, I could see the ghost of his physical form. The sharpened cheekbones, the deep hollows beneath his eyes. As if he was slowly decaying, turning from flesh into bone.

"I'm fine."

But he wasn't fine. I knew he wasn't, and I should have tried to do something about it then and there. I should have made him talk to me, tell me everything.

But I didn't. All I said was, "How about we go back to Earth? You can show me more of your favorite places."

192

He gazed at me with a combination of love and exasperation, a look I'd seen all too often from him. He glanced wistfully over his shoulder and said, "Sure, Abs. Let's do that. Have you ever seen the pyramids?"

I was relieved. Happy just to be with him. I wanted to believe I'd talked some sense into him, and he'd stay on Earth from now on. But deep down, I knew better, even then.

Chapter 37

Tuesday night. Time to copy another quiz key. I groaned as I climbed into bed and groaned again as my spirit left my body. I felt like I was trapped in a recurring nightmare, a hell of my own making.

Might as well get it over with. I zoomed off to the school and entered Mrs. Farkosh's room. After unlocking her desk, I flipped through the folders in the bottom drawer.

The Weekly Algebra Quiz folder wasn't there.

I stared into the drawer, unable to believe what I wasn't seeing. I flipped through the folders a second time, hastily, frantically. Then a third time, more carefully. Finally I found it. She'd misfiled it under A for algebra instead of W for weekly.

After giving my jangled nerves a minute to calm down, I slid the answer key under the door and out into the hall. I was almost to the office when a janitor's cart rolled out of a doorway up ahead, old Moe right behind it.

I froze, holding the answer key in front of me. Moe was trying to shove the push broom into its slot at the side of the cart, so he wasn't looking my way. If he turned his head, he would see that bright white sheet of paper floating in midair. I whooshed it down to the floor.

Moe turned sharply in my direction, which told me

he'd caught the movement from the corner of his eye. And, oh crud, now he was sauntering toward me, whistling softly, his bleary-eyed stare boring straight through me. I knew he couldn't see me, but that stare still creeped me out. I watched in dismay as he got closer. I flinched as his gaze dropped to the quiz key.

He bent down with a grunt and snatched up the paper. He glanced around as if trying to figure out where it had come from. After studying it for a minute, he turned and headed back up the hall. He dropped it into the trash bag mounted on his cart. Thank God he hadn't crumpled it up! Now I just had to get it back without letting him see.

I followed him to the next classroom. He parked his cart in a corner and ambled toward the wastebasket at the far side of the teacher's desk. If I didn't hurry, that quiz key would be buried under a fresh mound of trash, and I'd never be able to recover it.

I flew to the cart and peered into the garbage bag. The quiz key was perched atop the daily mishmash of trash—paper coffee cups, candy bar wrappers, used-up pens, balled-up wads of paper. I eased it up out of the bag and guided it toward the doorway. Moe was already starting to turn around, the wastebasket in his hands. In my hurry to get the quiz key out of sight, I moved too abruptly. The paper made a flapping noise as I whipped it around the edge of the doorjamb.

I cursed my own clumsiness.

In the hall I slid the paper up the wall next to the doorway and held it in place just below the ceiling. I heard Moe moving across the classroom, his footfalls heavy on the tile floor. He stepped into the hall and looked around, scratching the bald spot at the back of his head. To my relief, he didn't look up. After a minute, he went back into the classroom.

I didn't waste a second. I gusted off to the office to make my copy. Then I flew to Sophia's locker. As I was about to slip the quiz key inside, Moe stepped into the hall again. Hastily I shoved the paper through a vent. It hit the locker floor with a metallic twang that rang out like a gong in the silent building.

Moe stood there staring up the hall. He muttered, "Dang ghosts."

Moe thought the school was haunted? If I hadn't been so unnerved by everything that had gone wrong tonight, I would have found that hilarious.

I cannot keep doing this, I told myself as I flew home. I needed to have a chat with Sophia. Maybe it was time to let Brent Lamar take a stab at tutoring her.

The more I thought about it, the better I liked that idea. In fact, maybe I would suggest it to Sophia. The two of us got along fine when we were sharing a pizza or getting our nails done, but tutoring had become a major source of tension between us. Getting rid of that pain point would open the door to the friendship I wanted so badly.

It felt good to have a plan. Back in my body, I fell into a deep, peaceful sleep, never realizing what a devastating mistake I'd just made.

Chapter 38

It was Friday, quiz day, and Mrs. Farkosh was cranky. She'd been that way most of the week. She passed the quizzes out row by row, slapping the papers down on the front desks like she was swatting flies. People kept shooting her anxious glances.

I'd barely finished writing my name on my paper when I caught a movement to my right. It was Sophia, who sat two rows over and three seats up. She was staring at me with the frantic look of someone about to be burned at the stake. She held up her quiz and mouthed *What the hell?* I raised my hands in a *huh?* gesture. I had no idea what she meant.

"Sophia! Turn around and get to work," snapped Mrs. Farkosh.

I scanned my quiz. It seemed normal, no different from all the others. Five problems on the topics we'd covered this week. What was Sophia trying to tell me?

When the bell rang, I crammed my belongings into my backpack and hurried after Sophia. She was walking so fast, I didn't catch up with her till she stopped at her locker.

"Sophia, hey. What's going on?"

"What's going on?" she repeated, her voice trembling. "*You* tell *me*."

I shook my head, mystified.

"The answer key," she said impatiently. "You saw

it. You know."

"But I didn't see it. I never look at the answer key." It was my own brand of ethics. Although I was helping Sophia cheat, it was something I would never do myself. And the truth was, I didn't need to. "Just tell me what's going on."

"It's the *wrong key*!" Her eyes glistened with tears of fury. "You gave me the wrong answer key."

I gaped at her. "That's impossible. I got it in the same place as all the others."

She fumbled in her purse and thrust a small, fat paper square at me. "See for yourself."

She flounced off down the hall.

I unfolded the answer key and saw that she was right. This was the key to a whole different quiz. Same concepts, different problems.

I was dumbfounded. Why would Mrs. Farkosh replace this week's quiz with a different one?

It wasn't until American history class that I figured it out. I let out a horrified gasp that prompted Mr. Paxton to pause the lecture and say, "Does that surprise you, Abby?"—referring to some point he'd just made— and I said, in a voice that was a mere squeak, "I'm good. Go on."

I slumped in my seat, my eyes squeezed shut. I'd screwed up—big time. I'd been so distracted by Moe's presence that I'd forgotten to return the original quiz key to Mrs. Farkosh's desk. I'd left it in the photocopier, where one of the school office workers had undoubtedly discovered it Wednesday morning and traced it back to Mrs. Farkosh.

And since I'd never returned to Mrs. Farkosh's room, I'd also left her desk unlocked, her bottom drawer open. She knew someone had been snooping around. That was why she was in such a foul mood. That was why she'd trashed the original quiz.

My heart ticked fast as I worked through the ramifications of the situation. Mrs. Farkosh was bound to notice that Sophia, who'd aced every quiz over the past few weeks, had failed this one. What if she confronted Sophia? What if Sophia ratted me out?

I might as well have skipped the rest of my classes, because I didn't hear a thing any of my teachers said. At the end of the day, I raced up the hall to Sophia's locker, my purse spanking my right hip as I went.

"Sophia, listen."

"Go away." Those eyes. Toxic green, like a bad potato.

"Listen, I'm sorry about all this. Mrs. Farkosh must have figured out someone was getting into her quiz keys." I couldn't admit that my own stupidity was to blame.

"You think?"

I ignored the sarcasm. "I know you're worried about getting in trouble—"

She shook her head. "I'm not gonna get in trouble."

"But Mrs. Farkosh is going to wonder why you did so well on the last few quizzes but failed this one."

She slid one last book into her backpack and slammed her locker shut. "I'm not the only one."

"What do you mean?"

Her upper lip curled in a sneer. "Did you really think I'd keep those answer keys to myself? I shared them with some friends. And they might have shared them with *their* friends."

I clamped a hand to my mouth. "Oh, Sophia, this is

bad! This is very bad."

"No, it's good," she fired right back at me. "If it was just me, I probably *would* be in trouble. And so would you, because if I'm going down, I'm sure as hell taking you with me. Why should I be the only one to get in trouble? I didn't steal those answer keys—you did. This whole thing was your idea."

I stared at her in disbelief. "Because I was trying to help you!"

"Yeah. Thanks a bunch for that." She veered around me and strode down the hall.

Chapter 39

No surprise—Sophia failed the quiz. And she wasn't the only one.

Monday afternoon, the whole junior high got called to the auditorium for an impromptu assembly. A scowling Principal Whittaker told us that cheating in any form would not be tolerated. His booming voice, amplified by the microphone, rattled my eardrums. I'd never seen him so mad. He said, "You know who you are" four times and "If you have any integrity at all, you'll come forward" twice. Everybody in the audience looked mystified, though you could tell some people were faking it.

Apparently, the school authorities hadn't been able to figure out who had stolen Mrs. Farkosh's quiz key or how they'd done it, so the whole school was being warned. A technician had been brought in to make sure the security cameras were working properly.

Sophia and Emma were no longer speaking to me. On Tuesday, Sophia didn't stop by my locker with her usual "See you at my house" reminder, so I could only assume our tutoring session had been cancelled. Being ghosted was painful, but I didn't text Sophia to find out what was going on. Emma either. That would have only made them madder. I was giving them time to cool down, hoping our relationship could get back to normal once this whole quiz thing blew over. After all, friends got mad at each other all the time and then made up.

The question was, had we ever really been friends?

I gave it till Friday, and when Sophia and Emma stopped at Emma's locker after school, I offered a cheery "Hey, guys!" Sophia ignored me completely, but Emma glanced at me, which I took as a good sign. Sophia said something to Emma about walking home instead of taking the bus. It was an unseasonably warm day, and lots of people who lived in nearby neighborhoods were walking home. My house was farther than some, twenty-five minutes by foot, but I decided to join the walkers.

I mingled with a small crowd, concealing myself behind taller people. After Sophia and Emma turned the corner onto Galloping Ghouls Boulevard, I started to creep up on them. My plan was to invite them to the mall to get our nails done—my treat. I still had a lot of cash left over from my birthday bounty.

The toe of my shoe scuffed on the concrete sidewalk. Sophia swiveled her head around and spotted me. "What the hell," she said to Emma.

They stopped walking. Emma said, "Can we help you?"

"Uh…"

"Do you want something? Why are you following us?"

"I'm not—I just… I heard you say you were walking home from school, and I thought that sounded fun, so—"

"Shut up." Sophia waved her hands impatiently. "You want to walk home after school? That's fine. Do what you want. But you can't hang with us. We have things to talk about. Private things."

"Oh, okay. Sorry," I mumbled.

When I got home, my parents were still at work, so there was nobody to witness the meltdown. Blotchy face, swollen eyes, gasping sobs—it wasn't pretty.

It was time to stop lying to myself. Sophia and Emma had never wanted me as a friend. Sophia had needed a math tutor, and that was all I'd ever been to her.

By the time my mother got home, I'd gotten my face back in order, though my eyes were still puffy. Dad came home while she was cooking dinner, a quick and easy skillet meal consisting of ground beef and noodles in a reddish-purple sauce. I was sprawled on the couch watching a sitcom and trying to pretend I wasn't miserable.

Dad slammed the front door, which told me instantly that something was wrong. Dad never slammed doors. He handled everything in our house gently, to avoid expensive repairs. He marched into the kitchen without taking his jacket off and said, "What the hell, Leah?"

My mother looked taken aback. "What?"

"I stopped at the gas station after work, and I ran into your sister's friend, Jan what's-her-name. Brewer?"

The wooden spoon my mother was holding clattered to the floor, leaving a reddish-purplish splatter on the white tiles.

"She couldn't stop raving about what a wonderful experience she had working with her realtor—*my wife!*"

"Oh God," said my mother.

"Realtor?" Dad got right in her face. "You're a *realtor*? Is this true?"

"Just barely. I've only sold two houses," my mother said meekly.

"Unbelievable." Dad paced around the kitchen, leaving a trail of bloody footprints from the spilled sauce. "You would have had to take classes, get licensed, find a job. And you never said a word to me?"

"I was going to tell you eventually. I wanted to surprise you."

"Surprise me?" He was shouting now. "If you want to surprise me, wash my car. Make my favorite dessert. Don't change careers without telling me."

"You want to know why I didn't tell you?" my mother said, finally recovering her backbone. "Because I knew you'd try to talk me out of it. Going into real estate sales is risky. A realtor's income is based on commissions, not on a steady salary. Knowing how you are about money, I knew you'd never let me quit my job to—"

My dad gasped theatrically. "Quit your job? You quit your job? Your real job, the one with the regular paycheck?"

"Calm down. I did not quit my job, not yet anyway. I decided to sell real estate on a part-time basis to see if I was any good at it. And I am, Joe. I am. I've only been doing it for three weeks, and I've already made two sales. I could make a lot of money doing this— much more than I make at that awful nonprofit job, which I hate, which is sucking all the life out of me."

My dad glanced around the house. His mouth tightened as he spotted me. "Abby, go to your room."

"Why? What did I do?"

"Your mother and I need to talk in private."

"I'm hungry. It's dinnertime."

"Here," said my mother, pulling a plate out of the cupboard. "Get some food and eat in your room."

I loaded up my plate and shuffled off to my room. The conversation resumed before I was all the way there. I slowed my pace so I could hear more. My dad asked bitterly, "How'd you pay for the real estate classes? Took out loans, I suppose? Which we'll have to pay back."

"No loans. For the past nine months, I've been working in a real estate office on Saturday mornings, plus a couple of evenings during the week. I paid for everything out of those paychecks. I even managed to save some money."

"So all those Saturday mornings you said you were at the gym—"

"I wasn't. And those nights when I said I was working late at the Community Foundation? I wasn't doing that either." She sounded oddly triumphant, like she was proud to have pulled one over on old Joe.

"Damn," my dad said in a dazed voice. "So many lies. I don't even know you anymore."

I slipped into my room and eased the door shut. At least one thing made sense. Now I knew how my mother could afford to lend Cody a thousand dollars.

But I had to agree with Dad. I didn't know this woman at all.

Chapter 40

We celebrated Grandma's birthday in early March with a family party at her house. Not that I felt much like partying. I was still smarting from losing my two best friends, who hadn't even known they were my best friends and sure as heck didn't care. I'd heard that Sophia's parents had made her quit Galactic Scrimshaw and had set her up with an official math tutor through the school's tutoring program.

I'd given up trying to talk to her and Emma. They wouldn't even look at me.

I was also dealing with tensions at home. My parents were barely speaking to each other. They wouldn't tell me anything, so I'd taken to spying on them during OBEs. I'd found out they were seeing a marriage counselor and a financial advisor, which I supposed was better than divorce lawyers. Meanwhile, my mother was continuing to work part-time as a realtor, and nobody, she declared, was going to stop her.

Then there was the Logan situation, which was the most troubling of all.

Still, I managed to bare my teeth in a way that passed as a smile as I wished Grandma a Happy Birthday.

My mother had brought dinner—a ham-and-potato casserole—so Grandma wouldn't have to cook. Cody and Amy showed up with a beautiful bakery-made birthday cake, which I thought was a nice peace offering. But Grandma grabbed it out of Cody's hands without so much as a thank you and shoved it in the refrigerator so hard that the cake smashed into the side of the box.

Grandma didn't let go of grudges easily.

Between my parents' crisis and the Cody-Grandma situation, the air was almost as frosty inside the house as outside, despite the fact that Grandma had the heat cranked up to the usual seventy-five degrees. Amy spent most of the evening huddled at one end of the couch, her sleeves pulled down over her hands like she was having a physical response to the psychological chill. I hardly said a word, though there were so many other issues going on that nobody seemed to notice.

Over cake and ice cream, Cody announced that he'd be flying to Washington, DC, the next day for a week of job-related training. Dad started to ask for details but stopped when Grandma gave him the evil eye. My mother and I loaded the dishwasher, and after that, Grandma opened her presents. Then we sat in the living room staring at the walls while trying to think up conversational topics that wouldn't upset Grandma.

Cody caught me in the kitchen as I was sneaking a second piece of cake. I'd been doing a lot of stress-eating lately, and nothing was better for that than chocolate cake. "Minutia. How you doing?"

"Good."

"You look tired. Are you sleeping okay?"

"Yeah, why?"

"Just want to make sure my little Minutia is A-OK." He got a soda out of the fridge and flicked the tab open. He took a sip, staring soberly at me.

My melancholy mood spiked into something mean-spirited, and I said, "How are *you* doing, Uncle Cody? You managing to keep away from alcohol?"

"Oh, Minutia," he said, thumping a hand on his chest and staggering backward as if I'd shot him. "Ouch."

A blush of shame warmed my cheeks. *Lighten up, Abby.* "I mean, how do I know you've got cola in that can," I said, pretending to tease, "and not something stronger?"

He laughed. "You watched me open it. If there's anything stronger than cola in this can, the bottling company is going to have a lawsuit on its hands." He held the can out to me, inviting me to take a sip. I shook my head.

"Why'd you start drinking in the first place?" I asked.

"Why does anybody?"

"How would I know? I'm fifteen."

"It was a rhetorical question." He tilted his head back and took a long swig of cola. "Hard to get used to family gatherings without our Rump Roast."

"I know. I don't think I'll ever stop missing him."

"Same here."

"I'm so worried about him."

He looked at me sharply. "Worried? Why?"

My heart thumped in dismay. The words had slipped out—but, oh, what a dumb, dangerous thing to say! "You know, just because we're so far apart, because I never see him. I never know what he's doing, where he is, what's going on in his life." I cringed at the nervous, prattling sound of my own voice.

Cody set his soda can on the counter. "Minutia? Is there something you want to talk about?"

"No," I said, a little too hastily. I licked cake frosting off my lips, but it probably looked like a nervous gesture.

"You've been quiet all evening. You upset about something?"

"My parents are having...issues."

"Is that all it is? You know you can tell me anything."

"There's nothing to tell." I was starting to feel panicky, like a small animal caught in a trap. Cody was good at reading people. He knew I had something on my mind, and if I stayed here, he would try to get it out of me, and I sort of wanted to share my worries about Logan, but mostly I didn't, because that would mean telling Cody about our OBEs, and what if he couldn't be trusted? What if he told our parents? Logan would never forgive me.

"Come on, Minutia," Cody said, and there was so much compassion in his eyes and in his voice that my inner pendulum swung back the whole other way, and I thought maybe I should tell him everything, because the astral projection thing was such a heavy burden, especially now, with Logan off exploring the solar system, and it would feel so good to share it with somebody smart and caring who might know what to do.

Just as I opened my mouth to blurt out the whole story, Grandma barged into the kitchen.

"What are you two doing in here? Shame on you, Cody, if you're bending this poor girl's ear about computers."

"He wasn't," I told her.

"Well, come out and join the rest of us. We're going to play a board game."

"Oh, goodie," I said, even though Grandma owned the most boring board games on the planet. I scurried out of the kitchen without looking back at Cody.

Now that the moment had passed, I felt relief, not disappointment, that I hadn't shared our secret, mine and Logan's.

Chapter 41

I woke up on Wednesday morning feeling out of sorts. Restless, moody, my nerves jangling like discordant bells. Even school wasn't enough of a distraction. The feeling clung to me all day like an illness brewing.

After school, I went next door to play ball with Holly. On a whim, I decided to take her for a walk instead. I had a lot of nervous energy to burn off—and apparently, so did Holly. She kept straining at the leash, her short doggy legs moving much faster than my long human ones. I had to trot to keep up.

A shapeless sun glimmered behind gray clouds, offering no warmth, only light. And dim light, at that. I glanced around at the gaunt, naked trees, the olive-drab lawns. It was as if all the color had drained out of the world. Sodden brown leaves lined the street gutters like milk-soaked cornflakes at the bottom of a bowl. The vivid green of springtime was nothing but a promise, a distant memory.

Not that I minded. The drabness of the day matched the darkness of my mood.

Halfway down Shrieking Shadows Street, I came upon Sarah Palmer. She was in her front yard throwing a ball to a medium-sized dog—a schnauzer, I thought—who was almost as cute as Holly. I stopped to watch. It was a simple scene and yet one that radiated pure joy.

They both looked so in-the-moment. I wondered if I looked that happy when I was playing with Holly.

When Sarah spotted me, she waved a greeting and ambled over. Her jacket was partially unzipped, revealing a V-shaped patch of T-shirt underneath. I couldn't see the whole message on the shirt, just the word "Thy" centered on her chest.

She introduced her dog as if he were a person—"Abby, I'd like you to meet Cheddar. Cheddar, say hello to Abby." Holly and Cheddar sniffed each other and instantly became friends. They dashed around the yard while Sarah and I chatted.

"I didn't know you lived on Shrieking Shadows Street," I said. "Your house is really cute."

Sarah's house looked teeny-tiny from the front but went on and on in back, like a skinny lady with a big butt. It was a gray one-story with white trim and a bright red door that made me think of a lipsticked mouth.

Sarah wrinkled her nose. "There was this house on Devil's Reach Road I liked better, but my mom wouldn't even consider it. She was like, 'We are good Christian people. We cannot live on a street with such an ungodly name.' "

I laughed. "That's not the only 'ungodly' street in Eerie. Does she know about Hellfire Place and Dancing Demons Drive?"

"Yeah, she won't even drive up those streets. I'm surprised she agreed to move here. The town's history freaks her out. She's always burning sage."

"I hope she doesn't believe those old stories. I mean, levitating pots and pans, brooms sweeping by themselves..." I rolled my eyes to show how crazy I considered the old stories.

"She doesn't. She just thinks the town is—how'd she put it?—'too cavalier about celebrating evil.' Me, though, I'm totally into Eerie. It's like something out of *Harry Potter*. And the street names are so imaginative. Fanged Pansy Lane, Toxic Tallow Place."

"Bubbling Cauldron Drive, Hex Hollow Road," I added.

"I love the creepiness." She tossed the ball into the yard, and both dogs went tearing after it. Holly got there first and kept trying to grab it, but it was too big for her tiny terrier mouth. Cheddar barked furiously till she backed off.

"What street do you live on?" asked Sarah.

"Mystic Moon."

"Ooh, that's pretty."

"Not very creepy, though. My cousin used to live next door, and when he was, like, ten, he wanted to move to Viper Venom Way. He was going through a tough-guy phase, and he said he wanted a more dangerous address." My heart swelled nostalgically as I recalled the rub-on tattoos, the fake leather jacket he'd worn everywhere.

"Is that the cousin we called on the computer at your birthday party? The one who moved to Pittsburgh?"

"Yeah. Logan." To my dismay, his name rode out on a gulp that sounded a lot like a sob. I mumbled, "Sorry. I still miss him."

"Of course, you do." Sarah looked so sympathetic, I had to bite my lip to abort a full-blown meltdown. "Hey," she said, "if you're ever looking for something to do on a Thursday night, you should come to the youth group meeting at my church. We have a really great group."

"Oh, thanks." I shifted my gaze to the neighbors' yard, where a life-sized skeleton in a faded red Santa suit was propped against a tree, a remnant from holidays past. "But I'm not really—my parents and I don't—I mean, I believe in God and all, but…"

"It's cool. You don't have to belong to our church. You don't have to go to *any* church. This is just a bunch of high school kids getting together to talk and do fun things. Parties, roller-skating, go-carting. We do community service activities, too. Like, last fall, we walked up Galloping Ghouls Boulevard picking up litter. Oh, and there's a camping trip in the summertime, though I wasn't here for that last year."

"Yeah, wow, it sounds really great," I said. "I'll definitely try to make it sometime."

There was a long pause. Sarah kicked a small rock down the sidewalk and said, "A lot of people think youth group isn't cool, but it really is."

"I know. My grandma's church has a youth group," I said, as if that meant anything.

Sometime during our conversation, it had started to snow. Flakes were coming down in a lazy, crisscross pattern, with some angling to the right and others to the left, like out-of-sync dancers. Sarah shivered and zipped up her jacket.

"Well. I should probably get this pup home," I said.

"Yeah. I guess I'll go in, too." Now she just looked sad. "Bye, Abby."

I had to walk past my house to take Holly home. I puzzled over the sight of my mother's car in the driveway. She never got home from work this early.

When I opened the front door, the sound of sobbing stopped me in my tracks. I tried to tell myself it was coming from the TV, but I knew better. It was coming from my mother.

My heart dipped into my stomach. I tottered into the house on rubbery legs.

She was huddled at one end of the couch, hugging one of the designer pillows to her chest. Dripping tears on it. I tried to speak, to ask the obvious question, but I couldn't get the words out.

Her whole body jerked when she spotted me. She said something, but I couldn't understand it because she was crying so hard.

A chill much colder than the March air enveloped me. This wasn't *I wrecked the car* or *I lost my job* or even *we're getting a divorce.* This was catastrophe waiting to be unveiled.

The faces of all the people I loved flashed through my mind. Logan-Dad-Mom-Cody-Aunt Lisa-Grandma-Uncle Dirk. I'd never put my relatives in rank order before, never really thought about who I loved best. But there it was.

Please, God. Don't let it be Logan.

It took my mother a minute to pull herself together. She drew in a deep, trembling breath and blew it out like cigarette smoke. Then she said, in a thin voice, "Logan's in a coma, and the doctors don't think he's going to make it."

My knees buckled, and I sank to the floor, both hands clamped to my mouth. I was ninety-nine percent sure Logan was lost on the astral plane.

Chapter 42

"I need—I need to take a nap," I whispered.

My mother looked at me strangely, because that was a strange thing to come out of the mouth of a girl who'd just learned her cousin was dying. But at that moment I knew I had to get myself to the astral plane. I had to find Logan, to guide him back to his body. Doctors couldn't save him. Only I could do that.

My mother beckoned me over, her arms outstretched, her face contorted with fresh sobs. Reluctantly, I went to her and let her enfold me in her arms. I couldn't remember the last time we'd hugged. Her body felt bony and alien against mine, as if we were interconnecting blocks that didn't quite fit together.

I gave her a quick squeeze and tried to break away, but she wouldn't let go. I stiffened for a moment and then gave in, letting her hold me. And after a while, something happened. I started to feel comfortable in her arms. She was so warm and soft. She was wearing her signature perfume, a minty scent with a hint of coconut. I pressed my face into the nape of her neck the way I must have done when I was a baby. And felt the same primal comfort.

We stayed that way for the longest time, pressed together, sobbing softly, rocking ever so slightly. When we finally broke apart, she plucked two tissues from the box on the coffee table and handed me one. In a hoarse, toneless voice she repeated what Aunt Lisa had told her.

Logan's sleep issues had been getting progressively worse. There'd been a morning a week ago when she and Uncle Dirk had tried for fifteen minutes to wake him. They'd finally dragged him into a cold shower, and that had done the trick.

The same thing had happened today. After school, Logan had said he wasn't feeling well and lay down on the couch to take a nap. Aunt Lisa tried to rouse him at dinnertime but couldn't. She'd pinched him, slapped him, shouted his name. Even the cold shower didn't work. Uncle Dirk called an ambulance, and now Logan was in the ICU at a Pittsburgh hospital.

"Grandma's got her whole church praying for him," my mother said. She'd never believed in the power of prayer—she said it was no different from sitting on Santa's lap at the mall and making demands—but at that moment, she looked like she wanted to believe. "We haven't been able to reach Cody. He's in D.C. for job training and hasn't been answering his phone."

I said I was going to my room. Mom asked if I really wanted to be alone at a time like this, though maybe what she was really saying was that *she* didn't want to be alone. I said yes, I needed to be alone, just for a little while.

"Don't fall asleep and go into a coma," she called as I headed down the hall. It sounded like a joke, but I knew she was dead serious.

I lay on my bed and squeezed my eyes shut. I tried to lie still but couldn't. I flopped around like a dying fish. I could feel my heart pumping, the blood rushing through me like a flood-swollen river. Sleep was such a slippery thing. The harder I tried to catch it, the more it eluded me. I finally gave up.

Hang on, Logan. I'm coming to find you. I just can't do it right now.

I left my room. My mother was still on the couch, but now my dad was with her. I hadn't even heard him come in. She was leaning against him, her head on his chest. I walked over and stood in front of them. I said in a tremulous voice, "Maybe Logan's spirit left his body and got lost somewhere. Do you think that's possible?"

Mom raised her head and looked at me like I'd gone insane. "What are you talking about? Logan's in a coma."

Dad said, "The doctors are doing all they can, sweetie," which was a different conversation altogether.

Mom's response told me she didn't know about our family's freakish history. There was no point in laying that on her now. In her current frame of mind, she would never believe me.

It was well past midnight before I got to sleep. An OBE started almost immediately, and I zoomed into the sky. Because that was surely where Logan was. I went as far as I dared, farther than any human astronaut had ever gone. Earth was nothing but a bright dot in the distance, and I didn't want to lose sight of it. I was afraid of getting lost, like Logan. Afraid of falling into a coma. If that happened, I wouldn't be able to save him *or* myself.

I called his name over and over, hoping the sound of my spirit voice would guide him to me. The universe stretched out in every direction, black, infinite, merciless.

A movement caught my eye, and I turned eagerly toward it, but it turned out to be a car-sized gray rock floating by. It was shaped like a human skull, larger at one end than the other.

Logan! Logan!

Was God out here? If so, he could surely hear the desperation in my soundless cries. He had to see the love in my heart, the unbearable specter of Logan's death looming before me. Why wouldn't he help me?

Time passed, though I had no idea how much. Fatigue washed over me, and I knew my spirit needed a rest. Was my aura going dim? If that happened, I might not be able to get back to Earth on my own.

I had just decided to head home when I saw something new. Not an asteroid, but a feeble flicker of light, like a shimmer from a dying star. I called Logan's name again, and the flicker moved toward me, too lasting to be a meteor, too small to be a star. I watched as it got larger. I saw a shape emerge. And there in front of me was a person-shaped jellyfish.

Relief and joy bubbled up in me like cosmic gases as I rushed to meet him. "Logan! Oh, thank God. I've been so scared!"

"Me too." He shuddered, his spirit form rippling like a mirage. "I got lost. I couldn't find my way back to my body. My sutratma disappeared, and I had no idea where Earth was, which way to go—"

"It's okay," I said, "I'm here. I'm going to take you home."

"I've been out here forever, just floating around. I figured this was it. The end. I was never going to get back. Then I heard you calling me. Somehow I heard you—" He tried to smile, but his lips couldn't seem to stretch that far. "You saved me, Abs."

But he didn't look saved. I was shocked by his appearance. Of course, the Logan in front of me was just a snapshot of physical Logan, asleep in that Pittsburgh hospital. Still, I could see how pale he was, the dull eyes, the sunken cheeks. His aura was in even worse shape. It barely twinkled and had taken on a sickly grayish hue.

"You're in a coma," I told him. "You're in the hospital. In the ICU, actually."

His eyes went wide. "A coma? Seriously?"

"We need to get you back to your body. You'll be okay once you're back in your body."

"Let's go, then."

We flew past Saturn, unmistakable because of its rings. We passed Jupiter, where boys went to get more stupider.

Logan said, "Aren't you going to say 'I told you so'?"

"Eventually."

He sighed. "You were right, Abs. Too much astral travel is dangerous. I should have listened to you."

"We don't need to talk about that right now."

"I only pushed the limits because I was doing something important."

"Shh. Don't talk." The act of communicating was draining him. The light of his spirit was getting dimmer.

"I never stopped going to Mysterium. That's where I was just now. Before I went into the coma, I mean."

"Yeah, I figured."

"I'm sorry I lied to you. Sorry I broke my

promise."

"Me too."

"Do you want to know what I've been doing?"

"No," I said firmly. For months, I'd been obsessed with finding out what he was up to. Now all I cared about was getting him home.

"Saving a civilization—that's what I've been doing."

I gaped at him. Saving a civilization? I couldn't even get my head around that. I said, "You can tell me all about it later. Come on, we're almost home."

I watched Earth grow larger and larger, like a dilating pupil. Logan kept falling behind, and I had to wait for him to catch up. Finally, we were close enough to make out the shape of North America, floating like a seahorse in the dark ocean.

Behind me, Logan said, "Abs, stop. I need to rest."

"Okay, but only for a minute. How about if I tow you the rest of the way?"

I held out my hand, but he didn't see it. He was gazing at the Earth, with its marbled blues, greens, tans, and whites. "It's beautiful, isn't it? It's just so beautiful."

In the moment, I thought he was talking strictly about the look of the Earth, its swirling colors, so I said, "It's definitely prettier than the moon."

"Remember when we were little, how our parents used to let us run around in the rain in our bathing suits?"

"Of course, I remember. What made you think of that?"

"We'd go stomping through puddles, standing under rain spouts. It was like a free water park."

"Yeah, my dad really liked the free part."

"Remember that time we tried to toast marshmallows on the baseboard heater in my bedroom? We really thought that would work, but all it did was make a gooey mess that got us grounded. Oh, and the time we dug for treasure in Grandma and Grandpa's yard? Remember how Grandpa snuck out at lunchtime and buried that little box of coins at the bottom of the hole? Remember how excited we were when we dug it up? We thought we'd found actual buried treasure."

"Logan?" I said uneasily.

"All the times we've had," Logan mused. "Such good times."

"Hey," I said sharply. "Why are you talking like this?"

"People don't realize how good life is. Even when it's bad, it's good—you know?"

"Logan!" I wafted closer and nudged him. "Come on, let's get you back to Earth."

"Abby," he said. "Abby. Abby, I—"

And then his spirit went dark, like somebody had flicked a switch.

"Noooo!" I screamed, and that long, anguished syllable echoed across the astral plane. "Logan! Logan!"

But he didn't answer. He couldn't, because he was gone. His lifeless spirit drifted off into outer space.

Chapter 43

I awoke with a gasp, and already I was sobbing. Sobbing harder than I ever had in my life, harder than when Grandpa had died.

Logan was dead. My cousin, my twin, my best friend. People always talked about the finality of death, but suddenly I was feeling it, living it, staggering under its impossible weight. I would never see Logan's smile again. Talk to him. Hug him.

Had I ever told him I loved him? Probably not since we were little.

A collage of scenes ran through my head, Logan's life passing before my eyes. Our life, together.

Logan at age four, bringing me zinnias from my mother's flower bed, dirty roots and all, because I was sick in bed. At nine with a broken arm, insisting I had to be the first to sign his cast.

Our Halloween costumes over the years, always coordinated. Angel and devil, witch and warlock, salt and pepper shakers, astronaut twins.

Day trips with our parents to amusement parks, swimming pools, the science museum, the planetarium.

Riding boogie boards in the ocean. Our elaborate sand castles. Popsicle juice dribbling down our chins. Giggling over the rude shove of the waves.

Family picnics. Backyard badminton. Squirt-gun battles. Easter egg hunts.

The time we got the expensive video gaming system as a joint Christmas gift and he let me have it first.

Peewee soccer. Swimming lessons. Our week at horse camp when we were ten.

Sunburned noses. Skinned knees. The time I gave him a haircut. The time he gave me a haircut.

Our elaborate chalk mazes in the alley. Our matching milk moustaches. Counting mosquito bites to see who had more.

Neighborhood games: freeze tag and flashlight tag and dodge ball and hide-and-seek. Our joint adventures with my fashion dolls and his army dolls—tea parties in the jungle, fashion shows at the battlefront.

Camping out in the backyard. Gazing into the night sky and speculating about all the possible worlds orbiting those bright stars. Wondering if our parents would ever get divorced.

That grainy video of eighteen-month-old Logan patting seventeen-month-old me on the back to comfort me when I was crying.

Rubber snakes and tongue twisters and wiffle balls and armpit farts.

Lightning bugs in jars.

Laughter. Tears. Hugs. Love.

Logan.

He was right—it was all so beautiful. Earth. Life. Our shared experiences.

Chapter 44

It had been an eternity since Logan had died, and I hadn't moved. I'd been lying in bed like a corpse in my own right. Sick to my stomach, parched from crying, struggling to comprehend the incomprehensible.

He was gone. My smart, charismatic, larger-than-life cousin was gone.

It was starting to get light outside, but I didn't dare leave my room, because once I did, Mom would tell me the news, and then it would be official.

Better to lie here and pretend it wasn't true.

After another eternity, someone knocked on my door.

"Abby? You awake?" my mother called softly.

"Go away."

"I need to come in."

The door opened.

She looked awful. Her face was blotchy and swollen from crying. The dark circles under her eyes told me she hadn't slept much, if at all.

She sat on my bed. Sighed heavily. Wouldn't meet my eyes.

"Abby, there's something I need to tell you."

"I don't want to hear it."

"You have to. It's Logan. He took a turn for the worse."

"No." I squeezed my eyes shut.

"He started going downhill last night. Aunt Lisa called a little while ago. Logan's heart stopped beating."

I flipped over on my stomach and buried my face in my pillow.

"The doctors got it started again, but it took a while. Probably too long."

Her words hung in the long silence that followed. I replayed them in my head several times. Then I gasped. I flipped back over and stared at her. "They got his heart beating again? Is that what you said? So he isn't dead? Oh my God!"

I sat up. I laughed out loud. I threw my arms around her, dampening her shoulder with my fresh tears. "He isn't dead! Logan isn't dead!"

"No, no, Abby. Listen." She pried me away. "This is not good news. The doctors still don't know what's causing the coma. They don't expect him to live. And even if he does, he could have brain damage."

"But he's alive now! He didn't die!"

"Technically, he did die, but they brought him back. Unfortunately, he's in worse shape than ever. If his heart stops again, they probably won't be able to restart it."

She stood up, swaying like a tree buffeted by storm winds. Like me, she was weak and exhausted. We'd skipped dinner last night, the three of us, so sick with grief and worry that it hadn't even occurred to us to eat. "I'm going to book a flight to Pittsburgh. I should have gone last night. Lisa needs me."

"I want to come, too."

I was prepared to argue for my right to be with my cousin, but to my surprise she nodded. "Start packing."

She headed for the hall but then paused in my doorway.
"Bring clothes suitable for a funeral."

Chapter 45

"I'm coming with you."

"No, Ma, you're not."

"He's my *grandson*. I have a right to be there."

"I only got tickets for Abby and me. There's no more room on the plane."

"Then I'll take a different flight. As long as Joe can drive me to the airport—"

"He can't. He'll be at work."

I was in my bedroom with the door open, listening to this exchange as I packed. It had been going on for a while, as arguments between my mom and grandma tended to do. In terms of sheer stubbornness, they were evenly matched.

"Merciful savior," snapped Grandma. "Do you really expect me to sit home watching my toenails grow while my grandson is dying in a hospital?"

"Home is the best place for you. We'll call you if anything changes."

"But I might be able to help the doctors."

Mom snorted. "How are you going to help the doctors? You got a medical degree you never told us about?"

"I know something about kids not waking up. I used to have an awful time trying to wake Cody up for school. Sometimes it took twenty minutes or better."

"I don't remember that."

"It was during his teenage years. You were all grown up and out of the house by then. Whatever caused it, maybe it's some inherited thing that Logan got, too, except worse. I need to tell his doctors about it."

"I'll tell his doctors. If they need more information, they can…"

Mom's voice faded, while the echo of Grandma's words got louder, clanging in my head like an old-time school bell.

…awful time trying to wake Cody up…

…trying to wake Cody up…

…trying to wake…

I dropped the pair of socks I'd been holding and sat on my bed, trying to think of an explanation—a logical, everyday explanation—for why Cody would have been hard to wake up. Maybe he'd been one of those teenagers who stayed up too late on school nights. Playing video games, hanging out in Internet chat rooms, fixing sandwiches at two a.m.

Except that wasn't it.

The truth boomed in my chest like an amplified heartbeat: *Cody was an astral traveler.* It suddenly seemed so obvious. I might have realized it sooner if I hadn't been distracted by all the other things going on in my life.

Cody had been at our house that first night I'd been so hard to awaken. Ever since then, every time we'd been together, he'd peppered me with questions about my health, my sleep habits. He'd repeatedly encouraged me to talk to him about whatever I had on my mind. It was as if he suspected the truth behind that deep, fairytale-princess sleep and was trying to get me to confess.

Then there was the drinking. Alcohol was a depressant—I remembered that from eighth-grade health class—which probably meant it suppressed OBEs the same way sleeping pills did. If Cody was like me, there were nights when he was too exhausted to face a night of traveling. I used p.m. ibuprofen to prevent OBEs. Cody probably used alcohol.

I felt an urgent need to talk to my uncle, to tell him everything. Maybe he would know how to help Logan. I tried to call his cell phone, but he still wasn't answering. Frustrating! I left a message that was bound to baffle him if he wasn't an astral traveler after all— "Logan's lost in outer space. Can you help me find him?"

I zipped my suitcase shut and wheeled it to my doorway in time to see my mother stride across the hall and enter the bathroom. Grandma followed but stopped outside the bathroom door. I heard clattering, clinking noises as Mom gathered up toiletries.

"Why do you have to be like this? Don't you know how worried I am?" Grandma glanced my way, her eyebrows forming a bulldog frown, but she looked straight through me like I wasn't there.

"We're all worried."

"You can't stop me from coming. I'll book my own flight if I have to."

"You've never booked a flight in your life. You don't know how."

"I'll get Eliot next door to help me."

Mom stepped into the hall, her arms full of jars and bottles. "Dammit, Ma, you're not coming, and that's that."

"Why not?" Now Grandma sounded like a whiny three-year-old.

"Because you'd be more of a hindrance than a help. You always are."

"*What?*" The word whooshed out of her mouth, an outraged whisper.

"You have no filter," Mom went on. "You just blurt out whatever's on your mind. You'd only end up upsetting everybody. Stay home and pray—that's what you do best."

Grandma gasped and clutched her chest, like she was having a heart attack. My mother brushed past her and went into her bedroom.

Ouch, Mom. That was harsh.

"Rose? Hey, hey, take it easy." My dad, who'd just gotten back from putting gas in the car, came trotting up the hall. "I'm not going either, okay? We can keep each other company. I'll come to your house every day after work if you'd like. We can—"

"Don't try to placate me, Joe. If you care about me at all, you'll try to talk some sense into that wife of yours."

"I think Leah might be right. It's probably best if you stay home."

"And I don't even have the comfort of Cody living downstairs anymore," Grandma shouted, and then burst into tears.

She left our house in a teary huff.

Dad drove us to the airport and got out of the car long enough to give each of us a hug. When it was Mom's turn, the two of them clung to each other like they never wanted to let go.

Tragedy seemed to have brought them back

231

together. But how long would it last?

We'd been lucky enough to get seats on the same flight, though not together. I was in 21F, a window seat, while Mom was several rows up, sandwiched between a hefty older man and a college-age girl in headphones who was bopping along to tunes only she could hear. Meanwhile, my seatmates were a pre-teen boy and his mother, a pair so quiet and solemn that I wondered if they were on their way to a funeral.

The flight included a forty-minute layover in Chicago, though luckily we didn't have to leave the plane.

"I'm planning to sleep straight through," I'd told my mother, "so don't try to wake me in Chicago, okay? *Okay?*"

"Okay, okay!" she'd said.

I'd accepted the p.m. ibuprofen tablet she'd offered me, but only because I was too tired to think up an excuse for refusing. Of course, I had no intention of taking it. I just hoped I'd be able to nod off on my own.

As it turned out, I was so exhausted that I conked out shortly after takeoff, lulled by the drone of the plane's engines. One second I was strapped in my seat watching cars shrink into toys on the ribbony roads below, the next I was on the ceiling of the plane, staring down at dozens of tightly packed bodies, including my own. I shot into the sky like a bottle rocket and headed back to the spot where I'd last seen Logan.

He wasn't there.

I called his name, again and again. I crept closer to the edge of the solar system, until Earth was nothing but a luminous speck in my rearview vision. I scanned the depths of the galaxy, looking for a sparkly human-shaped jellyfish lurching toward me.

I saw nothing but perpetual dark relieved by a trillion twinkling nightlights.

My soul sagged with the futility of my quest. How could I hope to find one tiny spirit in a universe that went on forever?

I turned back toward Earth, a new plan forming in my mind. Cody wasn't the only person who might be able to help me. There was somebody else.

Jakob.

Now if I could just work up the nerve to approach him.

The plane had taken off a little before two p.m., which put the current time around eleven p.m. in Germany. I prayed I wasn't too late.

Rothenburg was a medieval-looking town surrounded by a wall so thick, people could stroll around on top of it. The town's architecture looked familiar, though I couldn't remember where or when I'd seen it. Maybe it had been the setting for a movie I'd watched?

I found Jakob's house the same way I'd found Logan's, drawn to it through the navigational magic of astral travel. The house was creamy white with brown trim, so much trim that it resembled a gingerbread house. A very tall gingerbread house—I counted four stories beneath the steeply gabled roof. Window boxes underscored all the windows, though none of them held flowers. It was late winter here, same as in Oregon.

I hovered outside, too shy to go in, trying to think of what to say.

After a while, a translucent being drifted out of a third-story window of Jakob's house.

"Jakob," I called, and the spirit stopped, but it wasn't Jakob. This guy was slightly older, with blond hair and Jakob's eyes. His spirit glowed purple, a deeper shade than Jakob's.

He wafted over and looked me up and down, a crooked grin on his lips. "Well, well. If it isn't Abby, all the way from America."

I stared at him in surprise. "How did you—?"

"Jakob'll be along shortly. Wait on the roof—he likes to go out through the chimney." He winked and flew off into the night.

When Jakob saw me, he swore. I thought he was swearing at me, but later I understood that he was swearing at the situation. He knew the moment he saw me that Logan had gotten himself into trouble. He'd been expecting it.

He looked at me with resigned eyes and said, "Tell me everything."

Chapter 46

"He might be on Mysterium," Jakob said as we shot past the moon.

"Why would he be there? The last time I saw him, he was almost home. Why didn't he keep going till he was back in his body?"

"Hard to say. Maybe he got disoriented from, you know, *dying*."

Dying. The brutal reality of that word rocked me again, like an earthquake's aftershock. My cousin had *died*. And yes, the doctors had brought him back, but time was ticking away, and he could die again at any moment. This time for good.

Jakob had drifted ahead of me. I hurried to catch up. "You know where you're going, right?"

The look he gave me made me wish I hadn't asked. I added quickly, "Mysterium's so far away. It seems like it would be hard to find."

"Not for me. You've never been there?"

"No." I told him about my disastrous first venture into outer space. "I'm kind of worried the same thing will happen today."

"It shouldn't. You're a more seasoned traveler now. You've strengthened that muscle. As long as we don't stay out here too long, you should be okay."

I didn't ask how long *too long* was. I had to find Logan no matter how long it took.

We were crossing the asteroid belt. I swerved around a rock the size of a tractor-trailer and rejoined Jakob on the other side. "How sure are you that Logan's on Mysterium?"

"Fairly sure."

"Like, ninety-six percent sure? Eighty-two percent? Sixty-seven percent?"

He shot me a sardonic look. "I'm *fairly sure*. Which falls between *really sure* and *not sure at all*."

I decided to call that seventy-five percent. "And if he's not on Mysterium?"

"Then he's lost in some distant corner of the universe and we'll never find him."

For a moment I was speechless—but only for a moment. I felt my spirit swell as fury rose up in me. "That's just mean! Why would you say that?"

"How is it mean? You asked, I answered. I'm not going to sugarcoat anything. Comas are tricky. They disable a traveler's instinctive navigation."

"Instinctive navigation? You mean that magical GPS thing?"

"Call it what you want. Not every traveler has it, but Logan does. So do I. You too, obviously—considering you found my house tonight. But if somebody goes into a coma while they're on the astral plane, they're flying blind. It's like their navigational system goes offline. And their sutratma disappears, so they're doubly screwed."

I chewed on that for a minute. "But how would Logan have gotten back to Mysterium if his navigational system wasn't working?"

"You said Mysterium was the last place he visited before the coma? Then he might have been able to retrace his steps. Same way you would if you were walking through a snowy forest on Earth and realized you were lost. You wouldn't be able to get to your destination, but you could turn around and follow your footprints back to where you'd been."

I gave him a dubious look. "But all the way to Mysterium?"

"It's possible. This is a bare-bones form of instinctive navigation, sort of like when your computer crashes and restarts in 'safe mode.' Of course, there's no way of knowing if it kicked in for Logan."

I said desperately, "But shouldn't *we* be able to find *him*, no matter where he is? I mean, considering you and I both have instinctive navigation?"

He let out a quiet sigh, one that said he hadn't expected so many questions. "Instinctive navigation helps you find *places*. What you're talking about is *spirit radar*—the ability to find spirits. Other travelers. I don't have that ability." He turned his cool gaze on me. "Do you?"

I said gloomily, "No." In all the months I'd been searching for Logan on the astral plane, I'd never once found him. "But maybe if I concentrate really hard—"

"Doesn't work that way. Either you have it or you don't. It's just like in the physical world—certain people have certain abilities that come naturally to them. My brother's good at dream-whispering. Another traveler I know can make herself appear to people in the physical world, like a ghost."

That was all very interesting, and I wanted to hear more, but not now. "I found Logan last night just by calling his name. But for some reason it didn't work today."

"He's obviously farther away today. Out of range. So let's hope he's on Mysterium, because if he isn't, we're not going to find him."

Anger flared in me again. "Why do you keep saying that? Are you trying to torture me? I know you don't like me, but…"

"What makes you think I don't like you?" His tone of detached amusement only made me madder. And why wasn't he denying it? That would have been the polite thing to do, regardless of how he actually felt about me.

"Because—because of how you acted at the Eiffel Tower. You were so rude! It was like you couldn't stand having me around."

"I couldn't. You were annoying."

"*I* was annoying?" I stared at him in wide-eyed indignation, but he wasn't looking back.

"I'd been searching for my friend for weeks. I finally found him, we had important matters to discuss, but *you* kept getting in the way. Butting in, making demands. And Logan clearly didn't want to talk in front of you. It was frustrating."

"I was worried! I just wanted to find out what was going on."

"So did I." He pointed up ahead, where a gray orb with a smear of red across its bottom was suspended in space like a magician's levitating ball. "There's Pluto if you're interested."

"I'm not!"

Even so, I watched the dwarf planet sail away behind us like a baseball someone had whacked into infinity.

"Well. I'm sorry if I seemed rude," Jakob said.

"You didn't *seem* rude," I said. "You *were* rude."

"Fine. Then that's what I'm sorry about."

"Fine." Feeling impish, I added, "I met your brother tonight. *Somehow* he knew who I was."

For the briefest moment, Jakob's lilac sparkles took on a fuchsia hue, as if his spirit was blushing. But when he spoke, his tone was nonchalant. "I might have told him about you."

"Might have?"

His eyes flashed defensively. "You were so annoying, I had to talk to someone about it!"

"I am not annoying! Stop saying that!"

"Calm down, you're turning orange." A corner of his mouth quirked. "You look like an angry carrot."

That did it. "Dude," I shouted, "why don't you go home. I'll find Mysterium by myself."

He snorted. "Good luck with that. You'll never get there."

"What are you talking about? I have instinctive navigation."

"That's not good enough." His tone was irritatingly matter-of-fact. "Instinctive navigation works fine when you're looking for places on Earth. But in space the distances are too great. The farther away a place is, the harder it is to find it."

"And yet you seem to think you can get us to Mysterium."

"Because I've actually been there. Multiple times. If you've visited a place at least once, instinctive navigation will take you back, no matter how far away it is or how long since you've been there. But finding a place for the first time, especially a planet as far away as Mysterium? We're talking needle in a haystack."

I opened my mouth to argue, because that was the mode I seemed to be stuck in. I shut it when I realized I had nothing to say. Jakob knew everything about astral travel. I knew next to nothing.

We flew on in silence while I cooled down. When I was pretty sure my orangeness had subsided, I asked, "How far away is Mysterium?"

"I don't know. A gazillion light years?"

"Gazillion isn't a real—"

"*I know.* My point is, it's very far away."

"I just want to calculate—"

"Well, you can't. It's impossible to measure the distance. Mysterium is definitely in another galaxy. Maybe another universe."

I arched an eyebrow at him. "Another universe? Dude, there's only one."

"Is there, *dude*?" His eyes, so alive in his ghostly face, glowed golden-brown. "Some people believe there are many. And Mysterium is just weird enough that I wouldn't be surprised to learn it's in a whole different universe."

"Weird how?"

That familiar smirk was back. "You'll find out soon enough."

I glanced behind us. I could no longer see Earth, and the sun was nothing but a small, bright flare, like a campfire burning on the far side of a lake.

I couldn't begin to guess how far from home we were. A gazillion miles at least. Once the sun disappeared from sight, I would have no way of getting my bearings, other than my sutratma, which had narrowed to the girth of my dad's garden hose.

The stars around me suddenly dipped and swirled

as a sensation like vertigo swept over me. I was falling, tumbling, tossed head over heels in a roiling ocean of blackness. I felt like my spirit was about to explode into a thousand jellyfish pieces that would float around the galaxy for eternity. This wasn't the same feeling I'd had the night Logan had brought me out here. I didn't feel sick or wobbly. But something was definitely wrong.

"Check out the nebula," Jakob said, pointing to a swirly orange and purple cloud in the distance.

"I don't care about the blinkin' nebula!" I shouted. "This isn't—I can't—I just—"

"Okay, whoa." He swerved in front of me, forcing me to come to a halt. "I was wondering when this would happen."

"When *what* would happen?" I was still yelling. Not audibly, of course, but the intensity was there.

"The outer space freakout. That moment when you realize how far from home you are and start worrying that you won't be able to get back."

"I think I have a good reason to freak out," I snapped, "considering what happened to my cousin."

"What happened to your cousin," Jakob said severely, "was his own doing. He came out here too often and stayed too long. You, though? You're going to be fine."

"I don't feel fine!" I'd never had a panic attack before, but I was ninety-nine percent sure I was having one now.

I wondered what was happening back on the plane. Was I moaning in my sleep? Convulsing? Was a flight attendant asking if there was a doctor in the house?

"It'll pass," said Jakob, sounding maddeningly unconcerned. "The same thing happened to Logan and me the first time we came out this far. You just need a distraction. Come on, we have to keep moving." He set off again. Reluctantly, I followed. "Let's talk about Mysterium. Has Logan told you about the situation there?"

"Um…" I had to think hard, because my hysteria was like thick black smoke clouding my thoughts. "He said he's saving a civilization. That's all I know."

"Well, then," said Jakob. "I have lots to tell you."

Chapter 47

"This whole thing started," said Jakob, "when Logan met an astral traveler from another planet."

I had never really processed Logan's revelation about saving a civilization. The implications of that hit me now.

Life existed on other planets.

Space aliens were real.

We were not alone in the universe. (Or universes.)

I didn't comment on Jakob's statement, because what could I say? *Oh wow*? Or maybe *holy shmoley,* like my grandpa used to say? There were no words tall enough, wide enough, deep enough to encompass a development this big.

Jakob continued, "Ed, the alien traveler, was seeking help, and Logan agreed to—"

"Whoa," I said. "The space alien's name is *Ed*?"

"Not really. That's what Logan calls him. Ed's language is very different from human languages—it's all clicks and whistles. We manage to communicate just fine on the astral plane, but names don't translate well."

"So you've met him. You've met this *Ed*." I couldn't stop picturing a bald, paunchy guy in a polo shirt.

"Logan introduced us the first time he took me to Mysterium."

My panic attack was subsiding, like flood waters

soaking into the ground. I was still apprehensive about what lay ahead, still worried sick about Logan, but I no longer felt like an impending explosion.

"How did Logan meet Ed?"

"You know how he loves to explore space, our Logan. One night he was hanging out at the edge of the galaxy, when along comes Ed. They got to talking, and Ed told him—"

"Wait a minute. You're saying two astral travelers from planets a gazillion light years apart just happened to run into each other in outer space? What are the odds of that?"

"Better than you'd think. Ed has spirit radar. He was probably drawn to Logan like a magnet." Jakob leveled a stern gaze at me. "You know, this story would go a lot faster if you'd stop interrupting me."

"Fine." I made a zipping-my-lips gesture. "Go on."

"Ed was looking for advice on how to save his people. There's this other group that's been eating them, and Ed was hoping Logan could—"

"*Eating* them?" My mouth dropped open. "Is that what you said? Holy crud!"

Jakob shot me an exasperated look. I said, "Sorry!" and rezipped my lips.

He continued, "Mysterium is a young planet. Intelligent life is just getting started, so the two groups are pretty primitive. They live on the same island."

"And the one group eats the other." I couldn't get past this gruesome fact. "Intelligent life my butt! That's something lions do to gazelles."

Jakob ignored that. "Ed's people are the Ishwees. The other group is the Jinnku. Those aren't their real names—just Logan's best translation of what Ed calls them."

Ishwees, Jinnku. I spent a moment memorizing those unearthly names so I wouldn't mispronounce them and earn a smirk from Jakob. "Can't the Jinnku dudes find something different to eat? Like, what do the Ishwees eat?"

"They don't really eat. They absorb liquids through their skin. Tree sap, crater gunk, rain."

"Crater gunk?"

"Gunk in craters."

I rolled my eyes at the unhelpful explanation. "Well, can't the Jinnku eat crater gunk, too? Or drink it or absorb it or whatever?"

"No. The two groups have totally different digestive systems. They're not just separate races. They're entirely different species."

Now I understood why Logan had felt compelled to return to Mysterium. He was helping a friend. But I was still smarting over the fact that he'd lied to me.

"How can Logan save the Ishwees?" I asked. "How can anybody?"

"Logan's been teaching them how to build boats. There's a bigger island half a day's travel away. Ed calls it Bigland. There are no Jinnku there. No predators of any kind, as far as we can tell. If the Ishwees can relocate to Bigland, they'll be safe from the Jinnku."

"But won't the Jinnku build their own boats and go after them?"

"Not likely. The Jinnku are afraid of the ocean. They won't go near it."

"How do you know that?"

"Ed told us. He's been observing the Jinnku during his OBEs. He's learned a lot about them."

I studied Jakob's profile because that was all he was offering me at the moment. There was a bump in the middle of his nose that changed the angle of its slope. I wondered if his nose had been broken in a fistfight. Was he that kind of guy?

I said, "You don't think Logan should be doing what he's doing on Mysterium."

"What makes you say that?"

"You made it pretty clear that morning we ran into you at the Eiffel Tower."

He got a little purpler. "I wouldn't be going back myself if Logan wasn't in trouble."

"But it sounds like he's doing something really good. Are you against it because traveling so far into space is dangerous?"

"Sure, that's part of it."

We were passing a solar system populated by twin suns. I watched it go by, wondering if the residents had to use extra-heavy sunblock. If in fact there *were* residents.

I asked, "What's the other part?"

He flashed a smile that had no humor in it. "It's complicated. We don't have time to get into it now."

"So you're just going to leave me hanging."

His glimmering eyes were unapologetic, though not unkind. "You'll find out everything eventually. Right now, we have to stop yakking and get moving. We need to ramp up our speed if we want to get to Mysterium in this lifetime."

We were already going faster than any Earthling had ever traveled by car, train, boat, or supersonic jet. I glanced uneasily behind us. The Milky Way galaxy was nothing but a bright smudge that was getting smaller by the second. I asked, "How fast are we talking about?"

"Can't say exactly. Much faster than the speed of light."

I gaped at him. "Is that even possible?"

"We're doing it right now."

"What!"

"But we need to go even faster. You ready?"

"Wait. What if we get separated?"

"We won't."

"But what if we do?" The panic was trickling back. My sutratma was thinner than ever and we weren't even close to our destination. How much farther could it stretch?

"Here, grab hold." Jakob held out his hand.

Hesitantly, I reached for him. As my spirit hand met his, I felt a tug and a grip and a pleasant zap, as if a mildly electrified mitten had slipped tightly over me. Not just my hand, all of me.

That zap. It felt intimate somehow. Like a kiss.

I glanced at Jakob to see if he'd felt it. His spirit was blushing fuchsia. He looked away as soon as my eyes met his.

He pulled me forward. "Get ready for the ride of your life."

Chapter 48

I felt a violent jolt as we took off. Suddenly I was inside a twisting tunnel of colors, shapes, lights, and textures. Whole galaxies whizzed by like headlights on a highway. We rocketed past colorful nebulae and bore straight through countless planets and at least one star. We might have even gone through a black hole (fifty-one percent sure).

And it was all over in a matter of seconds.

"You okay?" asked Jakob.

"I...yeah." The universe was still spinning around me, though it was slowing rapidly, like an amusement park ride coming to an end. "I just need a second to catch my breath."

"Which would be easier if you'd brought your lungs with you."

I grinned through my dizziness, because Jakob's joke seemed like an overture, a step in a friendlier direction, and I wanted to encourage that.

"It's okay," I said. "I'm okay." I checked my sutratma. It was still visible, though it was now as thin as my forefinger. I looked around and did a double take as I saw a huge, woolly green orb looming to my left. "What is *that*?"

"That," said Jakob, "is Mysterium."

"Why is it so fuzzy?"

"It's surrounded by clouds. You won't see the sun

on Mysterium—the clouds are too thick. It rains almost all the time because the planet is mostly water. And Mysterium is closer to its sun than Earth is to our sun, so evaporation happens a lot faster. It's a never-ending cycle of moisture going up, moisture coming down. Like on Earth, but faster, more intense."

"Why are the clouds green?"

"Because the water is green."

"Why is the water green?"

"Probably because of mineral content."

"Well," I said, "you were right. This place is different."

Jakob's mouth twitched. "Just wait."

I glanced down, suddenly aware that our spirit hands were still clasped. Jakob's gaze followed mine, and his aura flickered fuchsia. I wondered what mine was doing. Turning orange? Hastily we broke apart, and the warm buzz I'd felt from our contact vanished.

"Follow me," said Jakob.

We dove into the green clouds. A thunderstorm crackled around us, and when lightning struck me, I screamed.

Not because it hurt. I was just startled.

"You okay?" asked Jakob, coming to a halt.

"Yeah." Then, "Actually, I'm better than okay. I feel…"

"Energized? Like you just had a shot of caffeine?"

I looked at him in surprise. "You know about this?"

"I do lightning zaps on Earth all the time. Gives me a nice energy boost when I've been out on the plane too long."

The smile he gave me was unexpectedly charming.

I wondered suddenly if he had a girlfriend.

Then I wondered why I was wondering.

"How'd you figure *that* out?" I asked. "Like, one day you decided to throw yourself into a lightning bolt to see what happened?"

"Logan and I learned about it from Ed. I've found that it works if you go through electrical wires, too, though the effect isn't as strong."

"Weird," I said.

"Not really. Spirits are pure energy. It makes sense that we'd feed on other types of energy."

When the next lightning bolt flashed, Jakob zoomed over to catch the tail end of it. I watched his sparkles brighten, like lilac blooms lit from within.

The first thing I saw when we swooped below the clouds was a bottle-green ocean dotted with widely spaced islands in varying shapes and sizes. Each island was a scribble of gray-blue plant life, obviously jungle. No surprise there, considering how much rain the planet got. It was raining now, spattering down in green droplets that held metallic glints of purple, gold, and blue. The air around us sparkled as if decorated with bits of Christmas tinsel.

We soared over land and sea, following the curve of the planet. I stayed tight on Jakob's tail as he glided toward an island shaped roughly like a trapezoid. As we got closer, definitive shapes and colors emerged. The shapes and colors of an alien jungle.

I came to a halt in midair, staring. The area below me looked like a sprawling playground crowded with asymmetrical jungle gyms. Or a series of curved webs built by giant drunken spiders.

It took me a minute to realize that the bent, tangled

structures dominating the jungle were trees. They didn't stand tall, like Earth's trees. They weren't reaching for the sun. Instead, each tree formed an arch, a living bridge that curved up and over a section of jungle. The tips of the tallest branches were buried in the ground, just as the bottoms of the tree trunks were. Many of the trees crisscrossed each other, resulting in a pretzel-like jumble of entwined branches.

The gray-blue tree trunks contrasted with the pink sap that oozed out of cracks in the bark. The leaves, if you could call them that, were also gray-blue. They were long and bushy, like the tails of Persian cats. Thick purple vines spiraled up some of the trunks, tight as chokers.

Jakob, probably hoping to head off another annoying question/answer session, said, "Those shaggy leaves on the trees? They might look light and fluffy, but they're actually very dense. The trees start off growing toward the sky, same as Earth's trees, but as more and more leaves grow, the trees get too heavy to stay upright. Gravity pulls the treetops down. The trunks and branches are flexible, like rubber. If they weren't, they'd probably snap. Once the treetops touch the ground, they burrow into the soil and put down roots."

"Weird," I said.

I drifted closer to the ground, eager to see what other oddities the jungle had to offer.

All around me, silvery bushes tinkled musically as raindrops spattered their mirror-shiny leaves. Scattered about on the ground were rocks in different sizes, shapes, and even colors—butterscotch yellow, rusty red, eggplant purple. Some glowed. Half hidden behind a large red rock was a gray shrub, bumpy as cauliflower. The shrub was covered in inch-long gray hairs that wriggled continuously, like tiny, hyperactive worms.

The only things that looked remotely normal were the flowers. My eyes settled on the nearest one, a neon-orange bloom as big as a dinner plate. Layers of feathery petals were arranged in a circle and imprinted with an ornate design, the kind you might see on one of Earth's more exotic moths.

As I moved in for a closer look, the head of the flower popped off its stem. I sprang backward in surprise. The flower drifted past me and landed in a cluster of similar flowers a few yards away.

Jakob said, "Insects don't seem to exist here, so the flowers have to pollinate themselves. At least we think that's what they're doing. They mingle with other flowers and then come back and reattach themselves to their stems."

I watched as a second flower flew off to fraternize with a friend. Flower sex, who'd have thought?

"But how do they fly?" I asked. "They seem too heavy to float in the air, but somehow they're doing it."

"Couldn't tell you. It's just one of the mysteries of this place."

I flinched as one of the gravity-defying flowers floated up to me and hovered in front of my face like it was checking me out. I stared back, mesmerized. Was there a brain inside that feathery head?

"This place—!" I said, and the flower zoomed away as if I'd spooked it.

"This place," Jakob agreed.

I took another look around, barely able to believe I

was on an alien planet. Earth was far away, and my life there seemed even more distant. Hazy and unreal, like a dream. Fractured friendships, unrequited love, my parents' issues—my earthly problems crumbled away like the brittle pages of an old storybook.

"So where are the Ishwees?" I asked. "Where are the Jinnku? I haven't seen anybody yet."

"You won't see too many of either group in these parts. The Ishwees live in caves, and most of the caves are on the other side of the island. The Jinnku live over there, too, though they're a little farther inland."

"Is that where you think Logan might be—the other side of the island?"

"Yes. Ready to head over?"

I was and I wasn't. If Logan wasn't there, I didn't know what I would do.

Chapter 49

We flew up and over the jungle. When we reached the opposite shore, I saw the green ocean, its waves endlessly rinsing a shore of smooth, slate-like rock. I saw the green clouds churning above. But I didn't see Logan.

That panicky feeling was coming back. "Where is he? You said—"

"Relax. There are lots of places he could be."

Including *lost in some distant corner of the universe.* I hadn't totally given up hope, but at the moment I couldn't help imagining the worst.

"You said Ed has spirit radar," I said, flitting anxiously in front of Jakob. "If Logan isn't here, if he's somewhere else in the universe, would Ed be able to help us find him?"

"In theory, yes. *If* Ed hasn't been gobbled up by the Jinnku, and *if* we can find him in spirit form."

Those were two big *ifs.* I didn't even want to think about the odds.

I trailed Jakob to a cove surrounded on three sides by dense jungle.

"Damn," he said softly. "Looks like they did it."

A raft big enough for square-dancing rocked gently in the water. It was made of those shiny plant leaves laid across rubbery gray-blue tree branches, and the whole structure appeared to be glued together with tree sap. I could see the pink goo glistening between the leaves like messy mortar.

I felt a rush of cousin-pride. Mysterium didn't have hardware stores stocked with nails and hammers and clean-cut boards, so Logan had made do with the materials at hand. And under his direction the Ishwees had managed to build a serviceable raft.

Jakob was staring moodily at the raft. I said, "You still haven't told me why you're against this."

"It's complicated."

"Yeah, you said that. Maybe it's time you told me *how* it's complicated."

He gave a resigned nod. "Maybe it is."

But before he could begin, something flitted through the air to my right. At first I thought it was one of those flying flowers, but as it got closer, I saw that it was something much better.

Logan.

I gave a shriek of joy and flung myself at him. The warm buzz of spirit-to-spirit contact flowed through me. "Oh my God. Logan!"

"Abby! Is it really you?"

"I've been so worried about you!"

"I thought I was a goner!"

"I didn't think I'd ever see you again!"

"I can't believe you found me!"

"Let me look at you. How are you feeling?" I wafted backward, slipping out of that spirit embrace. "You look a little better than the last time I saw you."

A little was right. He was still gray around the edges, his ghost-face practically skeletal. But his sparkles had ratcheted up to medium-bright, and his jubilant smile gave an overall illusion of good health.

255

"I'm feeling...not bad. I spend a lot of time in the clouds, getting zapped by lightning. It keeps me going."

"You're still in a coma, though. Did you know that?"

"Yeah, I figured." His eyes softened. "How are you doing, Abs? You feeling okay? You're kind of far from Earth."

"I'm fine," I said. "Getting here, though. What a trip!"

He laughed. "If a roller coaster and a kaleidoscope had a baby, right?"

We grinned at each other, though I was closer to tears than laughter as I remembered how it had felt to lose him.

"How'd you end up here?" I asked. "The last time I saw you, we were almost back to Earth. Then you died. Do you remember dying?"

All the mirth drained from his face. "Yeah, talk about surreal. I felt myself kind of blink off. A little while later, I blinked back on. I was in space, floating around. You were gone, and I couldn't see Earth anywhere. My sutratma was gone, too. But it was peaceful. The stars looked so pretty, like a jar of glitter spilled across black velvet. And I got to thinking that if this was what being dead was, it wasn't so bad. I was fine with spending eternity just floating around the universe. Then Ed found me and towed me back to Mysterium, and I knew I wasn't dead."

"We need to keep it that way," I said. "And that means you can never, ever come back here again."

"I know."

"No more broken promises. No more lies. Outer space travel is too dangerous. It literally killed you."

"I know, Abs. I've already decided that if I make it back to Earth, I'm never leaving again."

"Well, then," I said. "Let's get you home."

I reached for him, but he backed away. "I just have a few things to finish up first."

"Logan, no. We need to go *now.*"

"Come on, Abby. If I'm never coming back, you can't expect me to just…" He trailed off as his gaze drifted to a spot behind me. His golden sparkles darkened to amber. A purple brightness loomed at my side.

"Hello, Logan."

"Jakob."

They eyed each other like alpha dogs meeting on a sidewalk. I could practically hear the snarling. I knew they couldn't physically hurt each other, but I inserted myself between them anyway.

"So you're going through with it," Jakob said tightly.

"Already have," Logan replied. "Most of the Ishwees are safely on Bigland. There are only a few left on the island, and they'll be making the final trip tonight."

"Damn!" said Jakob. "Can't you see what a big mistake you're making?"

"Not doing something would be the mistake, bro."

I waved my arms. "Excuse me. Will somebody please tell me what's going on?"

Logan replied, his icy gaze still on Jakob. "I'm saving a civilization."

"Yeah, I heard. What I want to know is, why are you guys fighting?" I turned to Jakob, whose aura had gone the shade of crushed blueberries. "Saving a civilization sounds like a good thing. Why are you so against it?"

Jakob spoke tautly. "It's not as simple as Logan makes it sound. He might be saving one civilization, but he's killing another in the process."

Logan's aura sparked angrily. "That is such an exaggeration! I'm not killing anybody."

"Not with your own hands. But people will die because of what you're doing." Jakob half-turned to me. "Here's the part you didn't know. The Ishwees are the Jinnku's only food source. With the Ishwees gone from the island, the Jinnku will starve to death. The whole species will go extinct."

That left me mildly stunned, but I recovered quickly. "Well, maybe they deserve it, considering what jerks they are."

Jakob looked at me like I'd just confessed to drowning puppies.

"You don't know for sure that they'll go extinct," said Logan. "They might find something else to eat."

Scorn flashed in Jakob's eyes. "The Jinnku have been living on this island for who knows how long. If they haven't found something different to eat by now, do you really think they're going to?"

"So we should just let them keep slaughtering innocent people."

"It's the only way to ensure both groups survive. Don't you see? If the Ishwees stay on this island, some will die, yes—but at least their species will live on. But take the Ishwees out of the picture, and the Jinnku die. All of them."

Jakob and Logan were circling each other now, like wrestlers about to begin a match. I was at the center of their orbit, getting dizzier by the second. I ducked out of that dysfunctional solar system and said to Jakob, "But what kind of life is that for the Ishwees? Being hunted like animals, constantly on the run…"

"It sounds barbaric, I know," Jakob said, bowing his head. "But that's the natural order of things on Mysterium. Earth is no different—it has a natural order. There are food chains. Rabbits eat grass, coyotes eat rabbits, cougars eat coyotes. In the ocean, big fish eat little fish. Nobody gets up in arms about that."

"Fish and rabbits aren't intelligent creatures," I pointed out. "They don't sit around thinking, 'Crud, I'm going to die at some point, and if I get caught by that animal with the sharp teeth that keeps staring at me, it'll be today.' But the Ishwees? They probably think those thoughts every day."

Something was simmering in Jakob's eyes, the same look I'd seen in Holly's gentle doggy eyes one day last summer when she'd nosed a bumblebee on a clover, just trying to be friendly, and ended up getting stung. An odd heaviness sank into my soul. We'd finally been getting along. Why did I have to go and ruin it?

And why did it bother me so much that I had?

"Abby's right," said Logan, wafting closer to me. "Put yourself in Ed's place. How would you feel if you were nothing but a food source for other creatures?"

Jakob was scowling now. "Not all Ishwees get eaten. Ed told us that himself. Some of them live long lives and die natural deaths, same as deer in the woods on Earth."

"Not very many," Logan said grimly. "And not for much longer." His eyes glittered triumphantly. "The

Jinnku have started farming Ishwees. They're breeding them like cattle." Seeing Jakob's shocked expression, he added, "You didn't know? I guess you haven't been here for a while."

Jakob tossed his head impatiently. "What do you mean they're breeding them?"

"It started maybe two months ago. An Ishwee fell into a pit and couldn't get out. That gave the Jinnku their bright idea. Now they herd Ishwees into pits and keep them there, like cows in a barn. We've had to rescue a bunch of them. If we didn't get all the Ishwees off the island, there'd come a time when none of them would be free anymore. They'd all be farm animals spending their whole lives in captivity, just waiting to be slaughtered."

Abruptly his gaze shifted toward the jungle. His sparkles brightened as he called, "Ed! Over here."

I turned and saw Ed for the first time.

Oh God. Ed.

Chapter 50

Jakob had talked about Ed and his *people*, so I'd expected him to look like a *person*. Not a middle-aged guy in a polo shirt, of course, but maybe the standard green space alien with an oversized head and large, slanted black eyes.

Ha. Not even close. Except for the aura, which was in fact green.

Ed was in spirit form, so I was seeing only the translucent image of his physical self. But, oh, Ed was not pretty. He looked like that hairy shrub thing I'd seen in the jungle, only bigger and with dangly appendages that looked like a cross between a root system and octopus tentacles. Ed had no head, which meant no face. No eyes, ears, nose, or mouth. Just an oblong, bumpy gray body the size of a large bed pillow.

How could I relate to this creature when I couldn't even make eye contact?

Ed's tentacles writhed in the air. I tried to count them, but it was tough with all the movement. There might have been twelve, though most were split into two or three branches, which made it seem like more.

Logan said, "Ed, I'd like you to meet Abby."

Ed flicked a three-pronged tentacle toward me. I edged backward, just out of reach, hoping my revulsion wasn't obvious. Ed was hideous, but I didn't want to hurt his feelings.

"Hi, there," I said, in a chipper tone that got me odd looks from both Logan and Jakob.

"Far travel difficult. Weary?" Ed's communication style involved disjointed words interspersed with images that he somehow projected into my consciousness. It took me a minute to get used to it, but once I did, I saw that it got the job done. I felt like I was reading a child's picture book.

"I'm good," I said. "But, yeah, a little tired." The lightning zap had worn off.

Ed said my aura was very lovely. I thanked him and said his was nice, too. And then I felt something wash over me, something that started out gentle and tentative but then swelled until it was a warm, bright light beaming friendship and understanding and goodwill. I could see straight into Ed's heart, all the love that dwelled there, and I was so moved, I wanted to laugh and cry and hug everybody in sight, most of all Ed.

I couldn't speak. The hint of a smile on Logan's face told me he knew exactly what I was experiencing.

While I pulled myself together, Ed told how he'd found Logan floating in space not far from Mysterium, his aura alarmingly dim. He'd towed him back to the planet and kept him in the clouds until lightning revived him.

Logan picked up the story. "Ed's plan was to get me zapped, let me rest, and send me home. He didn't know I couldn't see my sutratma anymore. Once he found out, he said he'd try to take me to Earth himself. The problem is, he's never been to Earth before. He's only been as far as the edge of our galaxy. He wasn't sure he'd be able to get me home."

"Doesn't he have instinctive navigation?" I asked.

"He does, but just a very basic form. It gets him to places he's already visited, but that's about it."

I thought for a minute. "But if he could get you to the edge of our galaxy, wouldn't you be able to find your way home from there?"

"Are you kidding? There are, like, four hundred billion stars in the Milky Way. It would take me four hundred billion years to find the right one. Anyway, we agreed it was too risky for us to try to get to Earth. I figured my best shot was to hang out here and hope my sutratma eventually showed up."

Ed said he was deeply sorry to have failed Logan.

"You didn't fail him," I said. "You're probably the reason he's still alive. Thank you for taking such good care of my cousin. I'm here now, so I'll take him back to Earth."

Ed said something along the lines of "Shucks, it was nothing," and then there was a sort of "Say what?" that I didn't understand, and then the conversation stalled.

Jakob smoothed away the awkwardness by sailing forward to greet Ed. While they chatted, Logan pulled me aside and said, "He doesn't understand, Abs. The Ishwees don't have that concept."

"What concept?"

"Cousins. Families. I don't even think they have males and females."

I frowned. "How do they make babies?"

"They shed these...seeds, I guess, that get pushed into the ground by the rain and grow into new Ishwees. Except most of the seeds never sprout. Conditions have to be just right—enough rain but not too much, the right temperatures, soil that's loose enough for the seeds to burrow down but firm enough for them to take root. They grow for a while, and when the time is right, they pull themselves out of the ground and wander off to find their people."

"Weird," I said. "So Ed is technically a plant?"

"I'm not sure what he is."

"Hey," I said, suddenly remembering something. "I think I saw one of them. An Ishwee, growing in the jungle. It was this shrub thing, but it looked a lot like Ed."

"Where'd you see it? We've been trying to dig up all the seedlings and replant them on Bigland. We must have missed one."

"It was kind of hidden behind a rock. I can take you there. Unless you think the Jinnku have already gotten it."

"No, it should still be there. Ed says the Jinnku never bother the Ishwee seedlings. Apparently, they taste bad when they're rooted in the ground. Some kind of evolutionary defense mechanism, I guess."

I was still trying to envision a society made up of self-harvesting vegetables. I asked, "How does anybody know whose kid is whose?"

"They don't."

"So nobody has parents? Who takes care of the babies?"

"They're not really babies. And nobody takes care of them. When they're in the ground, they get everything they need from the rain and the soil. Once they're out of the ground, they're totally self-sufficient."

"That's crazy." I tried to imagine not having

parents. As aggravating as my mom was, I knew she loved me deeply—maybe even more than she loved my dad. Without my two parents anchoring me to the world, I would have felt unmoored, unprotected, and far more isolated than I already felt.

"It's not crazy," said Logan. "It's just different. The Ishwees are like certain critters on Earth that lay eggs but don't hang around to take care of their young. Turtles, insects. The new Ishwees know right from the start what to eat, how to take care of themselves. They even know to keep away from the Jinnku."

"Seeds in the ground, though," I said. "That's a pretty weird way for intelligent beings to reproduce."

"Ed thinks the way we do it is weird."

I considered that. "He's not wrong."

Jakob wafted over to us. He and Logan directed stiff nods at each other, as if declaring a truce.

"Where's Ed?" asked Logan.

"Disappeared. Guess he woke up."

"Aw!" Logan's aura pulsed his frustration. "There are things I need to tell him. Now we'll have to wait till he comes back to us in spirit form."

I sighed. "Logan, come on."

"It shouldn't take long. The Ishwees take a lot of naps. Anyway, you need to show me that Ishwee seedling."

Jakob said, "Ishwee seedling? What Ishwee seedling?" He was giving me the same look I'd seen that morning at the Eiffel Tower, as if my very presence offended him. I figured he was mad that I hadn't agreed with him about the Ishwee-Jinnku situation.

"I saw it when we were in the jungle. It was hidden behind a rock. I didn't realize what it was till now." I hardened my expression to match his. "You want to see it? Come on, we're heading over there now."

The hostility in his eyes faded. "I'll wait here. Give you two some cousin time. But hey." He jerked his head toward the jungle. "Look around the island if you get a chance. There's plenty you haven't seen."

"She doesn't have time for that," Logan fired back. "Didn't you hear? She's in a hurry to get back to Earth."

He zoomed away. I hurried to catch up.

"Why didn't you tell me about this?" I asked as we wound our way through the jungle.

"Tell you about what?"

"Mysterium. The Ishwees. Why didn't you tell me what you were up to when you started coming here?"

"I don't know." His aura blinked gently. "I guess I was afraid you wouldn't approve of what I was doing."

We parted to swerve around a massive boulder, though we could have gone straight through. I still half-expected to have a painful collision every time I flew through a solid object.

"You're saving a civilization. Why wouldn't I approve?"

"Because I'm changing the evolution of the planet. Remember when we used to watch *Star Trek*? Remember how they had that rule that said they weren't allowed to interfere with alien civilizations?"

"Yeah, and they were always breaking it."

"Right. And every time they did, you'd get all fired up and say, 'Why can't they leave those poor aliens alone!' "

"That was just a TV show."

"Still. I was afraid you'd think I shouldn't be

helping the Ishwees. That's why I didn't want to tell you."

I threw him a sidewise glance. "But then you changed your mind. That night you tried to bring me here."

"I thought if you could just meet Ed, you'd understand."

"And I do," I said. "I do understand. Ed is amazing. So much love in his heart. I'm glad his people will finally be safe from those awful Jinnku."

Logan smiled, but in an oddly strained way.

"What I don't understand," I said, "is why you kept coming back. Once you taught the Ishwees how to build a raft, that should have been the end of it. You shouldn't have come back after that. If you'd just stayed on Earth, we could have avoided this whole cruddy nightmare."

Logan nodded heavily. "That's what I was planning to do. It just didn't work out. Building things doesn't come naturally to the Ishwees. They needed constant supervision, but I couldn't give it because I wasn't able to communicate directly with them. When I saw them making mistakes, I would have to wait for Ed to have an OBE so I could tell him, and then he would tell the others. And it always took them a bunch of tries to get things right."

Torment clouded his eyes. "I knew it was hurting me, being so far from my body for such long stretches of time. But I couldn't quit. I had to finish what I started. Because I was the only one who could save them."

Below us, three bumpy gray bodies slithered through the underbrush. Ishwees, probably on their way to the raft. I prayed they wouldn't encounter any Jinnku along the way.

"I get it," I said softly. "I don't like it, but I get it."

All around us, the never-ending rain poured down, a plinking xylophone of sound. It slicked the tree trunks and dripped across leaves and pooled in green puddles on the jungle floor.

"Tell me about Ed," I said, pushing past Logan to lead the way, because he was heading in the wrong direction. "How does he work?"

"What do you mean, how does he work?"

"I didn't see any eyes or ears or a mouth. Can he even see us?"

"Yes, he can see us—in his own way. From what he told us, those little hairs all over him are sensors. He doesn't see and hear and smell the same way we do, but he processes sights and sounds and smells through those hairs. Plus, he has a bunch of extra senses that we don't have."

"Like what?"

"No idea. He tried to tell me about some of them, but I couldn't understand. They're not like anything any creature on Earth has."

I said, "Weird."

Logan's mouth twisted. "You keep saying that. Ed's people aren't weird. They're just different. Their biology is actually better than ours in a way. Like, if our eyes get poked out, we're blind. But if a few of Ed's sensor hairs get damaged, it's no biggie, because he still has all the others. He doesn't lose any of his senses. And new hairs grow back to replace the damaged ones."

I nodded thoughtfully, like I was buying this. Then

I said, "Nope, that's just weird." I knew I was being ornery, but I couldn't help myself. I was exhausted from traveling, bowled over by Mysterium, and sick of this whole adventure. I just wanted to go home.

Logan said tightly, "You don't like Ed."

"No, I do like him. A lot. It's just—he's so different. I never knew anybody without a face before. And those tentacles! I mean, *octopuses* have tentacles."

"Octopuses do not have tentacles." I heard the scorn in Logan's voice before I saw the scowl on his face. "They have *arms*. Sheesh, we learned that way back in fifth-grade science class."

"Okay, whatever! I just thought Ed would be more, I don't know, *humanish*."

"Why would you think that? We're not on Earth anymore. We're on an alien planet far, far away. Why can't you accept and respect the people who live here instead of hating them because they're different?"

He sounded like a school principal. I felt like a chastised child. "I don't hate them," I mumbled. Then, as we followed the contour of the terrain down a small slope, "Forget it. We're almost there."

The Ishwee seedling was right where I'd last seen it. Logan hovered near the ground, examining it. He said, "I'll have to fetch an Ishwee to come dig it up."

"How are you going to do that? You're a spirit. It's not like you can talk to them."

"I use signals to communicate. The Ishwees are used to it—they know all about Ed's invisible friend. When I want somebody to follow me, I rustle bushes or bang sticks together to guide them. They're smart. They usually figure it out. You'll see."

"Actually, I won't. I'm going to take a quick look

269

around the island."

"Aw, don't do that, Abs."

His dismay took me by surprise. "Why not? Because it was Jakob's idea?"

"I just feel like we should stick together." He smiled feebly. "Cousin power?" He extended an arm for a spiritual fist bump, but I ignored it.

"I won't be long," I said. "I'll meet you back at the raft. You be quick, too, okay?"

I zipped away before he could charm me into staying.

Chapter 51

I headed back to the Ishwee side of the island. Enough of being a tourist. I wanted to see where the locals lived.

For a while, there was nothing around me but jungle. Plants, flowers, those strange bowed trees, the occasional snaking stream. Patchy mist hugged the ground like steamy puffs of breath.

I accidentally disrupted a flower pollination in progress, and two flower heads circled me like angry bees.

"Sorry!" I said. I seemed to be rubbing everybody the wrong way today.

I suddenly realized how quiet the jungle was. How still. Only the musical patter of raindrops broke the silence. There didn't seem to be any birds on Mysterium. No small animals scampering around. That struck me as sad, and a wave of homesickness swept over me. I missed Earth, with its abundant, chattering wildlife.

The jungle thinned out as the ground got rockier. The terrain grew steeper, too. If I'd been hiking on my own two feet, I'd have been starting to huff and puff. Up ahead the light was brighter. I sailed into a clearing and stopped in front of a rocky cliff that rose from the ground like a four-story building.

Now I was getting somewhere. Rocky cliffs often

housed caves.

I flew up and down the face of the cliff but couldn't find anything that looked like the mouth of a cave, only narrow fissures that split the rock like tight smiles. That was disappointing. The caves Jakob had mentioned must be somewhere else.

I was about to leave when I saw something gray and bumpy oozing out of a fissure. I watched in fascination as an Ishwee squeezed out and plopped to the ground.

Amazing, I thought, that those bulky cauliflower bodies could fit through such narrow openings. They must have squishable bones, if they had any bones at all.

The Ishwee scuttled into the underbrush. I followed it to a field pocked with shallow craters, their bottoms bubbling with a thick yellow liquid. What had created them? A meteor shower? Volcanoes simmering below the surface? The Ishwee slithered into one of the craters and sat there, like an Earth lady soaking in a bubble bath. I remembered Jakob saying that the Ishwees ate crater gunk. Through their skin. *Bon appetit, Ishwee!*

I returned to the cliff and flew through the narrow fissure the Ishwee had squeezed out of. Sure enough, a small cave was inside, clearly an Ishwee home. I flitted around, studying the crude furnishings. Flattened piles of twigs and grasses that probably served as bedding. A short table made of four flat rocks stacked on top of each other. On the table, a bowl-like piece of wood containing pink tree sap. Everything was either small or had started off in tiny pieces. Larger materials wouldn't have fit through that narrow opening.

The Ishwees might be a primitive civilization, but

it was clear they were advancing. That was bound to happen even faster on the bigger island, where they wouldn't have to spend all their energy trying to elude the Jinnku.

Back in the jungle, I floated around like dandelion fluff, not sure where to go next. Had Logan finished his business and returned to the raft? I should probably get back, too. I didn't want to delay our departure by a single second.

But I didn't return to the raft. There was something else I needed to see. My one and only visit to Mysterium was coming to an end, and if I didn't get at least a glimpse of the Jinnku, I would always wonder about them.

Did they live in caves like the Ishwees? In trees like birds? Out in the open like lions? Jakob hadn't said. I didn't even know what they looked like.

Until suddenly I did.

Chapter 52

I sailed out of a tangle of shrubbery and came face to face with a Jinnku.

It had to be a Jinnku. What else could it be?

I shrieked, temporarily forgetting that my spirit-self couldn't be harmed. Unlike the flying flowers, this creature gave no sign that he was aware of me.

In my fright, I'd rocketed backward, so I was far enough away to get a look at him in his entirety. Multiple oddities jumped out at me. The pale green skin, wrinkly as unironed linen. Four arms, three legs. Eyes on all sides of his head. He was a big guy, at least nine feet tall. But he looked more human than the Ishwees did. In one clawed, three-fingered hand he held a crude knife, honed to a lethal sharpness. It appeared to have been made from those shiny metallic leaves.

I moved closer to get a better look at those eyes. There were four in front, five in back, more on the sides and top. Not all were open at the same time, and they kept blinking in what seemed to be a deliberate sequence. He didn't have a neck to allow for head-swiveling, so I supposed he had to open and close eyes on different sides of his head depending on where he wanted to look at any given time. His bulbous eyeballs filled their sockets and glowed copper-pink, like new pennies.

I saw no mouth, nose, or ears. If he had them, they

were probably hidden within skin folds.

I trailed him through the jungle, fascinated by the complex rhythm of his gait. If I'd had an extra leg to deal with, I would've been tripping over my own feet. The Jinnku deftly navigated the horizontal tangle of trees, ducking under the highest arches, high-stepping over the low ones, and climbing over the densest ones.

When we reached the crater field, he zigged and zagged his way across, stopping to check each crater. The Ishwee who'd been feeding there earlier was gone.

Next, the Jinnku headed to the rocky cliff and spent several minutes peering into crevices. No luck there either.

We followed a stream that frothed creamy green where it bumped over rocks. Rounding a curve, we came upon two Jinnku gazing somberly downward. A third Jinnku was lying on the ground, obviously dead. His wrinkled skin was gray-white, like the sun-bleached trunks of long-dead trees. The Jinnku I was following stood next to the others for a few minutes, as if paying respects, before continuing on his way.

He stopped to stare despondently into a muddy pit. I suspected this was one of the pits the Jinnku used for trapping Ishwees. It was empty.

Eventually he arrived at a wide clearing where the ground was riddled with large holes. Irrationally, I pictured giant bunnies. When the Jinnku slipped into one of the holes, I followed.

Inside were several small, irregularly shaped rooms containing primitive furniture. Tree stump tables. Rugs woven crookedly out of dried grasses. Thicker, fluffier mats that might have been beds. I even saw what looked like rudimentary plates and food-preparation utensils fashioned out of those shiny metallic leaves. Centered on a tree stump like a piece of art was a shimmery green and purple rock.

Although Jakob had said the Jinnku were an intelligent life form, I'd pictured them as brutal wild beasts—specifically, lions. I'd imagined them pouncing on Ishwees, tearing them apart with their teeth, and then bedding down in the underbrush.

This home, with its comforts and its tools—and even art!—didn't line up with that notion. The Jinnku were far more than wild beasts.

The Jinnku laid his knife on a tree stump and plodded to a back room. I followed. A small Jinnku was sitting on the floor, listlessly scratching lines in the packed dirt with a clawed finger. When the little Jinnku saw the big one, he toddled over with a happy squeak. The big one picked him up. They tapped their heads together three times, their front-facing eyes blinking in unison. The big one rubbed the little one's back.

There were noises—squeaks from the little one, grunts from the big one. Jinnku talk. I imagined the conversation.

Where's the food? Did you bring food?
No, my darling. I'm afraid there isn't any food.
Why not? Where did it go?
I don't know.
But I'm hungry! You didn't bring food yesterday either.
I know, and I'm sorry. You've been so brave.
We need food! If we don't eat, we die. Isn't that right?
[No response.]
Are we going to die? Please, I don't want to die!

The big Jinnku slithered to the floor as if too weak to stand. Leaning against the dirt wall, he wrapped two arms around the child and stroked him with the third.

The child made keening noises that sounded to me like crying.

That was when I left. I was starting to feel sick, and I wasn't sure if it was a reaction to what I'd just seen or a warning from my Earth-bound body to get home before I ended up in a coma.

Chapter 53

I returned to the raft to find another argument in progress.

Actually, the same argument.

"I just think it's time you stopped playing God," said Jakob.

"I am not playing God," Logan said angrily. "I'm saving lives. No decent person would stand by and let this killing go on."

"No decent person would wipe out an entire species."

"Guys," I said. "Can we please go home?"

They ignored me.

"How about this," said Jakob. "We keep the remaining Ishwees on the island long enough for them to lay down some seeds. Then we leave the seedlings here for the Jinnku. That way, most of the Ishwee population will be saved, but the Jinnku will have at least a fighting chance at survival."

Logan's lip curled in a soundless snarl. "You just don't get it, do you? The whole point of getting the Ishwees off the island is to stop the killing. *All of it.*"

He swung his head toward me. "Abs? Help me out here?"

I saw the message in his eyes. It wasn't a threat, more like a plea, but I knew what it meant. Logan and I had always had each other's backs, and that was what he expected now. If I teamed up with Jakob, it would be a betrayal, one that could drive a wedge between us.

That was why it was so hard for me to say what I had to say.

I took the spiritual equivalent of a deep breath and blurted it out. "I've seen the Jinnku, Logan. I've been in a Jinnku home. And they're not monsters! They're normal, decent people with furniture and dishes and arms and legs and eyes, and kids that they love, and they don't deserve to die. They just don't."

I glanced at Jakob. He was nodding, his aura a lovely shade of lavender. This was why he'd told me to explore the island. He'd wanted me to see the Jinnku for myself, to reach my own conclusions. I had to give him credit for that. He could have tried to force his opinion on me during the trip to Mysterium, but he hadn't. He'd given a neutral account of the situation and hadn't said one bad word against Logan.

Logan's aura was a grim, dull amber, edging toward brown. "I can't believe this. You're flipping to his side?"

"I have a right to change my mind."

"But you said I was doing something good."

"That was before I saw the Jinnku." I eyed him coolly. "You didn't want me to see them, did you? That's why you tried to stop me from exploring the island."

He ignored that. He did an exaggerated *tsk-tsk* and said, "This is sad. I never thought I'd see you turn into Grandma."

"Grandma? What are you talking about?"

"Grandma thinks everybody should be like her. White, middle-class, Episcopalian. She looks down on

279

anybody who isn't those things. Hell, she won't even talk to the couple across the street because they're biracial."

That got me bristling. "Don't you compare me to Grandma. I'm nothing like Grandma! I don't have a problem with biracial couples."

"But you have a problem with Ed. Don't deny it—I saw your face when you met him. He makes you uncomfortable because he's different. And now you've seen the Jinnku, and they seem a little closer to human, so naturally you think their lives are more important."

Jakob said, "Abby, you're looking a little dim," but I only half-heard him.

"I don't think their lives are more important," I said. "I just happen to agree with Jakob. You shouldn't be playing God."

"I'm not playing God! I'm helping desperate people survive."

We stared at each other. I saw the fire in his eyes and felt the same fire in my own heart. Neither of us was about to back down.

Above us, the clouds were dulling from pale green to sage as nightfall approached. Below us, a small group of Ishwees slithered onto the raft, preparing to make the final trip to Bigland. I could hear the excited clicks and whistles of their conversations.

"Don't you understand," I said wearily to Logan, "the Jinnku never set out to hurt anybody. They're just trying to survive. And to do that, they have to eat. It's not their fault their only food source happens to be the Ishwees."

"But it's wrong!" Logan said passionately. "Don't you see how wrong it is for one life form to eat another?"

"But Logan," I said, "You do it. You eat cheeseburgers and chicken nuggets all the time."

His eyes glinted proudly. "Not anymore. I've gone vegan."

"Since when?"

"Since I met Ed."

"Wow," I said. Here was yet another fact I hadn't known about my cousin. "So you're not just risking your life for this guy. You're changing your whole lifestyle."

"He's my friend," Logan said, his eyes blazing. "That's what this all comes down to. Ed is my friend, and he asked me for help, and I agreed to help him. Wouldn't you do the same? Wouldn't you do whatever you could to help a friend? Oh, wait. You don't have any friends."

The cut happened so quickly, all I could do was gape at him as the knife sliced through me. Suddenly I was bleeding. Hemorrhaging. Of course, it was emotional bleeding, not physical, but maybe that was the worst kind.

Almost instantly, Logan's face registered horror. "No, no, Abby, I didn't mean that. I'm sorry! I only said it because I was mad."

"No," I whispered. "You said it because it's true."

Suddenly I was tired. Really, really tired. I lurched toward the jungle. Logan followed. I made a pushing-away gesture with my arms.

"Get away from me. I need to be by myself."

"Come on, Abs, don't be mad. I said I'm sorry. You can be so stubborn sometimes. I was just trying to make you see how..."

He was still talking, but suddenly his voice was muffled, fading out. The scenery around me darkened, and I felt funny. Flimsy, like a soap bubble about to pop.

From a great distance I heard Jakob shout, "Logan, grab her—she's going dark!"

And then I blinked off.

Chapter 54

I was in a strange netherworld where everything was dim and distorted. The clouds above and the ocean below were red, not green. The jungle was bronzed orange. Rain flowed from the clouds in ultra-slow motion, allowing me to see each individual raindrop.

But the rain wasn't just rain. Encapsulated within each droplet was a tiny creature, an amoeba-like splotch made of liquid metal, with a single bulging eye and a wide mouth. These creatures rode the rain down, and the ones that didn't get snagged by trees or bushes joined soupy communities on the ground. They were muttering in gruff voices, their words stretched and garbled like a recording played at the wrong speed.

A movement at the edge of the jungle caught my eye, and when I looked over, I saw a small group of flower heads bobbing there. One of them, a pink orb with spiky petals, detached itself from the group and drifted over to me. Hovering in front of my face, it whispered a secret, a truth so profound and glorious that I could only gape in wonder. Then it wafted away.

"Holy crud. Did you hear that?" I said, but I was talking to thin air. Logan and Jakob were nowhere to be seen. My sutratma was missing, too.

Was I dead or alive—or something in between? I was trying to figure that out when the bizarre interlude ended. I came back to myself with a snap, as if waking from a nightmare.

"Abs! Oh my God, are you okay?"

I nodded, too dazed to speak.

Logan told me I *had* gone dark, but only for a few seconds. He and Jakob had hustled me into the clouds, and there were so many lightning bolts flashing around that one caught me immediately.

"The rain is alive," I murmured. "The flowers know things. They said…" I tried to remember the incredible secret the pink flower had told me, but I couldn't. It had been wiped from my memory. And with every passing second I was finding it harder to remember there had even been a secret.

Jakob shushed me and said I should rest. He probably thought I was delirious.

"Don't move," said Logan. "We're going to hang out up here for a while, get you all charged up. We'll head back to Earth as soon as you feel ready."

"But you have stuff to finish up."

He shook his head soberly. "Getting you home is more important."

His sparkles were back to their usual pastel shade. So were Jakob's. Without saying a word, we knew the dispute was over. What was the point of arguing? It was too late to change anything.

Logan kept dropping to the bottom edge of the clouds to peer down at the raft. After he'd done that five or six times, he said, in a taut voice, "There are only twenty-seven Ishwees on the raft. There are supposed to be twenty-eight."

"Guess somebody forgot to set their alarm clock," Jakob said lightly, but Logan's frown only deepened.

"Be right back," he said, and swooped below the

clouds. He was gone for several minutes, and when he returned, his aura was flashing like a fire alarm. "It's Ed. Ed's missing."

Jakob said, "You can actually tell them apart?"

"For the most part. It isn't easy, considering they don't have faces. But there are differences in how they look. Their size and shape, how many tentacles they have, the way they move. Plus, Ed has this hump on his left side that makes him pretty easy to recognize." He sent another anxious glance downward. "Something's wrong. It's not like him to be late."

"You don't think—" I broke off because I didn't want to say it.

Jakob finished for me. "—the Jinnku got him?"

Logan winced. "That's what I'm afraid of."

"We have to look for him," I said.

"We don't have time," said Logan. "We have to get you home."

"It's okay. I'm feeling better. Come on, our friend needs help."

He looked at me gratefully. "You sure, Abs?"

"Hundred percent. I'm crazy about Ed. I can't leave without making sure he's okay."

We flew into the jungle, tight as a formation of Air Force jets. We stopped off at Ed's cave but found it unoccupied. Logan knew where all the Jinnku pits were, so we started checking them one by one. The first pit was empty, though several Jinnku prowled the jungle nearby, obviously hoping for the chance to snare an Ishwee.

The second pit was empty, too. And the third.

We flew over a stream and up and down a few rolling hills. At the bottom of the last hill, we found two

Jinnku peering into a pit. Ed was at the bottom, staring up at them.

"Oh no!" I said.

"It's okay. We can scare them away," said Logan. "Jinnku get freaked out by anything that moves. If we just rustle some bushes—"

"Hold on," said Jakob. "I think Ed is talking to them."

We floated closer to the edge of the pit. Ed was uttering noises that sounded a lot like Jinnku grunts. The Jinnku stood perfectly still, their front-facing eyes wide open as they listened.

"Oh wow, he's speaking Jinnku," Logan said. "He told me he'd picked up bits and pieces of their language, but I didn't know he could speak it."

"Probably didn't have a chance to try it out till now," said Jakob.

Ed continued grunting, and when he paused, one of the Jinnku said something. Then Ed spoke again. The two Jinnku stepped back from the edge of the pit and spent a minute in private conversation. One of them picked up a knife like the one I'd seen in the hand of the Jinnku I'd followed. He hopped down into the pit. Ed shrank into the farthest corner.

"I think it's time to rustle those bushes," said Jakob.

He picked up a rock and hurled it at the Jinnku in the pit. The Jinnku yelped and whirled around, looking for the source of the attack. Logan and I rustled bushes while Jakob continued to throw rocks. Both Jinnku howled in terror. The one with the knife scrambled out of the pit, and the two of them tore off into the jungle, leaves jingling in their wake.

"Don't worry, Ed, we're going to get you out," I called.

"He can't hear you, Abs. He's not in spirit form," Logan reminded me.

But Ed knew we were there. He raised a tentacle as if high-fiving us.

Jakob pulled a purple vine off a tree and tossed one end into the pit. He tied the other end to a tree branch. Ed clambered up like a monkey, arm over arm over arm.

"He'll never make it to the raft in time," Logan lamented.

"Won't they wait for him?" I asked.

"They can't. They have to leave as soon as it's dark. That's when the tide switches direction and flows toward Bigland. It'll take all night to get there, and if they don't leave on time, they won't make it by morning. The tide will turn, and they'll end up right back here. Or, worse, lost at sea."

The three of us glanced upward. The greenish glow in the sky was fading fast.

We hovered above Ed like anxious parents, watching him thrash his way through the jungle. His tentacles were a blur of movement as he scuttled under tangled tree branches and climbed hills. He sloshed through a wide creek and got swept ten yards downstream before making his way to the opposite bank. His tentacles got entwined in a jumble of vines, and Jakob had to swoop down to untangle him.

By the time Ed reached the shore, the sky was dark. He came to an abrupt halt at the water's edge, reaching one tentacle forlornly toward the horizon.

The raft had already departed. It was maybe a

hundred feet out in the ocean. The three of us stared after it in dismay.

"Can't they row back and pick him up?" I asked.

"They don't have oars," said Jakob. "Which seems strange, now that I think about it."

"We tried oars," said Logan. "They couldn't get the hang of rowing. They're not built that way. Anyway, they don't need oars. The current is strong—much stronger than the currents in Earth's oceans."

That was obvious. The raft was chugging along as if propelled by a motor.

"But how do they steer?" asked Jakob.

"They don't need to. The current will take them straight to Bigland. It's a big island—there's no way they can miss it. The return trip is iffier since this island is a smaller target. They've been sending the raft back after each trip so it can be used again, but it doesn't always make it back. The times it hasn't come back, they've had to build a whole new raft. Of course, this time they don't need to send it back, since it's the last trip."

"Oh wow, he's swimming for it!" I said.

Ed was plowing into the water, cheered on by his comrades on the raft. His tentacles churned like propellers. The raft was moving fast, but Ed was moving faster.

"Look at him go!" crowed Logan.

It didn't take long before Ed was bobbing just behind the raft. Two of his comrades flung tentacles into the water and hauled him aboard.

The three of us cheered. Ed must have figured we were watching from the shore, because he waved a tentacle in our direction. Or maybe he was waving goodbye to his homeland. We watched until the raft was a speck on the horizon.

Jakob suggested we get one last lightning charge before heading home. Both he and Logan were looking a little dim, and their worried glances told me I was, too. A mega-bolt crackled through me, energizing me instantly. But I knew it was a false buzz, the same kind a strong cup of coffee might provide. I felt shaky to my very core, and I knew that getting back in my body was the only thing that would cure me. Same for the guys. But for now, getting zapped was our best option, and we had to hope it would be enough to get us home.

We dipped below the clouds to take a last look at Mysterium. The blue-gray jungle, the bottle-green ocean. The air filled with that endless, shimmery rain. I didn't feel the least bit nostalgic, but I could tell Logan did. His aura quivered like a violin bow playing a sad tune. When Jakob said, "Let's go," we soared up through the clouds and into space.

We went slowly at first, warming up our space-travel muscle. We had barely moved past Mysterium's solar system when something came barreling toward us.

Ed.

Logan and Ed spun in a circle, doing a friendship happy-dance. Ed said he'd been so exhausted from getting captured by the Jinnku, making that mad dash through the jungle, and swimming out to the raft that he'd fallen asleep. He was very glad an OBE had followed, because now he could thank us for saving him.

Logan told him we wouldn't be coming back to Mysterium. The trip was just too hard on our bodies. Ed said he understood. He was giving up space travel, too, for the same reason. It saddened him to know we would never see each other again, but he would never forget us and would always consider us dear friends.

He and Logan drifted away for a private talk. I eyed them anxiously. Now that we'd left Mysterium, I was eager to get that wild roller-coaster ride over with. At the same time, I could tell that Logan and Ed were having a meaningful conversation, their last ever, so I let them be.

Jakob wafted over to me. "Still feeling okay?"

"Okay enough to get home, I think. You?"

"I'm good."

We regarded each other solemnly. Soon we would be back on Earth, going our separate ways. A strange sadness welled up in me, and I wanted to hug him. I wanted to say I would miss him. But I didn't do either of those things. I just didn't have the nerve.

Instead, I said, "Thank you for saving Logan."

"Glad I could help."

"You did more than help. I never would have found him without you."

"That's probably true."

"I'm just sorry I had to drag you the whole way across the universe to do it."

"Technically, I'm the one who dragged you."

"But don't worry—this will never happen again. Logan and I are staying on Earth from now on." I shuddered, remembering the dark moments of our journey. "Actually, I think I'm going to take a break from astral travel for a while. If I do have OBEs, I'll stay close to home."

"I'll be doing the same."

Our eyes had been locked together throughout this

exchange. His suddenly seemed to burn into mine like unfiltered sunshine. Flustered, I shifted my gaze to Logan and Ed. They were still talking. Two of Ed's tentacles were waving earnestly, as if he was making an important point.

I started to say, "I wonder what they're talking about," but Jakob spoke at the same time, and what he said was, "When we do get back to traveling, maybe we could hang out."

A clot of breath lodged in my throat. Not really, but that was how it felt. "You want to hang out with me?"

"I could show you Versailles."

"But I'm so annoying."

"I'm getting used to it. I barely notice it anymore."

"The time difference, though—it's, like, nine hours."

"We'll make it work. We could also call and text each other. Meet up on social media. You know. Interact in the real world."

Holy crud. Me—hot all over. Which was crazy, because getting hot was a physical sensation, which I couldn't possibly be having.

"Um, yeah," I said. "We can definitely do those things."

"Abby, I'm sorry," Jakob said abruptly.

"For what?"

"For being a jerk sometimes. Like that morning at the Eiffel Tower."

"You already apologized."

"That wasn't an apology. Not a sincere one, anyway. You deserve more. An explanation."

He glanced at Logan and Ed as if to make sure they

were still occupied. Then he turned back to me. "Sometimes I act too much like my father. He's a total ass. Rude, crabby, always looking for something to be mad about. Drinks too much, too. Broke my nose when I was fourteen because he tripped over my bookbag. His own father was an alcoholic, so he didn't have the best role model growing up. Guess he never learned how to be a dad."

And I'd thought my family had problems.

Jakob went on, "When I get tense and frustrated like I was that morning in Paris, I tend to channel my father. When I should be channeling my mother. She was the opposite of him—kind, cheerful, warm."

"Was?" I said uneasily.

His aura throbbed like a heartbeat, its hue as dull as a sprig of dried lavender. "She died three years ago. Grandmother moved in with us afterward. She knew my father would be useless as a single parent."

"Jakob, I'm so sorry."

"I need to try harder to be the person my mother wanted me to be. 'Treat people the way you want to be treated,' she used to say. 'Think before you speak.' 'Always wear sunscreen.' "

"Good advice, all of it."

"She'd be disappointed in me, how I acted that morning in Paris."

"Maybe not. Looking back, I guess I *was* kind of annoying."

"Oh, you definitely were. But I didn't have to be so mean about it."

I planted my hands on my hips in mock indignation. Jakob grinned.

We'd been drifting closer and closer, and now we

were practically touching. When Logan flew over, we broke apart guiltily.

Logan looked from me to Jakob and back again. "Wow, you guys are such pretty colors."

I hadn't even noticed Jakob's bright fuchsia tint. I was probably blushing, too. It didn't take a genius to sum up the situation, but Logan didn't tease us. He clearly had something else on his mind.

He said, "You won't believe what Ed just told me."

Ed, I saw, was gone.

"You can tell us later," said Jakob, sounding so brusque and businesslike that I had to look twice to make sure he was the same guy I'd just been talking to. "We need to get moving."

"Trust me, you're going to want to hear this."

"*Later*," Jakob said firmly. "We've been out here way too long. If we don't get home soon—"

He interrupted himself with a strangled cry. "Damn it—no!" Then, speaking so fast I could hardly understand him: "Abby-it'll-be-okay-you-can-do-this-just-remember—"

And then he disappeared.

"Jakob!" I screamed. "Jakob, no!"

But he was gone.

Chapter 55

"I guess it's morning in Europe," drawled Logan. "Jakob's grandmother must have swept him out of bed with her broom."

"It can't be morning already," I moaned. "We haven't been out here that long!"

"Time works differently on the astral plane. It's unstable. Sometimes it speeds up, and sometimes it slows down. I think it's because we're technically not in the physical world, but we're still connected to it through our bodies. It's like time doesn't know what to do with us."

"How can you be so calm about this?" I screeched. "Now we'll never get home!"

"Sure we will. You have your sutratma to guide you."

"No, no, that's not good enough!" I flew around him like an agitated bird, unable to keep still. "I can't count on my sutratma. It went away when I blinked off. What if it goes away again?"

"It won't. You're all charged up."

"We have to go much faster than the speed of light. I don't know how to do that."

"Sure you do. You might not realize it, but you do."

I stopped flitting and looked at him desperately. "You've been to Mysterium and back a lot more than I have. Can't you lead the way?"

"No, Abs. I still can't see my sutratma."

"Oh my God, we're doomed!" I clutched my head, trying to quash this new panic attack.

"Abs, stop. You can do this. You're *going* to do it because you have to."

I gazed into his eyes, mesmerized by the trust I saw there. The confidence. He totally believed I could get us back to Earth.

So maybe I needed to believe it, too.

"All right. Okay. Just give me a minute," I said shakily.

"While you're working up your nerve, let me tell you what Ed said. I think you're going to like it."

Logan said Ed had known that the Ishwees were the Jinnku's only food source. And although Ed's first obligation was to save his own people, he couldn't stop fretting over the Jinnku. He felt the tragedy of their impending extinction in every corner of his heart.

Knowing what kind of guy Ed was, I wasn't surprised to hear this.

As Mysterium's only astral traveler, Ed knew his planet better than anyone. In recent weeks, he'd taken to exploring the ocean and had found it teeming with life, far more life than the islands supported. Among its various life forms were creatures that looked a lot like the Jinnku. Three legs, four arms, multiple eyes. The only differences seemed to be their rubbery skin and flipper-like arms and legs.

The diet of the water-based Jinnku consisted of several varieties of plants that grew on the ocean floor. Ed suspected that the land-based Jinnku could eat those same plants. They would just have to go into the ocean to fetch them.

That was what he'd told the two Jinnku who'd captured him.

"This might be a dumb question," I said, "but how can the Jinnku go in the ocean to eat plants? Won't they, like, *drown*?"

"Actually, they should be fine. Ed figures they're descendants of the water Jinnku. He thinks they evolved to live on land but still have the ability to breathe underwater."

My eyes followed a passing asteroid as I thought that over. "So Ed wants them to go back to living in the ocean?"

"No. I mean, I guess they could do that, as long as they can still breathe underwater. But the ocean has predators that go after the water Jinnku. Ed thinks that's why they migrated to the island in the first place—they were trying to get away from those predators. And it's why they're scared of the ocean to this day. Stories got passed down through the generations about the horrible sea monsters that eat Jinnku."

"Oh. So you're saying they would go into the ocean only when they needed to get food. The ocean would be like their grocery store."

"Exactly."

"But what if Ed's wrong? What if they can't breathe underwater?"

"They still might be okay. Those same plants grow in the shallow water closer to shore. Don't get me wrong—they'd still have to learn how to swim, how to dive. They'd have to get over their fear of the ocean. But if they can do those things, they should be able to survive."

"Well," I mused, "I guess it's a good thing Ed happened to get captured."

"Except he didn't 'happen' to get captured. He went to see the Jinnku on purpose."

"What! Is he crazy?"

"Crazy?" For a second, I thought Logan was going to yell at me again for insulting Ed. Instead, he smiled a wistful smile. "No. Just selfless in a way you and I could never understand. He figured it was a suicide mission, but he told me he wouldn't have been able to live with himself if he didn't at least try to save them. So he hung out in Jinnku territory till he ran into two of them."

He gave a rueful laugh. "Of course, the first thing they did was herd him into that pit. But when he started talking, they listened. They thanked him for the information and said they'd tell the others. And then they said they were very sorry, but they were going to have to kill him. Their children were starving, and they couldn't afford to let such a fine specimen of fresh meat go."

I shrugged. "Well. At least they apologized."

Logan grinned sympathetically. "I get where you're coming from, Abs, I really do. And you're right. The Jinnku aren't monsters. They're just trying to survive, like everybody else in the universe."

My gaze drifted to the solar system where Ed lived. This seemed like a happy ending for the Jinnku, but it wasn't really. It was nothing more than a chance, a possibility, one that might or might not save them. Either way, we would never know.

"Ready to go home?" asked Logan.

I nodded in resignation and lined myself up so my

sutratma was centered in front of me like a guide rope. I reached for Logan as he reached for me and felt that mittenish zap as our spirits connected.

"Hang on tight," I said.

And then we took that wild ride in reverse. It was very much like the first trip—whizzing lights, colorful nebulae, possible black hole. Logan was right—I knew how to go impossibly fast without even thinking about it.

Once the post-trip dizziness subsided, I took a look around.

I could hardly believe it. Somehow I'd gotten us back to the place where Jakob and I had been before that first roller-coaster ride.

I laughed, giddy with relief. "Look where we are! See that bright splotch way up ahead? That's the Milky Way." My sutratma, nearly as thick as a garden hose, stretched toward it.

"What'd I tell you? I knew you could do it!" Logan's aura was a dreamy, creamy gold. He gazed at the Milky Way, still a gazillion miles away and yet finally within reach. "It's just so beautiful. Isn't it beaut—"

"Don't start," I warned.

Arm in arm, we sped toward that bright splotch.

We had just entered our galaxy when I started to feel funny. Not like a soap bubble about to pop. Not sick and wobbly. A different kind of funny.

My whole being shuddered as if an earthquake was rumbling at my core. Or as if someone had grabbed my shoulders and was shaking me. Too late, I realized what was happening. I didn't even have time to scream.

I felt a rapid unfurling as I was wrenched away

from Logan.

My mother's face loomed in front of me.
I was back on the plane.

Chapter 56

My mother was hysterical. Gasping, sobbing, hiccupping. Her blotchy face, inches from mine, radiated heat.

"Abby, Abby, oh, thank God!" She threw her arms around me, her hot tears drenching my neck. "I thought you were in a coma!"

I spat a strand of her hair out of my mouth and peered past her head. All the other seats were empty. The plane had a settled feeling, as if it had landed quite some time ago. I wondered how long my mother had been trying to wake me.

Gently, I pushed her away. A flight attendant materialized behind her. "Here," she said, handing me a small bottle of water. "Drink this."

I sucked the whole thing down in a few swallows. Meanwhile, my mother had plopped into the seat next to mine and was crying so hard, I thought she must be having some kind of breakdown. The flight attendant fetched her a bottle of water, too.

"I wasn't in a coma," I said. "You have to stop thinking like that. When I sleep, I sleep hard—that's just how I am. Plus, I didn't get much sleep last night. Then you gave me that p.m. tablet." Which I hadn't taken, but that was a detail she didn't need to know. "What did you expect?"

Eventually, her sobs transitioned into soft gasps.

"It's just—this is how it started with Logan. If the same thing happened to you—I couldn't bear it. I just couldn't."

"Mom, seriously, I'm fine." I patted her hand.

"Ma'am?" said the flight attendant. "The paramedics are here."

"Paramedics?" I glared at the flight attendant, then at my mother, not sure who to blame. "I don't need paramedics. I'm fine."

I got up and tried to leave the plane, but the flight attendant blocked my way. My mother said I wasn't going anywhere until I got a medical checkup. The two paramedics, a man and a lady, came striding down the aisle. The man took my pulse, temperature, and blood pressure while the lady peered into my eyes, looked down my throat, and listened to my heart. They said my blood pressure was a tad low, my heart rate was slightly elevated, and I was moderately dehydrated, but overall my vital signs were good.

"Drink extra fluids for the next day or two," the lady paramedic said crisply. "Get lots of rest. Follow up with your family doctor."

My mother accompanied the paramedics to the front of the plane, and while they chatted, my thoughts turned full-force to Logan. I bit the sleeve of my sweatshirt to keep from screaming. We'd been so close to home—*so close*—and yet he was still out there, floating around like space debris. I tried to beam him an order to stay put until I could come get him. Maybe I'd be able to nod off during the taxi ride to the hospital. All I needed were a few minutes of sleep and a solid OBE.

But I was too keyed up to sleep in the taxi, plus my

mother wouldn't stop squeezing my arm and patting my leg, as if she needed constant physical contact to assure herself that I was okay.

I moved on to Plan B. Once we reached the hospital, I would slip away to a visitors' lounge for a nap.

The taxi dropped us off at the hospital's main entrance, and we hurried inside, rolling our suitcases behind us. A lady at the front desk directed us to Logan's room.

As we neared his door, my mother thrust out an arm, stopping me in my tracks. "You need to prepare yourself. You've never seen anybody close to death before. It might come as a shock."

But when we entered Logan's room, the shock we got wasn't the one we were expecting.

Chapter 57

Logan was sitting up in bed, pale as the moon but alert. Aunt Lisa stood on one side, spooning soup into his mouth. Uncle Dirk was on the other side, watching raptly, as if slurping soup had become the world's most fascinating spectator sport.

"Logan!" I cried, abandoning my suitcase to rush across the room. "You made it back!"

Logan flashed me a warning look, and I hastily corrected myself. "You woke up!"

"It happened less than an hour ago," Aunt Lisa told us. "It was very sudden." Her smile was radiant, though tears glistened in her eyes. "It was like his alarm clock went off and he was getting up for school."

Uncle Dirk added, "The first thing he said was, 'I'm starving!' " He said it loudly and with a laugh, though emotion brimmed in his eyes, too. He ruffled Logan's hair in a that's-my-boy way.

Mom whipped out her cell phone and called Grandma to tell her the good news. Grandma wanted proof, so Mom put her on speakerphone and let Logan say a hoarse hello. Grandma said merciful savior, it was good to hear his voice, and it was surely all the prayers from the good people in her church that had brought him back from the brink of death. Once he was feeling better, he might want to send a thank-you note.

Logan and I looked at each other and rolled our

eyes. That was *so Grandma*.

A nurse stuck her head in the door. "Is there an Abby here?"

"I'm Abby," I said.

"Phone call for you. Guy's been calling every ten minutes. I'll forward the call over."

"Guy?" said my mom, a thousand question marks popping out of her eyes.

I shrugged like I had no idea who would be calling me at a Pittsburgh hospital, even though I was ninety-nine percent sure I knew.

My heart rate was elevated, but it had nothing to do with my physical condition.

When Logan's bedside phone rang, I snatched up the receiver. A male voice said, "Abby? Is that you?"

All eyes were on me. Luckily, the phone was cordless, so I took the receiver into the bathroom and shut the door. "Jakob?"

"Abby! Are you okay? Did you and Logan get back safely? Is he out of the coma?"

"Yeah...Logan, he—both of us—we're good," I said, suddenly stammering, suddenly shy. On the astral plane, communication took place without vocal cords or eardrums. Jakob's voice, with its deep timbre and fluctuating tones, its particular stresses and inflections, and its moderate German accent was the voice of a stranger. It would take some getting used to.

"Logan's out of the coma," I added, finally managing to untwist my tongue.

"That's what I was hoping to hear! Sorry I left so suddenly. Grandmother—"

"—swept you out of bed with her broom? Yeah, we figured."

I told him what had happened after he'd left. He offered a hearty "Fantastic!" when I told him about Ed's conversation with the Jinnku. Then I asked, "How did you find me?"

"I phoned Pittsburgh hospitals until I found the one that had Logan registered as a patient. The nurse wouldn't tell me anything about his condition, though, because I'm not family. I had to keep calling till you showed up."

"What time is it there? Shouldn't you be in school?"

"Should be, yes. I'm skipping today. Too exhausted to do much of anything."

"Yeah, me too."

Silence fell, the kind you get when a steady wind suddenly dies down. There were so many things I wanted to know about him, but this wasn't the time for questions.

I said, "You speak English."

"That surprises you?"

"Not really. It's weird to hear your voice, though."

"It's weird to hear yours. The way it goes up at the end."

"What?"

"Everything you say sounds like a question, even if it isn't."

"Dude," I said, flabbergasted and appalled, "I do not do that!"

"Dude, you totally do that. Relax, I like it. It's very American."

I knew plenty of uptalkers, but I'd never realized I was one of them. I vowed to kick the habit.

Jakob said, "I've been thinking back on our crazy

trip across the universe."

"You mean *universes*."

"How we saved Logan. How we saved Ed. I think we have good teamwork."

"It makes the dream work," I said lightly. Jakob's voice was growing on me by the second. It was a good voice, well-modulated but slightly edgy. A voice fit for reading bedtime stories, especially exciting ones.

"My brother and I, we've been doing something on the astral plane. A crusade. I was thinking maybe you could join us."

"What kind of crusade?"

Before he could answer, a mighty disturbance erupted at his end of the line. I heard a raspy female voice squawking words I couldn't understand. German words. Jakob cried, "*Nein, Oma—nein!*" There was a scuffling noise that suggested Jakob's phone was involved in a tug-of-war. Then more squawking, followed by shouted retorts from Jakob. Next, a clatter that suggested something—a lamp?—had crashed to the floor. Finally, the woman's voice receded, though I could still hear angry muttering.

"Abby!" I jumped when Jakob's voice collided with my eardrum.

"Jakob! Is everything okay?"

"I'm so sorry. Grandmother says if I'm too sick to go to school, I'm too sick to talk on the phone. I have to hang up."

"You were going to tell me about your crusade."

"That'll have to wait. Quick, give me your personal phone number before she comes back and snatches my phone away."

After we hung up, I stood there for a minute,

hugging the phone to my chest. Real conversations were so much better than imaginary ones.

Chapter 58

The second I emerged from the bathroom, Mom pounced on me. "Who was that?"

"A friend of Logan's," I said, "calling to see how he's doing. Jakob says hi," I told Logan. The look of smug amusement in his eyes told me he knew what was going on. I blushed hard, confirming it.

A nurse came in to take Logan's temperature and blood pressure. On his way out, he high-fived a doctor in blue scrubs who was coming in. She introduced herself as Dr. Chen and said to Logan, "Welcome back to the world, young man," which I thought was pretty funny.

We left the room while Dr. Chen examined Logan. When the doctor came back out, Mom and Aunt Lisa and Uncle Dirk followed her down the hall for an in-depth talk. I wasn't invited, so I went back to Logan's room and plopped into his bedside chair.

Gazing at him, I suddenly felt tongue-tied. Awestruck. I was looking at a miracle, somebody back from the dead. Logan's eyes, looking back at me, were bright, a startling contrast to the dark circles beneath them.

"How'd you get back?" I asked.

I was expecting to hear "My instinctive navigation kicked in," or "Ed flew across the universe to save me," because that was exactly the kind of thing Ed would do.

Or maybe even "Jakob came back to rescue me," though that seemed less likely, considering that Jakob hadn't mentioned it during our phone call.

But what Logan said was, "Cody."

I gaped at him. "Cody?"

"Gotta love a plot twist, right? He said you texted him about me being lost in outer space."

"Oh crud." I palm-slapped my forehead. "I totally forgot about that. And I never turned my cell phone back on after we landed." I fished my phone out of my purse and turned it on. There were three text messages from Cody. The first one said, "I'm on it!" The second one said, "Mission accomplished." The third one said, "Call me when you get to the hospital."

"So you knew?" said Logan. "You knew Cody was an astral traveler?"

"I was, like, ninety percent sure. I was so desperate, I would have tried anything."

I brought up Cody's name in my phone contacts and tapped the little icon for speakerphone. Cody answered on the second ring. "Minutia! Hey, sorry it took so long for me to see your text message. We aren't allowed to take our cell phones into the training area."

"That's okay. Your timing was perfect, actually. Great news—Logan's out of the coma."

"I know. After I got him back in his body, I hung around and watched him wake up. How's our boy feeling?"

"Feeling pretty good," said Logan. "Thanks for rescuing me, Uncle Cody."

"My pleasure, Rump Roast."

"Was it hard to find him?" I asked Cody.

"Not too hard. I have this special ability to home in

on other spirits."

I sucked in a breath. "You have spirit radar? You're so lucky!"

"I know. It comes in handy sometimes."

"I can't believe you're an astral traveler," said Logan. "I bet you have lots of interesting stories to tell."

"Yeah, and not all of them are good."

We waited, but Cody didn't elaborate.

Logan said, "You can't say something like that and not follow through."

There was a long silence at Cody's end. Then a resigned sigh blew out of my phone. "Okay, okay. Long story short—a couple of years ago, there was this guy at work who used to pick on me. One night during an OBE, I decided to get back at him. I ended up scaring him so bad, he ran into the street and got hit by a car."

"Holy crud!" I said.

"Yeah. He wasn't killed, but the accident left him with chronic headaches and a permanent limp. Thirty-two years old, and he had to walk with a cane. I ended up quitting my job. I couldn't take it, seeing that guy day after day. Knowing I tormented him almost to death—literally."

I caught Logan looking at me, and I knew he was thinking about Lanie. I shuddered. I was lucky she hadn't thrown herself out her bedroom window the night I'd spooked her.

"Is that what made you start drinking?" asked Logan.

I thought that question was a little too personal, but Cody answered without hesitation. "Yep. I decided I was done with astral travel. I didn't want to hurt anybody ever again. I'd found that drinking suppressed OBEs, so I'd have a couple of beers every night before bed. Or something stronger—mixed drinks, shots of whiskey. Of course, I eventually came to realize what a stupid, self-destructive habit drinking is. I kicked the habit over a year ago, though I would still have a nightcap every now and then when I needed a solid night's sleep."

"Like at my birthday dinner," I said.

"Yes. But now that I've learned how to prevent OBEs naturally, I've decided to give up alcohol for good."

Logan sat up straighter. "You know how to prevent OBEs? Can you teach us?"

"Sure. It's simple, really, though it takes a little practice and self-discipline. When your OBE starts, you force your spirit to stay close to your body. The spirit is like a dog—it wants to roam. If you don't let it, it gets bored, and the OBE ends. After a while, an OBE won't even start unless you want it to."

"Where'd you learn that?" asked Logan.

"In my astral travel training class."

"Astral travel training class!" Now I was the one sitting up straighter. "That sounds amazing. Sign me up!"

Cody gave a sympathetic laugh. "Sorry, Minutia—not possible. The class is part of the job training I'm taking in Washington, DC."

Logan and I exchanged bewildered glances. Logan said, "You work in IT security, Uncle Cody. Why are you taking an astral travel training class?"

"It's not for my IT job. It's for a different job. A new one." He lowered his voice. "You can't tell

311

anybody about this, okay? I'm working for the government. As an astral traveler."

"Whoa!" said Logan. "So you're, like, a spirit-spy?"

Cody didn't reply. I pictured him smiling a mysterious smile.

"Does anybody else in the family know you're an astral traveler?" I asked.

"Nope, just you two. Grandpa knew, but only because he was a traveler, too."

"Grandpa!" I wasn't totally surprised, but hearing it confirmed made me think of my grandpa in a whole new light.

"He never actually told me," Cody said. "I found out by accident. We ran into each other on the roof one night when he was coming home and I was going out. I was shocked to see my dad in spirit form, but he didn't seem surprised to see me. He just said, 'Hello, son. You too, huh?' "

"Does Grandma know about him?" asked Logan.

"God, no. Grandma can be a bit of a blabbermouth. Grandpa knew that if he told her, the whole neighborhood would end up knowing, not to mention everybody at church."

I had so many questions. I'd just opened my mouth to ask one when Cody said, "Listen, guys, I hate to cut this call short, but I need to get some shut-eye. I have an OBE homework assignment due first thing in the morning, and I haven't even started on it. We'll talk again later, okay?"

We said a quick round of goodbyes, and Cody clicked off.

I poured Logan a fresh glass of ice water and

reclined his bed to a thirty-degree angle so he could rest. We regarded each other somberly. Tears seeped into my eyes.

"Abby? Are you crying? What's wrong?"

"It's just—I can't believe what a jerk I've been." I used my sleeve to blot the tears away. "You're such a good person, and I'm...not. You used your powers to save a whole civilization. I used mine to get back at a mean girl. I helped people cheat on quizzes."

If Logan was shocked by the quiz confession, he didn't show it. "Don't beat yourself up. I've done bad things, too."

"The prank with Dad's jacket? That wasn't so bad. What I did to Lanie was worse."

"Yeah, maybe. But I've done other things, too."

I waited for him to tell me about the other things, but he didn't. I supposed I could live with that. We were allowed to have secrets from each other.

"Eventually I realized I should be using my power to help people. I know that sounds like a cliché, but it's true. And I think that's why I went to so much trouble to help the Ishwees. Why I literally risked my life. I was trying to make things right with the universe."

He sounded so serious, so grown up. And looked it, too. His eyes seemed darker, like something weighty was casting shadows behind them.

"I bet everybody who has OBEs goes a little crazy at first," I said.

"Sure. Astral travel is so wild, all the possibilities of it. You're going to do some things just because you can. But if you're basically a good person, you eventually come to your senses and start using your power for good."

"But if you aren't basically a good person—" My eyes met his. "Do you think there are bad astral travelers? People who use OBEs for evil purposes?"

"I'm sure there are."

Logan's bedside phone rang. The nightstand was beyond his reach, so I answered the call. His best friend, Charlie, was on the line. Aunt Lisa had texted him the good news, and Charlie couldn't wait another second to talk to his buddy.

"It's Charlie," I said to Logan. His face went pink as I handed him the receiver. I blew him a kiss and left the room.

Chapter 59

Logan was in the hospital for five days, because that was how long it took to get his heart rhythms stabilized. He spent another two weeks recuperating at home. He slept a lot, up to sixteen hours a day, which freaked his parents out at first. But he was always easy to awaken, which assured them that he wasn't slipping into another coma. Every afternoon Charlie brought his homework assignments to the house so he wouldn't fall behind at school.

I slept a lot, too, those first few days, and by the weekend, I was feeling like myself again. It was amazing what a couple of nights of solid sleep could do for a person. Both Logan and I had quickly mastered the OBE-prevention technique, which meant we could now control when—and whether—to have an OBE, and without the use of drugs. I was perfectly content being OBE-free for a while.

I told my parents about Jakob a few days after Mom and I got back from Pittsburgh. I had to—they wouldn't stop bugging me. Why was I spending so much time on the phone? Who was I talking to? Was it somebody I didn't want them to know about—maybe someone I'd met online? Did I know that child molesters often posed as teenage boys on social media?

And why was I smiling so much?

I fessed up with a story that was four parts truth

and one part lie. I said I had a special guy-friend (truth), his name was Jakob (truth), he was from Germany (truth), and he was seventeen (truth). I said we'd met as pen pals (lie). We'd started corresponding a few months ago—I'd gotten his name through a program at school—and had really hit it off. I introduced them to Jakob via a video call, and they liked him instantly. My dad praised his bilingual skills and said his manners were "Euro-peccable."

My mom was ecstatic. I could see how, in her eyes, this was the best possible scenario because, number one, it proved I wasn't a social misfit after all, and number two, since our relationship was a long-distance one, she didn't have to worry about me doing something stupid, like getting pregnant.

Her bliss level shot to the moon when, a few weeks later, I announced that I had a best friend. The best friend was Sarah Palmer.

Nobody was more surprised than me. Who'd have thought I'd end up being besties with Number Two?

I'd been doing a lot of soul-searching since the trip to Mysterium, thinking back on all the awful things I'd done as an astral traveler. If there'd been a Cruddy Person of the Year award, I would have been a serious contender. So I took Sarah up on her invitation to attend the youth group meetings at her church, thinking maybe a dose of religion was what I needed to set me straight.

I ended up enjoying the meetings far more than I'd expected to. There was always an outing or a party or a game or a deep discussion, and I went home in high spirits every Thursday night. Sarah and I grew close and started spending our free time together. We went to the movies, roamed the mall, took Holly and Cheddar for walks, or hung out at her house or mine to talk.

Sarah also persuaded me to attend Sunday morning church services with her, which made Grandma both happy and disappointed. Praise the Lord, I'd seen the light—but why did it have to be a United Methodist church? Wasn't Episcopalian good enough for me?

An even bigger surprise came shortly afterward when Lanie and I became friends. It turned out that Lanie was a member of Sarah's church, and sometimes she and Sarah and I would go out to lunch after church on Sunday. Lanie started coming to our youth group meetings, and pretty soon the three of us were a thing. Not a clique—just three friends who enjoyed hanging out together.

Lanie was still with Austin, but that no longer bothered me. I had Jakob now. Anyway, Lanie was a good person, and I knew I was blessed to have her as a friend.

In early spring, to everyone's surprise, the Sophia-Emma alliance fell apart. Sophia and Emma liked the same boy, and he ended up choosing Emma. Around the same time, the junior high choir director quit her job to have a baby, and the guy who took her place gave somebody else, not Sophia, the big solo in the spring concert.

Karma, baby.

I didn't feel at all sorry for Sophia. Whereas Lanie had become kinder and humbler after the lipsticked-mirror scare, Sophia's misfortunes had only made her meaner. She was like an angry hornet buzzing around, constantly looking for somebody to sting.

One day at school, when Sarah and I were walking down the hall, Sophia was passing by, and she deliberately bumped into Sarah. Sarah had just given a pencil to a new student, and Sophia had witnessed the transaction.

Sophia's green eyes bored into Sarah's brown ones as she said, "Thou shalt not hand out religious doodads in school."

Sarah's mouth trembled, but she didn't say anything.

I blocked Sophia as she tried to walk away. "Dude, seriously? That mean-girl stuff is getting old."

Sophia made a noise like she was spitting in my face. "Nobody says *dude* anymore—*dude*."

"I do, *dude*." I shot her sneer right back at her. "You are truly tragic," I said, thinking how my English teacher, Mrs. Kelly, would appreciate the alliteration.

That wasn't all I had to say. I paused, trying to choose between *Sung any solos lately?* and *Don't Emma and Kyle make the cutest couple?* But before I could decide which would cut deeper, Sarah grabbed my arm and yanked me down the hall.

I started to protest as I stumbled along behind her. Then I shut my mouth. I bowed my head. I said, "Thank you."

Sarah was helping me become a better person.

I still had a ways to go.

Chapter 60

On a pre-dawn morning in mid-May, Logan, Cody, and I met up at the Eiffel Tower. Jakob had been with me earlier and had been planning to join us, but then his grandmother had swept him out of bed with her broom. Or so I figured, considering how abruptly he'd vanished.

The spirit of the dead white-haired man was with us, flitting around like a pesky mosquito. We had to keep moving out of his way.

This was the first time I'd seen Cody in spirit form. His aura was pale blue, like the daytime sky viewed through a chiffon-thin layer of clouds. I couldn't stop staring, lulled by that cool, soothing color.

We were at the tippy-top of the Tower, bobbing around like buoys in the ocean. We chit-chatted for a few minutes, then Cody said, "So what have my two favorite astral travelers been up to? We haven't talked for a while."

I opened my mouth to reply, but Logan beat me to it. "Abby's become a crime-fighter."

Cody whistled softly and asked for details.

I laughed modestly. "Logan makes me sound like a superhero."

"You kind of are," said Logan.

"But I don't have superpowers."

"Unless you count invisibility," said Logan.

"And telekinesis," said Cody. "And the ability to fly."

I threw my hands up in surrender. "Fine, I'm a superhero. Anyway—yeah, I've been fighting crime with Jakob and his brother. We hang out in high-crime areas, and when we see somebody doing something bad, we scare them away. Like, three nights ago, we stopped two muggings in Chicago and a burglary in London."

Because of the time difference, I didn't get to join Jakob on the astral plane as often as I would have liked, but we had a standing date every Friday night. I conked out super early, helped along by a mug of warm milk, and Jakob went to bed late. That put our OBEs more in sync, giving us a couple of hours to work on our crusade or, sometimes, to go on a just-us spirit-date.

"Fighting crime!" Cody said when I'd finished talking. "Minutia, I'm blown away."

"The whole thing was Jakob's idea. He's always saying we should use our powers to make the world a better place."

"Have I told you how much I like Jakob? You really picked a winner for your first boyfriend."

"He's not my boyfriend," I said automatically. I'd been saying that for weeks, but I knew I was sounding less and less convincing. Earlier tonight Jakob and I had kissed for the first time. It probably wasn't as good as a physical kiss, not that I would know, but it had rattled the entirety of my spirit in a very pleasurable way. Jakob had an after-school job and was saving up for air fare so he could visit me in person over the summer.

Of course, he wasn't perfect. Sometimes he still channeled his father. When I noticed him getting snappish or withdrawn, I would say, "Okay, Dieter"—which was his father's name—and he would apologize and try harder to be nice.

I was helping him become a better person just like Sarah was helping me.

"Not your boyfriend. Got it," Cody said with a wink. I was probably blushing, but neither Cody nor Logan commented on it.

"How about you, Rump Roast?" Cody asked. "You back to exploring the world?"

"Ha, no. This is the farthest I've gone since the coma. There's always this thought in the back of my mind…" His aura took on that somber brassy tone I'd seen before. "I'm half afraid I'll get lost again. I think I have astral travel agoraphobia!" He tried for a light-hearted grin, but it devolved into a grimace. I could tell this was really bothering him.

Cody nodded sympathetically. "You're suffering from PTSD. Totally understandable, considering what you went through. You'll get past it, though. And don't worry about getting lost. As long as you stay on Earth and don't overdo the traveling, you'll be fine."

"I know. It's getting better all the time." Logan wafted backward, deftly dodging the dead spirit. "And it hasn't stopped me from doing stuff on the astral plane. I've been trying to help people, too—in my own small way."

"I wouldn't call it small," I said.

"It's not as good as what you're doing."

"Sure it is. It's just different."

"I don't get results as fast as you do."

"But you get them. Plus, you have a special gift that not many people have."

Cody said, "Guys, the suspense is killing me! What is it you've been doing, Rump Roast?"

Before Logan could open his mouth, I said, "Logan's a dream-whisperer."

"Get out! For real?"

Logan blushed, a lovely silvery-gold color. "Yeah. I communicate with unconscious people. After I came out of the coma, I didn't travel for weeks. When I started up again, I stayed close to home. I kept going back to the hospital. I don't know why. Looking for closure, maybe? One night I met the spirit of a lady who was in a coma."

Cody said, "Ah, another traveler who stayed out of body too long."

"Actually, no. She wasn't an astral traveler. She'd been in a car accident, and it was the coma that put her on the astral plane. But she didn't have the powers we have. She could barely move—she was stuck above her body like a balloon on a short string."

I shuddered, imagining how awful that would be.

"I used to visit her every night," Logan went on. "We'd talk for hours. I counseled her. I told her to focus all her energy on healing her brain injury. After a couple of days, she woke up. The doctors were amazed. They didn't think she'd ever come out of the coma."

Cody, who'd been listening to Logan's story with his mouth hanging open, said, "Rump Roast, I have to agree with Minutia. You have a very special gift. And you're using it in the best possible way."

Logan waved away the praise. "I can't save everybody, though. Some people have too much brain damage. But I did help a guy in Philadelphia wake up. And a teenage girl in Baltimore." His aura was now a brilliant white-gold, a happy color I hadn't seen in a long time. "Anyway, that's my thing now—helping people wake up from comas."

Cody glanced from Logan to me, admiration shining in his eyes. "You two are something else. When I was your age, all I did was spy on the neighbors."

"Yeah, I've done that, too," said Logan.

"Me too," I said. I was fine with confessing small crimes as long as I wasn't the only one doing it.

A pink blush lined the eastern horizon, a promise of the coming day.

"I should probably take off," said Cody. "I have an astral travel job assignment to wrap up. Are you guys heading home soon?"

"I think I'll hang out here for a while," I said. "I want to watch the sun come up."

"I'll watch with you," said Logan.

"Well, then. Minutia, Rump Roast—it's been great seeing you. Let me know if you ever need anything. Advice about astral travel, about romance"—another wink at me—"how to deal with Grandma, anything. Just no more outer space rescues, okay?" With a smile and a wave, Cody flew off in a northeasterly direction.

"I wonder where he's going," Logan mused, staring after him. "Maybe Russia—it's up that way."

We hovered in companionable silence for a few minutes, watching the pre-dawn pinkness seep across the sky like a spilled strawberry milkshake.

Logan asked, "How's everything at home?"

"Good. Mom quit her job at the Community Foundation. She's selling real estate fulltime now."

"I heard. And your dad's okay with that?"

"Totally. Your coma really shook everybody up.

323

They're like, 'Life's too short to be working a job you hate.' Dad said if selling real estate is what makes his wife happy, he's all for it. I think they're going to be okay."

"That's great."

The first golden sliver of sun peeped up over the horizon, like a child playing peekaboo. The dead spirit wafted past us yet again, close but not dangerously so. His face was mostly turned away from me, but I thought I glimpsed a small indentation in his cheek, possibly a dimple.

Was he smiling?

I said, "I guess we won't be seeing much of each other on the astral plane. You have your thing. I have mine."

"Still. Every once in a while we should arrange to meet up."

"Definitely."

"And we'll still call and text and email each other."

"And do video calls."

"And visits. You should come to Pittsburgh for a week or two over the summer. If your dad will spring for the air fare. I'll take you to all my favorite places, introduce you to my friends."

"I'd love to meet Charlie."

We exchanged mirror-image grins. People always said we had the same smile.

A movement from above caught my eye, a far-off plane inching its way across the sky. I watched it go, knowing that no matter where it was heading, I could get there faster. I would probably never stop marveling over the magic of astral travel.

"Abby?" said Logan. "Did you happen to see

where our friend went?"

The dead white-haired man! I'd been trying to keep track of him—because the last thing we needed was a collision with a dead spirit—but in that brief plane-watching interlude I'd lost him. I spun in a circle, glancing up and down, left and right. Logan was doing the same.

He was gone. The spirit who'd been wafting so insistently among us for the past half hour was suddenly nowhere to be seen.

Logan and I turned toward each other at the same time.

"What the—?"

"Where did he—?"

"Do you think he—?"

This was the Jinnku situation all over again. We would probably never know for sure whether that lost soul had found the elusive portal to the next world. If we saw him in the future, we would know he hadn't. But if he never showed up again, that wouldn't necessarily mean he'd moved on. It might only mean our paths hadn't crossed.

"Huh," said Logan, and the half-smile on his face told me he was choosing to believe that the man had found his happy ending. I wanted to believe it, too, but I wasn't a hundred percent sure. Eighty-eight percent was the best I could do.

The sun rose higher, burning away the shadows below us. A siren blared from a great distance, a tiny sound that belied its urgency. Traffic crept along like a procession of nanobots. Paris was starting its day.

"Pretty sunrise," said Logan. "I'm glad I stayed to watch. I guess I'll head home now."

"Are you okay going by yourself?"

"Yeah. My sutratma is lit up like Christmastime." He saluted me, solemn as a sailor about to depart on a long voyage. "Bye, Abs. Love you to Mysterium and back."

"Same."

We grinned at each other, but this goodbye somehow seemed weightier, more final, than any other goodbye we'd ever said. We were heading in opposite directions, like two meteors on different trajectories. Those blissful days of cousin power were behind us.

No more silly riddles.

Side-by-side snow angels.

Shared crayon boxes.

Laughing so hard we snorted milk out our noses.

Of course, those days were always going to end. Hadn't I known that?

After I watched him fly away, I stayed for a while longer, taking in the world spread out below me. The bustling city, the blue-green forests on the horizon, and, beyond that, out of sight, the ragged mountains, the broiling deserts, the roiling oceans. Other continents, other cities. The whole world teeming with people living their lives, doing their thing, loving each other.

It was all so beautiful.

A word about the author...

Kimberly Baer wrote her first story at age six. It was about a baby chick that hatched out of a little girl's Easter egg after somehow surviving the hard-boiling process. Nowadays she writes in a variety of genres, including young adult, middle-grade, and adult romantic suspense. She lives in Virginia, where she likes to go power-walking on days when it's not too hot, too cold, too rainy, too snowy, or too windy. On indoor days, you're likely to find her hard at work on her next novel or curled up on the couch with a good book and a cup of tea.

You can call her "Kim." All her friends do. Visit her at www.kimberlybaer.com.

Milton Keynes UK
Ingram Content Group UK Ltd.
UKHW022053190224
438095UK00016B/525